I glanced up when the bell jangled. Samuel let the door shut behind him, but he didn't hang up his coat. He caught my eye and beckoned for me to join him. I set down the coffee carafe and hurried in his direction.

Adele's beau was nearly eighty-five, and his face bore the lines to prove it. Right now the furrows on his brow were extra deep. One leg jittered, and he jammed his hands into his pockets as if to calm them.

"Samuel, what's the matter?" I asked. "Is Adele all right?"

"She's not ill or hurt, if that's what you mean."

My shoulders slumped with relief.

"But, Roberta, I have awful news." He swallowed. "I found a man dead in her pasture this morning. Stone cold dead . . ."

Books by Maddie Day

Country Store Mysteries
FLIPPED FOR MURDER
GRILLED FOR MURDER
WHEN THE GRITS HIT THE FAN
BISCUITS AND SLASHED BROWNS
DEATH OVER EASY
STRANGLED EGGS AND HAM
NACHO AVERAGE MURDER
CANDY SLAIN MURDER
NO GRATER CRIME
BATTER OFF DEAD
FOUR LEAF CLEAVER
DEEP FRIED DEATH
SCONE COLD DEAD
CHRISTMAS COCOA MURDER
(with Carlene O'Connor and Alex Erickson)
CHRISTMAS SCARF MURDER
(with Carlene O'Connor and Peggy Ehrhart)

Cozy Capers Book Group Mysteries
MURDER ON CAPE COD
MURDER AT THE TAFFY SHOP
MURDER AT THE LOBSTAH SHACK
MURDER IN A CAPE COTTAGE
MURDER AT A CAPE BOOKSTORE
MURDER AT THE RUSTY ANCHOR

Local Foods Mysteries
A TINE TO LIVE, A TINE TO DIE
'TIL DIRT DO US PART
FARMED AND DANGEROUS
MURDER MOST FOWL
MULCH ADO ABOUT MURDER

Cece Barton Mysteries
MURDER UNCORKED
DEADLY CRUSH
CHRISTMAS MITTENS MURDER
(with Lee Hollis and Lynn Cahoon)

Published by Kensington Publishing Corp.

Scone Cold Dead

MADDIE DAY

Kensington Publishing Corp.
kensingtonbooks.com

KENSINGTON BOOKS are published by

Kensington Publishing Corp.
900 Third Avenue
New York, NY 10022

Copyright © 2025 by Edith Maxwell

All Kensington titles, imprints, and distributed lines are available at special quantity discounts for bulk purchases for sales promotion, premiums, fund-raising, educational, or institutional use.

Special book excerpts or customized printings can also be created to fit specific needs. For details, write or phone the office of the Kensington Sales Manager: Attn.: Sales Department. Kensington Publishing Corp., 900 Third Avenue, New York, NY 10022. Phone: 1-800-221-2647.

KENSINGTON and the KENSINGTON COZIES teapot logo Reg US Pat. & TM Off.

First Printing: April 2025
ISBN: 978-1-4967-4228-5

ISBN: 978-1-4967-4229-2 (ebook)

10 9 8 7 6 5 4 3 2 1

Printed in the United States of America

For Risa Rispoli and Jay Roberts, two special fans, who have boosted my books—as well as my ego—in all kinds of different ways but have never met each other. Thank you, friends.

ACKNOWLEDGMENTS

Many thanks to my longtime friend Jennifer Yanco for lending me a few of her grandmother's quirky expressions to put in the mouths of characters like Samuel, Adele, and Buck. Others who suggested phrases I used include Amanda Beachum, Max Carter, Amy Connolley, Jessie Crockett, Julie Hennrikus, Madeline Spangler, and Erica Voolich.

Fictional midwife Risa Ferguson takes inspiration from two awesome nurse midwives I am honored to be friends with, Risa Rispoli and Ann Ferguson. Thank you for your decades of ushering babies expertly and safely into the world, ladies. In addition, I'm grateful to Risa for checking the pregnancy and birth references in the manuscript.

Thanks to Hoosier friend Tim Mundorff for the photo of an abandoned farmhouse in Franklin County, Indiana. It was the inspiration I needed to move beyond a blessedly brief period of being mildly stuck as I wrote this book.

Marisa Young was high bidder in a Bouchercon charity auction for the right to name one of my characters. I was delighted to include Marisa's mystery-fan friend Juanita McWilliam as an Indiana state police detective. Any shortcomings in the fictional detective's character have no relation to the real Juanita, who I hope loves her new career.

Most of my fans know that I (as Edith Maxwell) wrote seven historical Quaker Midwife mysteries featuring midwife Rose Carroll. Earlier in the Country

Store series there is mention of Robbie's great-grandmother Rose, who had been a midwife, and it comes up again in this book. Yep—that Rose is indeed Rose Carroll, and I loved connecting the two story lines.

I'm grateful once again to Amy Glaser for giving the story a deep read and suggesting a slew of much-needed improvements. Thanks always to Jennifer McKee for help on the promotional side, and to my talented Wicked Author pals: Barbara Ross, Liz Mugavero, Julie Hennrikus, Sherry Harris, and Jessie Crockett. We've been together since the beginning, and I couldn't have navigated this path without you all. Readers, please find us at wickedauthors.com.

Thank you, always, to my agent, John Talbot, and to John Scognamiglio, Larissa Ackerman, and the rest of the amazing and hardworking crew at Kensington Publishing, who have fostered this series since well before book one—*Flipped for Murder*—released ten years ago.

Love and fierce hugs to my family: Allan, Alison, and Ida Rose, John David and Alex, Barbara, Janet, and David, and my Hugh. I am a lucky woman.

Finally, I am enormously grateful for the devoted fans of this series who have stuck with Robbie and friends for all thirteen books and several novellas. Thank you to Hoosiers who are delighted to have books set in their home state of Indiana and who tell everyone they know about fictional South Lick and the shenanigans that go on there. Blessings to the librarians and booksellers who talk up the series to readers. I'm deeply indebted to all of you.

CHAPTER 1

As I walked—well, waddled—to South Lick's First Savings Bank that mid-November morning, I was still aglow from the surprise baby shower our friends and family had thrown for my husband, Abe O'Neill, and me last evening. Our little one was due in two weeks, pretty much on Thanksgiving, and we had most of the basics. The fun, personalized gifts we received yesterday from our loved ones more than completed the list of what we needed and desired.

I had nothing to do before the due date except to stay calm and healthy. I also wanted to make sure my country store restaurant kept running smoothly, and hopefully I wouldn't get dragged into solving any more murders. I'd somehow become something of an amateur sleuth in the last few years, but South Lick and surrounds hadn't had a homicide on the books since May. I crossed my fingers that it stayed that way.

After I deposited the considerable till from the weekend and yesterday, I headed for the exit. My trajectory took me past the bank manager's office. In the open doorway, a man with short-cropped hair stood speaking with manager Carter Kingsley. Kingsley had started at the bank in the last year or two, and I basically only knew him from the name plate on his desk. I was sure he hadn't been a bank employee when I'd opened my business and personal accounts over five years ago.

The short-haired man looked near Kingsley's age, maybe in his early sixties, with plenty of gray in his hair, and the back of his neck was tattooed. I didn't think I'd ever seen him before. He certainly wasn't a regular in Pans 'N Pancakes, the popular country store breakfast and lunch place I own and run. Being a curious person, I slowed to watch their interaction.

Kingsley knit his brow and pressed his lips into a flat line. He shook his mostly bald head.

The visitor opened his hands to the sides. "I think it's something you should do." His voice was low and gentle.

"Not going to happen, Sheluk."

The man shrugged and turned. I whipped my face forward and resumed my waddle, pretending I hadn't stopped to take in their interaction. From the glare Kingsley shot me, I doubted I fooled either of them.

Sheluk nodded at me. "Let me get the door for you, ma'am." He hurried to the century-old Art Deco door, original to the building, and pulled it open.

"Thank you so much." I smiled at him.

He followed me out and let the door ease shut. He had a weathered look about him, as if he'd been through tough times. His work boots were well-worn, as was his navy pea coat. He didn't smile, but his kind eyes did. "Looks like you'll be a mama soon."

"Yes." I couldn't help wrapping my hands around my beach ball, otherwise known as a baby. My coat didn't close, but luckily the weather hadn't turned too chilly yet. "In a couple of weeks, more or less. It's our first."

"Good. I can tell you'll take good care of that little child," he murmured.

"I'm planning on it, sir."

He opened his mouth, then shut it, giving his head a little shake. "You have a good day, now."

"You, too." I watched him trudge away. What had he been about to say? I'd found, ever since becoming visibly pregnant, that total strangers seemed fond of giving unsolicited advice. Perhaps this guy had wisely stopped himself before he did the same. At least he hadn't reached out to touch my belly as others had, which was totally unacceptable.

I would be glad for many reasons to have our little one safely born and in our arms. But one reason was so people would stop thinking it was okay to lay a hand on my body and by extension my baby's.

What request from Sheluk had Kingsley been refusing to honor? I'd probably never know. I had found Sheluk's wording curious. He'd said he could tell I would take good care of my baby. How could he know that?

When a gust of cold wind blew a strand of hair in my eyes, I smoothed it back into my pony tail and tucked my hands into my pockets. I might have wrongly assessed the weather, I thought, as I began my waddle back to my livelihood.

CHAPTER 2

Business was bustling in Pans 'N Pancakes an hour later, just how I liked it. It wasn't yet noon, but the early rush kept today's crew of Danna Beedle and Turner Rao busy, one at the grill, one delivering plates full of lunch and busing tables after diners left.

I was busy, too, although I'd stopped taking a shift cooking. I couldn't easily belly up to the hot grill and stay safely away from the sizzling oil of an occasional popping sausage or sputtering beef patty. Instead, I took and delivered orders, poured coffee and kept the carafes full, accepted payment, and checked with diners to be sure they were happy.

In September we'd celebrated five years since I'd first opened to the doors to the country store, where I sold antique cookware plus local food and craft items, and the breakfast and lunch restaurant filling the rest of the space. I found it hard to believe we'd been open for half a decade.

I'd already been working as a chef here in the hills of Brown County, Indiana, but I'd dreamed of owning my own restaurant. When my aunt Adele brought me to this rundown country store that winter during my grief at the sudden death of my mother, we noticed it was for sale. I used money my cabinetmaker mom had left me to buy the store, and I employed the carpentry skills I'd learned from her to fix up the building. We opened later in the year.

The business now operated in the black and had also become a real community gathering place. People came not only to enjoy a delicious hot meal but also to socialize, share news, play board games, and more. Our awesome online reviews often lured in busloads of tourists from neighboring states as well as visitors from other countries. The three B&B rooms I'd created upstairs were popular, too.

Danna had been my right-hand person since the beginning, and Turner had come on about six months later. Len Perlman now helped out a few days a week, especially subbing in on weekends. They were a good team who worked well together, and I felt comfortable leaving the place in their hands so I could take a couple of months of maternity leave.

Right now I was still on the job, though. My seventy-something aunt wandered in holding a big cloth bag that looked full. I hurried over to greet her and kissed her smooth but lined cheek.

"Morning, Roberta."

"What's in there, Adele?" I gestured at the bag.

"Skeins and mittens. Folks are already shopping for Christmas, you know." She headed over to the display where she sold the yarn and knitted items made from the wool of her own sheep.

What was up with her? She hadn't smiled or asked how I was. She was one of the few with permission to lay her hands on my belly. She loved touching the baby and feeling it kick and squirm about in the increasingly tight space. My aunt hadn't reached out to touch my midsection upon greeting me, either. She frowned now as she arranged the new merchandise in the retail section of the country store.

I followed her. "What's up?" I murmured, sidling in close.

"Nothing." She didn't meet my gaze.

I shrugged. She'd tell me when she was ready. I started to make my way back to the kitchen, but when the door opened anew, I detoured in that direction. The newcomer was Frederica O'Neill, otherwise known as my mother-in-law. An energetic cellist in her early sixties, Freddy had organized last night's baby shower, with Adele's help. Now she beamed and held out her arms for a hug.

"Wasn't last evening fun?" She stepped back, blue eyes bright.

"It was. Thank you so much for putting it together, Freddy."

"Gifties for my first grandbaby? It was my pleasure. And there's my partner in crime. Hey, Adele." Freddy moved to Adele's side.

Again I followed. "Are you both here for lunch?"

Adele nodded without speaking.

"I'm absolutely starving." Freddy had an amazing ability to put away food despite being petite and shorter than my five foot three.

"You can grab that two-top near the kitchen area." I pointed. "It's one of the last free tables."

"Thanks, hon," Freddy said. "Shall we, my friend?" She took Adele's arm.

They hadn't known each other before Abe and I started spending time together, but now we often had joint family gatherings. The two, both independent-minded and interesting older women, had found much in common. Adele might open up to Freddy. Maybe I could quiz her later on what was troubling my aunt. Or ask Adele myself.

CHAPTER 3

Two hours later, Turner pointed to our big soup pot. "Just ran out of the curried lentil soup special, boss."

I checked the big wall clock, which had formerly told time in an elementary school. "That's okay, it's already one thirty. I'll erase the soup from the board."

We tried to offer a special dish at breakfast and lunch every day, but our regular menu was a good one. It wasn't a big problem when we ran out of the day's addition, although today's creation had been a tasty one, thanks to Turner. I had grabbed a bowl when I returned from the bank. My team was nothing if not good at reminding me to sit down and eat during lulls.

The antique cow bell on the door jangled. I glanced over. And blinked. It was the man from the bank. I ambled in his direction.

"Welcome to Pans 'N Pancakes." I smiled.

"We meet again, miss." He smiled slightly but didn't show his teeth, and he sounded a bit out of breath, as if the work of climbing the front steps had been taxing. "My, it smells good in here."

It did. The air was fragrant with the scents of onions and meat browning on the grill, along with apple fritters crisping in the deep fryer. The mildly spicy smell of curry also lingered.

"Thank you," I said. "Did you come to eat?"

"If I might." He unbuttoned his pea coat, revealing a plaid flannel shirt under a brown sweater. He pulled off a watch cap and stuffed it in one coat pocket.

"Of course. We're open until two thirty." I turned and surveyed the restaurant. "There's a table right there." I gestured to one at the near side of the restaurant.

"Ah. I would rather sit at that table in the back, miss."

The one he pointed to was the two-top where South Lick Police Chief Buck Bird liked to eat. It let him sit with his back to the wall and afforded him a good view of anyone coming and going. But Buck wasn't here.

"That'll be fine. I'm Robbie Jordan, by the way." I folded my hands over my now-ample midsection. I didn't like to shake hands while I worked with food.

"My name is Ivan Sheluk, Ms. Jordan."

"Good to meet you, Ivan. Please call me Robbie, and you're welcome to that table. The menu is on your place mat, and I'll be over in a minute to get your order. Would you like to start with coffee?"

"No, thank you."

He moved gingerly to the table, as if something hurt. I hadn't noticed him walking like that this morning. He shrugged out of his coat and hung it on the back of the chair, then sat facing the room. Just like Buck.

It took me a couple of minutes to get to the newcomer, what with taking diners' cards or cash and pouring from two full carafes. Ivan asked for a grilled cheese sandwich on whole wheat, a biscuit with vegetarian gravy, and a glass of chocolate milk.

"You got it." I began to turn away.

"Robbie," he said. "Your last name is Jordan. Would you happen to know an Adele Jordan?" His tone was casual but had an edge to it.

"Yes." Aunt Adele was my only living relative on this continent, not counting Baby Jordan-O'Neill. My mom's older sister, the former South Lick mayor, lived outside of town proper on her sheep farm, which surrounded her cottage.

"Do you know how I can contact her?" he asked.

This dude was a stranger to town. If he'd come in earlier, he would have encountered Adele, but she and Freddy had eaten and left, unfortunately without my learning what was troubling Adele. I wasn't about to give out my aunt's phone number or the location of her farm. It was public knowledge. If he really wanted to find her, he would.

"I can tell her you were asking, though," I said. "Do you want to give me your cell number or email address?"

He winced when I said the word "cell." *Why?*

"Thank you." He relayed an email address but not a phone number. "Please tell her I am in the area and would like to speak with her at her convenience."

If he wanted to speak with her, why didn't he let me

know how she could call him? Unless he didn't have a
phone, but someone walking around without a cell was
too crazy to contemplate. I jotted down his email address on my order pad and stuck the slip in my back
pocket.

"I will," I said. "Let me go put your order in."

He clasped his hands on the table and closed his
eyes. Praying? Possibly. Or meditating. Maybe just resting his eyes. Whatever he was doing, I left him to it.

CHAPTER 4

Buck Bird drifted in ten minutes later. The cold wind must have picked up, because his cheeks were pink under a navy knit police-issue hat. I headed over to greet South Lick's chief of police.

"You haven't been in all day." I smiled up at him. Way up, since the skinny man was more than a foot taller than me. He sometimes ate two meals a day here. And they were never small ones.

"Been busy. And busy means I'm hungrier than a elephant being starved by a tapeworm."

I groaned at the latest in a long string of exaggerated descriptions of how famished he was. "That's a particularly unpleasant image, my friend."

"Sorry, hon. But can I get me a hearty lunch sometime soon?" He looked around the room. "Why, lookie there, you up and gived away my table." He gave Ivan

Sheluk a careful once-over with his gaze. Ivan didn't glance up.

"We've been through this, Buck. You never want me to put a Reserved sign on your two-top. The table is fair game, and this customer wanted to sit there."

"Looks to be a newcomer to town, am I right?" He gestured with his chin.

"Seems that way. I've never seen him before today."

Buck seemed extra interested in Ivan, but I couldn't figure out why he would be. We had lots of visitors to our scenic village, including tourists who stopped by and people from the state's flagship university in the next county who often wanted to explore our area.

"About lunch," I said. "A few other tables are open. Take your pick."

"Will do, Robbie." He switched his focus to me. "Hey, you feeling in the pink?"

"I feel great, thanks. Does a double cheeseburger, a biscuit with sausage gravy, fries, and two apple fritters sound good?" I knew his legendary appetite well.

"Just about heaven. And a cocola, if you please." Buck had grown up right here in Indiana near the Ohio River, but he loved using phrases from farther south.

"You got it."

He raised his index finger. "Happen to have any brownies on hand or them chocolate cookies?"

I wrinkled my nose. "We might have run out. Hope was supposed to bring more but she hasn't been in yet." Exhausting our dessert supply was why Turner had whipped up the apple fritters so we had at least one sweet on offer.

"Hope's the new baker lady?"

"Yes." My regular dessert guy and friend had moved away last spring. Abe's teenage son Sean, who loved cooking and baking, had filled in over the summer, but he was now back in school and living in Italy as an exchange student.

I was lucky to find Hope Morris. A local woman, she'd been an occasional customer in the restaurant for the last several years. One day last summer when she'd complimented the brownie she ordered, I mentioned my baker was leaving. Hope said she wasn't a half-bad amateur baker and was looking for additional work.

At around the same time, someone had recommended her when Sean was packing to leave for his year abroad. After a session sampling her wares, it didn't take us long to work out a satisfactory arrangement. So far she'd brought tasty brownies and cookies every other day as planned and hadn't presented any kind of problem with either quality or prompt delivery—until today.

As if summoned, Hope backed through the door carrying a covered half-sheet pan. A woman in her late fifties with auburn hair that probably came from a bottle, she always met the world with eyebrows drawn together and deep furrows between them.

"Ah. I spoke too soon," I said. "It looks like you'll have your brownie." I took his order to Danna at the grill.

"I see Buck finally got his hungry self in here." Danna flipped a turkey patty and pushed around a pile of golden onions on their way to being nicely caramelized.

My mid-twenties co-chef today embodied the season in a long rust-colored sweater, leggings patterned with yellow and orange leaves, and a green scarf tying back her reddish-gold dreadlocks. At six feet, she was hard to miss, but I liked her style. The blue store apron over it all almost spoiled the look. I still tied an apron on every morning, but it was kind of ridiculous, since the strings barely tied around me.

"You're dressed as Fall, am I right?" I asked.

"How'd you guess, boss?" She grinned. "Can you plate up those two cheeseburgers, please?"

"Sure." I glanced at the slip and added a scoop of potato salad to one plate and fries to the other, plus pickle spears for both. I hit the ready bell for Turner to deliver the order and smiled at my longtime right-hand person.

Hope reached our area and set her pan on the counter. "Sorry I'm late. Car trouble."

"It's okay." I pulled back the plastic wrap to see a double layer of rich, dark brownies that smelled better than heaven and made my mouth water. Buck would be happy.

Hope muttered something about having more in the car and hurried away. I headed to the door to hold it open for her return. She stepped through holding two big trays, one stacked on top of the other, and I let the door close behind her.

Hope's face paled as she stared into the restaurant. I twisted my head to see what she was looking at. Ivan stood at his table, an empty plate in front of him. He shrugged into his coat.

Hope swore under her breath. The desserts started to

wobble. I extended my hands in a dessert-rescue move, but she gripped the trays again.

"What's he doing here?" Her voice rasped.

"He ordered and ate lunch," I said. "Do you know him?"

"I used to. Here." She shoved the trays at me and disappeared back outside.

I glanced at Ivan. He gazed at where she'd stood. I'd never seen such a sorrowful look on a man's face.

He squared his shoulders and caught my eye, raising his hand. I set down the pans on the kitchen counter and made my way over, fishing his check out of my apron pocket.

I handed him the slip. "Did you enjoy your meal, Ivan?"

"Very much. Thank you." He handed me a twenty. "I don't need change."

"We appreciate that." The six dollar overage would go straight into the tips jar for Danna and Turner.

"Please don't forget to tell Adele I'd like to speak with her."

"I promise. Do come back." I smiled at him.

He nodded, then trudged out, his shoulders weighed down by an emotion only he knew.

CHAPTER 5

I stacked Ivan's dishes and cutlery as I considered what his past with Hope might have been. It seemed he also had history with Adele. Who in the world was this stranger?

Corrine Beedle strode in. The mother Danna got her height from, Corrine was also the current mayor of South Lick and a bigger-than-life force of nature. Not only was she over six feet tall in the heels she usually sported, she wore her hair big, loved deep red lipstick, and didn't take fools lightly. Her big heart was the frosting on the cake.

In her full mayoral garb of heels, pencil skirt, and blazer, she stood rooted in place, staring back at the door. I delivered my busing to the kitchen.

Danna looked puzzled. "What's Mom doing here? I thought she had a meeting in Indy all day."

"Maybe the meeting was canceled or ended early. It's already after two o'clock."

"I'll ask her. In the meantime, Robbie, can you take Buck his lunch?" Danna asked. "And I need a break, ASAP."

"I'll sub in at the grill." Turner straightened from adding plates and mugs to the dishwasher.

"Sounds good, thanks." I loaded up my arms and made my way to Buck's table, where Corrine had joined him. "Here's lunch, Buck."

"Thank you. I am emptier than a scraped-clean stew pot." He squirted ketchup over his fries and under the top bun of the burger.

"Corrine, do you want to order?" I asked.

"Afternoon, Robbie," she said. "I am a bit peckish, but first off I want to know who that man is, the fellow who just left."

"I only met him this morning. Do you know him from somewhere?" I asked.

"Might could be." She twisted her lips to the side. "Know what he's called?"

"He told me his name is Ivan Sheluk." I glanced around. Nobody seemed in urgent need of service, so I pulled up a chair and sat. A sigh slipped out. It felt better than good to get off my feet.

"That's him, all right." Corrine rapped the table with one exceedingly long red fingernail. "It's been a couple few years, though. Or decades, more like, and he's changed."

Buck wiped a smear of ketchup off his chin. "Where all do you know him from, Corrine?"

"Here and there. Long story." She plucked a French fry off Buck's plate and popped it into her own mouth.

"Hey, now, don't you go stealing my food," Buck protested.

"Fine." She rolled her eyes, but with a fond expression. "Robbie, can I please get me a double cheeseburger with fries and two brownies? Plus coffee."

"Absolutely. Danna said you were supposed to be out of town for the day."

"Dang statewide mayors' meeting up and got itself canceled." She reached for another of Buck's fries, but he swatted her hand away.

"What was going on with Hope Morris and the Sheluk fellow?" Buck asked.

"I have no idea," I said. "When she saw him, she reacted as if he was a ghost. I asked her if she knew him, and she said she used to. Then she left."

Corrine's expression changed. She stared at the table with hooded eyes. Her gaze shifted back and forth as if she was remembering something.

"Huh." Buck glanced at the door.

"And he got the saddest look on his face after she disappeared through the door," I added. "You seemed to be keeping a close eye on Ivan, Buck. Do you know something about him?"

"Can't say that I do. He has a look about him, though, makes me think he's been in the criminal justice system. And not on the side of the law."

An interesting observation. I didn't have any experience with prisons, if that's what Buck meant, but Ivan did have a look about him, in addition to the tattoos. He was worn, weathered but not from the weather, not as if he was a farmer or made his living outdoors. It was more like life had worn him down. But he hadn't seemed bitter. His voice was gentle, his manner kind and polite, and he hadn't acted the least bit aggressive. I could easily imagine someone of his age who'd endured years of hardship becoming hardened to empathy, unable to think of others and taking their resentment out on strangers and loved ones alike.

I stood. "I'll give Turner your order, Corrine."

"Thanks, doll." Corrine seemed to shake off her mood. She raised her palm to Buck. "Before you start asking, Bird, I'm not going to lay out the whole story about how I knew Ivan for you right now. Later sometime. Maybe."

Danna emerged from the restroom. Corrine gave her a wave.

"Hey, Mom," Danna said when she reached the table.

"I can see you're curious why I'm here, sugar," Corrine said. "They postponed the dang meeting. I was halfway there when I got the call." She wagged her head. "Waste of time and gasoline."

I made my way to the kitchen and stuck Corrine's order on the carousel, then waddled about clearing and delivering checks and wiping down tables. Thinking all the way. Corrine made the third local who'd known Ivan, none of whom seemed happy about seeing him again. Four, if you counted Adele. It was going to be an interesting week.

CHAPTER 6

By three o'clock, all customers were gone, including Buck and Corrine. The door was locked, and we'd nearly finished cleaning up. Turner scrubbed the grill while Danna vacuumed. I sat rolling silverware into blue cloth napkins, once again glad to be off my feet. I'd put on thirty-one pounds so far, which my midwife assured me was a healthy weight, but hauling around an interior bowling ball was starting to get old.

My team joined me at the table after a few minutes. Turner helped with the napkins, and Danna restocked the condiment caddies. This was often our routine, and I enjoyed the quiet time with these two longtime employees I now counted as friends.

"I was thinking we could do scones for a breakfast special tomorrow," I said. "How does pecan and cinnamon sound?"

"Like heaven," Danna said.

"Like I want one right this minute," Turner added.

"You guys ate today, yes?" I asked. They were always welcome to eat whatever they wanted.

"I always eat." Danna pointed at Turner. "And I saw this one chowing down a major veggie burger when you were at the bank."

"So I did." Turner finished the last napkin. "You're the one who needs to remember to eat, Robbie."

"Yes, Dad." I smiled at him. "But your telling me reminds me, or rather, hearing from Roberto this week gave me an idea for a lunch special." Roberto being my Italian father, whom I hadn't learned about until a year after my mother died. We were now in touch regularly and had met several times over the past four years.

"Lemme guess, something Italian?" Danna asked.

"Exactly. We have ground beef, plus chicken stock and spinach in the freezer. Let's make up an Italian wedding soup for tomorrow."

"I've had Italian wedding soup. It's delicious," Turner said. "Good idea, boss. We have orzo and white beans to go into it."

"And rosemary in the pot out back," Danna added. "But who eats soup at a wedding?"

"I looked up the name," I said. "It's called wedding soup for the marriage of greens and meat, not because it's served at wedding feasts."

"Makes sense." Turner headed to the walk-in refrigerator, which included a chest freezer. "I'll get the stock out to defrost."

Turner returned. In one hand he held the gallon container we'd frozen the stock in. The other carried the basket we used to ferry ingredients out from the cooler.

Right now it contained five pounds of ground beef, a pound of butter, and two dozen eggs.

"For breakfast prep." He laid the butter and eggs on the counter. "I'll make up the meatballs now."

"Thanks," I said.

"Robbie, what was up earlier with Hope and the dude with the tats?" Danna asked. "She totally freaked out when she saw him. She, like, almost fainted. Turn, did you see what went down between those two?"

"I did." Turner beat eggs and added them to the meat in a big bowl. "She really reacted to seeing him."

"Do you know why, Robbie?" Danna asked.

"It's a good question, but I don't know the answer. Hope apparently knew him at some time in her past. That's the only information I got out of her before she split."

"Buck was keeping an eye on him, too," Turner added. "The guy isn't from around here, is he?" He measured breadcrumbs, Italian seasonings, and ground Parmesan into the meatball mix and mixed it all with his hands.

"I don't think he is," I said. "At least not recently." I told them about meeting Ivan in the bank and his interaction with the manager. "His name is Ivan Sheluk. He was asking about Adele, too."

"Adele?" Danna asked. "Dude is like the mystery man."

"I read this awesome book about the hero's quest." Turner began rolling the mix into orbs the size of table-tennis balls. "A stranger who comes to town is a classic opening."

"We get lots of strangers in here." I gazed from him to Danna. "We feed them lunch and never see them again, right? I'm sure that's all this is. Maybe Ivan lived here a long time ago, and he happens to be passing through."

"Maybe." Danna arched an eyebrow. "I'm going to go spruce up the restrooms."

After they both were done, I shooed them out and sent them on their way home. I loved being in here alone after we closed. I always prepped the biscuit dough and pancake mix for the next day, and I usually got ahead by dicing peppers and onions for omelets and cutting melons into cubes to get ready for tomorrow. Having my hands busy let me think about life, and occasionally about murder.

The latter not being the case today, I streamed a Three Tenors concert to the speakers and let the opera wash over me and my little girl.

Abe and I had told pretty much no one we were having a daughter. Despite the gorgeous voices singing in Italian, the lyrics of a song my grandmother had sung to me came to mind. Would our girl be pretty? Would she be rich? Would she have rainbows day after day? "Whatever will be, will be. *Que será, será*," was always the answer.

All I wanted for our baby was to be healthy, and happy—with a few rainbows thrown in for joy.

CHAPTER 7

By five o'clock I was home and sitting at the dining table next to Abe with our tablet propped up in front of us for our video chat with Sean. Cocoa sat on his haunches next to Abe. By now the chocolate Labrador retriever knew that when we got set up like this, he would hear his favorite human's voice.

Abe had hurried in at the last moment. Five was early for him to leave his job at Brown County State Park, but we needed to visit with Sean before he went to bed six hours east of here. Even talking now made the hour late. Abe had kissed me before he opened a beer and slid into his seat.

After Sean came on, we went through our greetings, including yips from Cocoa. Sean told the dog how much he missed him and asked if he'd been a good boy. Cocoa barked and panted but stayed seated. The first couple of times we'd done this, he'd tried to lick the screen, although by now he seemed indifferent to the video. Abe held up Sean's black cat, Maceo, who was disdainful and paid no attention to his two-dimensional human. One hundred percent cat.

"How's my baby sister?" Sean was the only other person besides Adele and our midwife who knew we were having a girl.

"She's lively and getting enormous." I stood and gave him a profile view.

"Wow, Mombie." Sean looked stunned. "How do you even walk around like that?"

I laughed. "It's getting harder every day."

"How's the language going, Seanie?" Abe asked.

One of the many things I loved about Abe was his affection for his son. Sean had never objected to his dad still using his childhood nickname. And the boy himself had come up with the hybrid name Mombie for me, his stepmother. Abe and Sean's mom had been divorced since he was a toddler, but she'd died last year. After Abe and I married, I never asked the boy to call me Mom, but I was delighted he'd combined Mom and Robbie into a nickname for me.

"*Ottimo*," Sean said. "Which means very well. I'm still stoked I got Italy instead of Greece."

He'd been disappointed last summer when the exchange organization assigned his second choice of country, but his destination had abruptly reverted to his first choice a few weeks before he left at the end of August. We chatted for a few more minutes about his Italian, school, host family, and politics in Europe.

"The food is to die for," Sean added.

"Let me guess," I said. "Simple and fresh and hand-made."

"Exactly. The father in this family goes to the market every day."

"He does more of the cooking?" Abe asked.

"All of it. The mother is a doctor and she works long hours, and he's like a stay-at-home dad, which is pretty unusual around here. I've been picking up recipes from him." Sean covered a yawn.

"Go to bed, honey," Abe said.

"Okay," he said. "But you'll let me know the minute the labor starts, right?"

"I promise." I smiled at him.

After we all exchanged a few more words, he ended the call. I leaned my head on Abe's shoulder.

"I miss him," I murmured.

"We all do." He stroked Cocoa's head, then kissed mine. "How was your day, my sweet?"

I sat up and faced him. "It was a little odd."

"Are you sure she's okay?" His expression slid to worried, and he laid his warm, strong hand on my belly.

"Our daughter is fine. As I told Sean, the baby is moving and definitely seems to still be growing. That wasn't what I meant about the day." I filled him in on what I knew of Ivan and the various people whom he seemed to know. "Are you familiar with the name?"

"I might have heard it. Let me think about where." He threw his head back and laughed. "That baby girl just kicked me."

"She's so strong. I think she's trying to kickbox her

way out." I pushed up to standing, a maneuver entirely different from what it used to be. "Back in a flash. I'm off to empty my tablespoon-sized bladder."

"I'll get dinner started." Abe rose and kissed me.

Tuxedo cat Birdy trotted along with me down the hall, but then peeled off to bat around a plastic ball with a bell inside, one of his favorite toys.

I returned to find my man aproned up and rubbing Mexican spices into boneless chicken thighs. "Ooh, is it burrito night?"

"No. I hope fajitas are a reasonable substitute."

"Even better. Let me help."

"Not a chance. You sit and let me feast my eyes on your lovely face."

"Yes, sir." I perched on a stool at the counter between us.

"I think I remember where I heard about Ivan Sheluk." Abe seeded a green pepper and sliced it into ribbons. "He's somewhere in his sixties, yes?"

"I'd say so."

"My dad might know him, or know of him, at least."

"Should I call Howard?" I was super fond of both my in-laws. I knew Howard, father of two sons and grandfather to one, would be over the moon to soon have a grandgirl to dote on. He'd told me more than once how happy it made him I was in Abe's life. Howard thought the world—and his younger son—needed more female energy. He was going to go nuts over a granddaughter.

"Hmm," Abe began. "I think he's in Chicago visiting his brother until tomorrow. Uncle Zeke is pretty sick."

30

Maddie Day

"I'm sorry to hear that. He's the one who's a lot older than Howard."

"He is." Abe finished slivering an onion. He sniffed and wiped his eyes from the volatile oils the slicing released into the air. "Actually, do you mind making the guacamole?"

"Set me up."

A moment later he brought me a cutting board, fork, spoon, sharp knife, and all the ingredients. I set to work mashing avocado in a bowl. I added lime juice, chili powder and cumin, a little medium-heat salsa, a few drops of hot sauce, and salt and pepper. Guac was so easy to make, I didn't understand why anybody ever bought it ready to eat.

But then, I was a mid-coast Californian. I'd grown up in a place where people with avocado trees in their backyards sometimes let the fruit rot on the ground because they couldn't find enough people to take their harvest. The delicious green topping was probably the first thing my mom had trusted me to make in our Santa Barbara kitchen.

This South Lick kitchen was now redolent with the smells and sounds of onions and peppers frying. Abe wrapped a half dozen flour tortillas in a damp dishtowel and set them in the microwave. I sampled the dip.

"Taste test?" I held out a forkful of the guac.

"Mmm." He savored it on his tongue. "A smidge more salt, I think. And a few more drops of lime juice?"

I nodded my agreement as I corrected the seasonings. "I'm a little bothered by Ivan's connection to

Adele. Before he showed up at Pans 'N Pancakes, she and Freddy ate an early lunch together."

"I love that Mom and Adele have become such good friends." He smiled.

"I do, too. They didn't come in together but your mom appeared right after Adele. Anyway, my aunt seemed worried about something. You know how she's always so even-keeled and cheery?"

He nodded, scooping the vegetables onto a plate. He turned up the heat and added a bit more oil to the cast-iron skillet.

"Well, she wasn't today," I said. "And she wouldn't tell me what was going on."

"She will, honey. Maybe her knee was bothering her." He carefully laid the chicken in the skillet.

Maybe it was her knee. But Ivan had asked about Adele. *Shoot.* I'd forgotten to let her know. I would give her a call after dinner.

Given the interaction I'd witnessed between him and Kingsley, plus Hope's reaction and whatever past with Ivan Corrine didn't want to talk about, I had to wonder how Adele knew the stranger. I hoped nothing bad would happen. Nobody in South Lick needed something bad to go down, me included.

CHAPTER 8

Last month, Turner had started taking my early-morning shifts. He now opened the restaurant at seven o'clock with Danna, which gave me leeway to start my workday at eight. I had gentle prenatal stretches and exercises to do every morning, and this allowed me time not to rush through them.

Those two figured out between them who would get there at five thirty to start the coffee and the biscuits and do all the other things, and who didn't have to come in until six thirty.

Still, I tried to arrive early for my shift. When I pulled open the door at seven forty-five today, the place was hopping and smelled like scone heaven. I quickly washed my hands and tied an apron over my bulk.

"It's a good thing you made up extra scones," Danna said from the grill. "They're going fast."

I had made a lot yesterday, including a few dozen I'd popped into the freezer.

"Glad you're here, Robbie." Turner hurried up, his arms already full of bused dishes from the earliest customers. "Can you take over coffee and orders, please?"

"You bet." I picked up the carafes and headed out. I'd just emptied them when I passed our biggest table, which Adele's boyfriend, Samuel MacDonald, always reserved for his Wednesday morning men's prayer group.

I had called Adele last evening to see if I could find out what was bothering her, but she hadn't answered her landline, which I knew she preferred speaking on. She didn't reply to my text, either. I might be able to squeeze in a visit to her after the restaurant closed.

At the big table, a half dozen men were already seated. Three had Bibles open, one read on his phone, and two sat with hands folded and heads bowed. Samuel wasn't among them, though. Well, it wasn't quite eight o'clock yet, and the Faithful Fellows, as I thought of them, usually didn't order until they were all present.

"All set with coffee?" I kept my voice soft so I didn't disturb the ones praying.

"We're good, thank you, Robbie," the youngest in the group said. A good-looking Black man about my age and a newer participant in the group, he had a big smile and a possible resemblance to Samuel. I'd never met any of my former baker Phil's siblings, but I wondered if this was a brother or a cousin, making him another of Samuel's grandsons.

I moved on, pouring and taking requests for eggs in all forms, pancakes, biscuits with or without gravy, hash browns, and today's scones. We also always offered oatmeal, fruit, and all the breakfast meats: sausage, bacon, and ham, plus turkey bacon and chicken links. I'd also sourced a remarkably tasty non-meat sausage for our vegetarian diners.

Danna was still on grill duty as I added several order slips to the carousel.

She used a low voice. "I asked Mom last night about that Ivan dude."

My heart quickened. "And? What did she say?"

"Zip. Said she didn't want to talk about how she knew him."

"Too bad."

"Yeah. But later I saw her pick up and stare at that small photograph of Marcus's dad she keeps in a frame in her bedroom." Marcus was Danna's older half-brother, a baby whose Black jazz-musician father Corrine had fallen in love with before she was twenty. But he'd died in an accident before Marcus was born, and she'd given up the newborn boy for adoption.

"You're thinking she knew Ivan Sheluk through Marcus's birth father?" I asked.

"It was a thought. Ow!" She jumped back as a sausage popped. "I'm okay, but I need to focus here. I shouldn't have brought it up."

"Is your hand all right? You can swap out with Turner any time."

"It'll be fine." She brought the back of her left hand to her mouth for a moment. "I'm good."

I busied myself making two fresh pots of regular coffee and one of decaf as I thought.

A couple of years ago Marcus had tracked down Corrine and Danna and had shown up at the restaurant one day. He and Corrine had blessedly had a happy reunion, engineered by Danna. She, an only child whose father was also deceased, had been ecstatic to acquire a sibling, and a big brother at that. Marcus lived in Bloomington in the next county, and he and Danna hung out from time to time.

Maybe Ivan was a musician, or had been in the past, and that was how Corrine knew him. If he came in again today, I'd figure out a way to ask.

I was about to cycle back to the Faithful Fellows—a name I thought sounded better than the Pious Parishioners or the Godly Guys—at a few minutes after eight. On my way, I glanced up when the bell jangled. Samuel let the door shut behind him, but he didn't hang up his coat and proceed to the group. He caught my eye and beckoned for me to join him. I set down the coffee carafe and hurried in his direction.

Adele's beau was nearly eighty-five, and his face bore the lines to prove it. Right now the furrows on his brow were extra deep. One leg jittered, and he jammed his hands into his pockets as if to calm them.

"Samuel, what's the matter?" I asked. "Is Adele all right?"

"She's not ill or hurt, if that's what you mean."

My shoulders slumped with relief.

"But, Roberta, I have awful news." He swallowed. "I found a man dead in her pasture this morning. Stone cold dead."

CHAPTER 9

I gaped at Samuel and his news. "You found a man's body in the sheep field?"

"I did." He shook his head. "I went outside because Sloopy was barking up a storm early this morning, after I'd opened his doggie door. Why, it wasn't even light yet. The dog was barking at the electric fence, the one that keeps the rams apart from the other sheep."

I nodded. I knew the ram pasture well. Adele usually had only one or two rams, and they had to be kept separate from the ewes and their lambs. She had a nifty lightweight woven fence system that could be electrified and repositioned where she needed it.

"I took myself over there," he went on. "I'd thought to grab a flashlight in the house, and I shone it around here and there until I saw a shape on the ground. I approached, and that's when I realized the shape was a man. One doesn't expect to encounter a body in the rams' pasture. I called to the fellow but he didn't respond."

"What did you do?" I asked.

"I went to the barn to turn off the electricity to the fence, except I found the power hadn't been on. Then I notified Adele. I needed her to help me move the enclosure so the poor gentleman would be outside of it instead of in."

"The sun doesn't come up until seven thirty. What time was this?"

"Six thirty, I do believe. I'm always up well before the birds at this time of year, having my tea and doing my devotional reading. In any event, we moved the fence. I knelt at the man's side but he was colder than cold. Clearly deceased, with his soul released to God's loving arms. I used my cellular telephone to call the authorities."

"Good."

"I'll tell you, Robbie, it was odder than Dick's hatband." Samuel rubbed his forehead.

I blinked. I'd never heard that expression before. Despite not knowing Dick or what his hatband looked like, it wasn't hard to understand the meaning.

"What was odd?" I asked.

"Why, Adele appeared to know who the fellow was, and she became stricken with a strong emotion. I couldn't make out whether it was grief or anger. Perhaps both."

Uh-oh. "Tell me more about what the man looked like. Age, distinguishing features, hair?"

"Let me think. A white man, probably over sixty years of age. Short cropped dark hair with a fair few white hairs mixed in. Rather tall, although most men are taller than I in recent years. I'm afraid I have been reduced to a height of barely five foot six these days."

"You're super observant, Samuel." So far he'd described Ivan Sheluk—a man who'd been asking about my aunt.

"I think it's important to be aware of the smallest details around us." He held up his index finger. "I believe I spotted a tattoo on the back of his neck as he lay there."

The body was Ivan's, all right, and Adele had recognized him. I exhaled.

"What about a wound?" I asked. "Could you see how he died?"

"Sadly, no. Nothing was obvious. I knew not to touch him beyond ascertaining that he had passed away."

"You said you called the police."

"Yes, dear. When I left the house, Chief Bird himself was questioning my beloved, with a separate team out in the field doing whatever they needed to do."

The youngest Bible dude approached us. "Is everything all right, Brother Samuel?"

Maybe he wasn't Samuel's relative.

"I'll be right with you, Brother Justin." To me, Samuel murmured, "If you can find a way to get out to the farm, Adele will need your comfort."

"It's going to be hard to get away, but I'll see what I can do."

Samuel followed Justin to the group table. I turned away. At the desk in the nook, I pulled out my phone. Adele didn't answer either the house phone or her cell. I texted, asking her to please call me. I mentioned Samuel had given me the news.

Was there any way I could get away from here?

SCONE COLD DEAD 39

Zipping out to the farm during our mid-morning lull was the only possibility, but I wouldn't be able to stay long. Today was Wednesday. I was pretty sure my part-timer Len, an Indiana University undergrad, was tied up in classes all day. This place ran a lot better with three of us on the job instead of only two.

With Samuel's earth-shattering news, I'd shut out the ambient noise of the restaurant. Now it all returned, with a vengeance. The ready bell dinged. Cutlery clattered. Bacon fat spattered. Laughter, voices, and calls of "Excuse me, miss?" intruded on my consciousness as Baby Girl O'Neill-Jordan kicked me in the ribs.

Back to work I went. I jotted and poured, smiled and nodded, delivered and cleared. I checked my phone every ten minutes, but Adele hadn't called back. Danna was making final adjustments to the soup.

"Want to taste test, Robbie?" Danna pointed at the soup pot.

I ladled a little soup into a small bowl and used a spoon to taste it. "Mmm. This is great. What do you think? A touch more rosemary and maybe a few grinds of black pepper?"

"Agree." She slid over to the grill.

I added pepper and the chopped herb to the soup, then savored a bite of a scone. Crunchy chopped pecans went perfectly with the buttery pastry, and the cinnamon inside and coarse sugar on top were the crowning touch.

"I guess we hit it out of the park with these," I said.

"You bet. A recipe worth repeating."

Nine o'clock came and went. The Faithful had eaten, prayed, and discussed the scripture of the week.

Samuel and Justin remained at the table with one other man, deep in conversation.

I made another round with the coffee carafe, but all three men declined. Samuel gave me an inquisitive look.

"She isn't returning my call or text," I told him.

He rubbed his thigh. "I would offer to relieve you in your duties here, but my gimpy hip is acting up. And I'm off to my shift as a greeter at the senior center soon."

"I'll go see her as soon as we close, I promise," I said.

Justin gazed up at me. "I understand my friend's beloved companion is in need of comfort. I have quite a lot of experience in the restaurant trade, Ms. Jordan, and my morning is otherwise unoccupied. Might I volunteer my services for a few hours, if not the rest of the day, so you can pay Sister Adele a call?"

Where did this guy my age learn to talk like someone from the past? Still, it was a kind offer. I thought about it for about three and a half seconds.

"Justin, are you sure?" I asked. "It can get pretty crazy around here."

"I can do crazy." He had the biggest, sunbeam-flashing smile I'd seen in a long time.

"Well, thank you. It's a lovely offer, and I'll take you up on it. When you're ready, I'll introduce you to Danna and Turner, and then I'll head out. I shouldn't be more than two hours."

"I'm happy to help, Ms. Jordan."

I smiled. "Please call me Robbie."

CHAPTER 10

On the rural road leading out to Adele's farm, I passed an ambulance heading in the other direction. A quiet, dark ambulance sadly going the speed limit as it carried the corpse.

I parked at the foot of Adele's long drive, now clogged with several police cruisers and official SUVs. On my way to the cottage, I skirted the Brown County Sheriff's team working at the fence line.

This man's death had been unattended, with his body found outdoors. I knew by now that the authorities had to investigate it. He might have died of a heart attack or another natural cause. But the end of his life could have been a homicide at the hands of someone malicious.

The day was chilly, and I snugged my big scarf tighter around my neck as I watched the team. On the other side of the fence, Aries III, the current ram, munched what grass he could find. He only occasionally lifted his impressive set of curled horns to focus his wide rectangular pupils on the humans as they worked.

I made my way into Adele's kitchen. She sat at her beloved kitchen table, the place where everything happened. Today, however, she wasn't sipping tea, kneading bread, or carding wool. A petite woman in her fifties sat across from my aunt. A pair of turquoise reading glasses perched atop her ear-length head of full, wavy hair with striking streaks of silver through the dark strands.

"Good morning." I kissed Adele's temple and squeezed her shoulder, then sat next to her.

"This here's a state police detective," Adele muttered, nodding her chin at the woman.

"Detective Sergeant Juanita McWilliam, ma'am." She extended a hand across the table.

I shook it. "Robbie Jordan. I'm Adele's niece."

"Ma'am."

The time was now after ten o'clock, and Samuel had said he'd found Ivan's body at six thirty. How long had McWilliam been questioning Adele, if questioning was what she was doing?

"How'd you get free of the store, hon?" Adele asked me. Her slate-gray pageboy hung listless and looked whiter than the last time I'd seen her. Her face bore more lines, too. "You should be at work, not out here looking after me."

"A young friend of Samuel's offered to sub in for me for a couple of hours. I took him up on it."

"Brother Justin?" Adele smiled, but it was a wan one. "Isn't he just the sweetest piece of pie around?"

The detective cleared her throat. "Your aunt and I are just finishing up."

Good. She seemed polite enough, but I didn't want to spend any more time than necessary with a homicide detective under any conditions.

"While you're here, may I ask if you happened to know someone named Ivan Sheluk?" McWilliam asked me.

"Is he the deceased?" I asked.

The detective nodded.

"He is," Adele whispered.

"I met him yesterday for the first time," I said. "We exchanged pleasantries in the South Lick First Savings Bank in the morning." Had I just uttered the words "exchanged pleasantries?" Now who sounded like someone from the olden days? "And he ate lunch in my restaurant in the early afternoon."

"What is your restaurant?"

"I own Pans 'N Pancakes on Main Street in South Lick, nearly downtown."

Adele twisted her head to look at me. "Ivan came in after I left?"

"Yes," I said. "He asked about you. Didn't I text you about that?" I hoped I had. I'd meant to, but foggy pregnancy brain was a real thing. I thought back. Yes, I'd texted her after dinner last night, in between yawns, when she didn't answer her phone.

"You did, hon, last evening. I was out at my book group, and I didn't see your message until late." Adele rubbed her brow. "And now it's too late."

McWilliam had been following our back-and-forth. "Ms. Jordan, I will ask you one more time. How did you know Ivan Sheluk?" Her dark brown eyes stared at Adele.

Adele shifted her gaze to me, then stared at the table. "It doesn't matter. It was a long time ago."

"And you have no idea why he was looking for you?" the detective asked.

Adele slowly traced a shape with her index finger on the table but kept silent.

McWilliam stood. She laid her business card in front of Adele. "Please don't hesitate to call when you are ready to share that information. Good day to both of you."

Adele didn't lift her head.

"I'll walk you out." I stood and followed the detective down the back steps and away from the house a few yards.

She stopped and faced me. "Do you know what she's refusing to tell me?"

"How Adele knew Ivan? No. She's never mentioned him to me. I'll let you know if she does." *When* she did, if I had anything to do about it, although I would tread lightly and as gently as I could. "What can you tell me about how he died?"

"Blunt trauma seems to have been involved, but it could have been accompanied by natural causes."

I shuddered at the first two words, but I forged on. "What kind of blunt trauma?"

She gave me that look law enforcement officers are so good at, the one that means No Way Am I Telling You.

"You have a good day, Ms. Jordan," the detective said. "I hope you can convince your aunt to share any and all contact she had with the victim, both recently and in the past." She turned away and headed for the crime scene team, pulling out her phone as she strode.

I heard barking from the barn. Samuel or Adele must have shut Sloopy in there so the border collie wouldn't try to run around herding the police officers or worse, sniff around the body.

What kind of blunt trauma would Ivan have gotten in a sheep pasture, and who delivered it? I hoped it hadn't been Aries III, although rams were known to be bullies. Possibly more important, why had Ivan come to the farm in the night? How had he arrived at the property? I didn't see any unexplained vehicles parked nearby. The stickiest question was, what prompted him to venture inside the fence?

I trudged back to the house with yet another question. I wondered if McWilliam had noticed Adele tracing the shape of a heart on the table.

CHAPTER 11

When I arrived back in Adele's kitchen, a mixing bowl and a two-cup glass measuring cup sat on the table. She turned toward me from the shelf where she kept her gallon jars of flour.

"There you are," she muttered.

"Here I am. Are you planning to do some baking?"

"Why, yes." She set the jar of white flour down on the table with a thud. "Got a problem with that?"

I blinked. Who was this cranky woman, and where was my loving, sweet aunt? I shook my head.

"A person has to eat, you know." She hauled a dozen eggs and a half gallon of milk out of the refrigerator.

I feared for the eggs when she slammed the carton on the table. For Adele, as for me, baking was normally a comfort. Creating delicious, warm, homemade biscuits or bread, pies or pastries, cakes or cookies for oneself and others was also a way to let hands and mind be busy at the same time. It didn't seem right now as if the process was comforting her at all.

I sidled over to her and gently laid my arm on her shoulders. "Adele, you don't have to bake. Let me make you breakfast." I spotted a half loaf of home-made bread on the sideboard, and the eggs were al-ready out.

"But I . . ." Her voice trailed off.

"But nothing. Please sit down. Let me take care of you."

She sagged, as if deflated. I guided her onto the chair. Her aging white cat Chloe trotted up and sat next to Adele, purring like there was no tomorrow.

Adele leaned down to stroke the cat's head but gave her head a sad shake. "I should be taking care of you, Roberta. Feeding that grandniece of mine. Making up something to take to those police people out there."

"The only 'should' right now is to take care of your-self, Adele." I put away the flour, large bowl, and mea-suring cup, and lit the burner under the tea kettle. "You had a terrible shock earlier. How does eggs and toast and tea sound?"

She nodded. "Good. But only if you eat with me."

"It's a deal."

Ten minutes later we sat with full plates of the promised breakfast, including a thick slice each of fried ham and Adele's homemade raspberry jam on the toasted bread. We feasted in silence for a few minutes. I was afraid she wouldn't have an appetite, but she tucked into the food as if she'd skipped breakfast. I was sure she had. I hadn't missed a meal earlier, but I fell to this one like a woman who was growing an ever-larger child inside her.

While I ate, I tried to figure out how to ask her about Ivan. As it turned out, I didn't have to.

"You said Ivan was asking about me," she began, tentative and no longer cranky. "How did he seem?"

I swallowed my last bite of scrambled eggs with cheese. "My overall impression was that he'd had a hard life. But he seemed gentle. Kind and soft-spoken, including in the bank earlier in the day."

"What happened there?" She forked in a bite of ham.

"He was speaking with the manager. It appeared Ivan had asked Carter Kingsley to do something he didn't want to. Ivan stayed calm and then left at the same time as I did."

"Mmm." Adele took a bite of toast. "I'm not surprised."

"His death has shaken you. I mean, beyond just finding a random person's body on your land."

Her eyes filled.

"Will you tell me about him?" I kept my voice soft.

"Maybe." She stood up. "Except not now. With an afterclap like that, I need to have me a lie-down, hon, and that's a fact. I feel like a boiled owl."

"I don't know about a boiled owl, but you do look tired." I rose. "I'll clean up."

"Thanks. Lock the door behind you when you leave, please." Stooped, Adele trudged out of the room.

I picked up my mug of apple-spice tea. Cradling it

in my hands, I moved to the window overlooking the
ram's pasture. The team continued their work, although
the detective seemed to have left.

My heart broke for Adele. Judging from her reaction to the death, she and Ivan must have been close, or
possibly lovers, although she'd never spoken of him to
me. I had to think she was feeling worse at having
missed seeing him by only a day or perhaps hours. I
knew Ivan's body was gone, but I imagined him lying
on the cold ground, wounded, unable to move.

My breath rushed in. Samuel had said someone had
turned off the electric fence. Adele never would have.
She always kept it on at night, both to make sure her
livestock didn't go wandering and to prevent predators
like coyotes or foxes from getting in and attacking the
sheep. She didn't usually keep the barn locked against
two-legged intruders, though. Someone, whether Ivan
or another person, made sure the fence was breachable
and wouldn't deliver a shock.

I drained my tea and headed back to the promised
breakfast cleanup. I didn't have time to think about rams
and fences, villains and victims. Right now I needed to
return to my job and relieve my generous volunteer.

Samuel said he'd be home by two o'clock, which
was good. I didn't think Adele should be alone for too
long.

CHAPTER 12

The restaurant was full to overflowing by the time I got back at a little before noon. A dozen diners milled around near the door, every one of them looking hungry. A loud crash of plates falling and breaking didn't help.

I shed my coat in the little office area and hurried to wash my hands.

Turner was working the grill. "That one was a mixed bag," he muttered. He made a subtle gesture toward where Justin knelt in front of a pile of broken plates, gingerly lifting shards onto the tray he'd dropped.

"Sorry about that." I tied an apron loosely around me.

"Not your fault he was clueless as well as clumsy." Turner flipped three meat patties. "We're glad you're back, though."

Danna shot a look my way, then handed the broom and dustpan to Justin.

"I am too," I said. "How's the soup moving?"

Danna approached. "Popular and holding up. I extended it with more stock, the last of the meatballs, and more beans a few minutes ago."

"Thanks." I gazed around the room. "Should I resume doing orders and coffee?"

"That'd be great," Danna said. "And gently dismiss our volunteer dweeb, would you?"

I laughed. "I'm sure he meant well." But Turner describing Justin as clueless and clumsy made me wonder what our helper's extensive experience in the restaurant business had actually been. I slid an order pad and pen into my apron pocket and headed toward Justin.

He glanced up. "I'm so sorry, Robbie. I'll have this cleaned up in a flash."

"Thanks, and I do appreciate you helping out. But I'm back now, so your shift is up. Please stay and have lunch on the house, if you'd like."

His gaze flickered over to Danna and Turner for a second. Justin swept the last of the broken dishes into the dustpan and straightened.

"I need to get going, but thank you."

"The offer stands for another day." I scribbled *One Free Meal* on an order slip and signed it. "Here. Use this in case I'm not here."

"Thank you, Sister." He gave me a chagrined smile.

"Hey, none of that Sister stuff. You make me sound like a nun. I'm just Robbie, okay?"

"Got it." He made his way to the tall waste can. After he quickly shed his apron, he headed for the door. I didn't miss the look of relief Danna gave Turner.

I busied myself with taking payments and organizing dirty dishes into piles to be bused. I jotted down orders, delivered them, and brewed more coffee.

After about an hour, all the waiting diners had been seated and served. Several tables were empty and clean, ready for more hungry customers. A fifty-something man in a sweater and jeans came in and glanced around.

"Welcome to Pans 'N Pancakes," I said. "One for lunch?"

"Lunch, yes, and I might be just one. I'm supposed to be meeting someone but he's not here yet."

I took another look. This guy was Carter Kingsley. Out of the context of the bank and his manager's blazer, I hadn't recognized him. I didn't think he'd been in to eat before. Maybe he was new to town or lived a distance away from his workplace. It was a bit odd he was in casual clothes on a Thursday, but perhaps he had a weekday off because he worked Saturdays.

"That's fine, Mr. Kingsley. Please follow me."

"Wait a second, miss." He frowned. "How do you know my name?"

That was an odd question. "I use your bank. I'm Robbie Jordan, and this is my business." I hadn't had many dealings with him, and he was one of maybe four managers at the bank, but his was a public-facing job. He shouldn't be surprised I knew who he was.

"Ah, yes, yes. Nice to meet you, Ms. Jordan, and the bank is happy for your trust." He looked around again. "Has a man a little older than I been in at all? Short grizzled hair, a few tattoos?"

Uh-oh. "Not today, no." Despite my being away for

a couple of hours, I was quite sure the person he expected to meet had not come through our door.

Kingsley shrugged. "I'd still like to get something to eat."

"You can have the empty two-top near the big table, if you'd like." I didn't need to escort him over there. It was the only open table in that area.

"Thank you."

"Would you like coffee?"

"Please." He pointed himself toward the table.

I turned when the door opened again and smiled to see Buck amble in. He greeted me, but it wasn't with his usual warm expression.

"'Spose you heard about the goings-on over to your aunt's farm," he murmured as his gaze roamed over the diners.

"I did. Samuel was in for breakfast and told me."

"It's a sad state of affairs, Robbie, and that's a fact."

"I went out there a little while ago to see if I could help Adele," I said. "Juanita McWilliam was still grilling her."

"Did she have any luck?"

"Adele refused to tell McWilliam how she knew Ivan." I shook my head. "She wouldn't respond to my questions about him, either, and then she insisted she had to go lie down."

"Huh. How'd you know the victim's name?"

"He was in for lunch yesterday. You saw him, and this morning McWilliam asked if I knew him."

"It's an odd thing, Robbie. A stranger comes to town. Somebody who seems to have a past with at least one local. And then he ends up dead the very next day."

"Odd and tragic. I don't suppose you know any more about how he died?" I turned away from the customers and spoke as softly as I could. "The detective said something about both blunt trauma and natural causes."

"Now, hon." Buck lowered his chin to gaze down at me. "You know it's too early for them kind of questions."

"Sorry. I do know, but it was worth a try. Listen, I need to get back to work. I will tell you that yesterday morning I overheard Carter Kingsley having a disagreement with Ivan in the bank."

"Is that so? The bank manager."

I nodded.

"Well, butter my biscuit." Buck gestured with his chin. "The man's setting right over there with an empty chair opposite."

"He might have arranged to have lunch with Ivan," I said. "He was asking if a man fitting that description had been in."

"I know old Carter from my strolls around town. I think I'll mosey me over there and see if he wants my company. You and me both know his date ain't never going to show up. Death is nothing if it ain't finacious."

"Whatever that means. Yes, Ivan won't be joining Carter, although I didn't tell him so, and I don't think Carter was faking not knowing about the death."

"Gotcha." Buck shrugged out of his jacket.

"I'll be right over to take your orders."

I never encouraged Buck to question people over a

meal in my restaurant. In this case, clearing Adele's name was more important than anything.

After I grabbed a full coffee carafe, I made my way to their table. More than one diner tried to get my attention as I went, but I said I'd be right with them. Serving a roomful was tricky. If I stopped to help each person asking for my time, the coffee I'd promised Kingsley would be cold by the time I got there. I'd already spent too much time talking with Buck.

"Do you know what you'd like to order, gentlemen?" I asked once their mugs were full.

"The special soup and a grilled cheese and ham on rye for me, please," the bank manager said.

"Now, Robbie, you know me." Buck grinned. "Hit me with the works, chef's choice."

"Will do," I said.

He looked at the specials board. "But none of that there soup. I'm happily married to a fine American woman, and I intend to keep it that way."

"Got it." I suppressed a giggle. He was, in fact, married to a fine person I'd finally met last spring. Melia Bird was a pediatrician, and Abe and I had agreed we couldn't think of anyone we'd want to look after our baby's health more than her.

"Carter, you know our Robbie here?" Buck asked.

"Not exactly, but Ms. Jordan does her banking with us."

"Get over that Ms. nonsense," Buck said. "In these parts we're all friends, am I right, Robbie?"

I nodded.

"Please do call me Carter, Ms. . . . I mean, Robbie."

The manager shifted in his chair and looked uncomfortable.

Whether his discomfort was from Buck's insistence on first names or the fact of Buck's presence at all, I couldn't tell.

"Thank you." I turned away. Behind me Buck was saying it was too bad Carter had been stood up by his lunch date. I inwardly cringed.

I moved on. Yes, I wanted to clear Adele of suspicion, but nobody wanted a roomful of unhappy customers. I had a business to run.

CHAPTER 13

Alone in the store at four o'clock, I cut butter into the dry mix for the next day's biscuits. Bless her heart, Danna had stayed after cleanup was finished until our food order for the next few days had arrived. Our delivery person was excellent, but her duties didn't extend to schlepping boxes and bags into the walk-in. By now, hoisting anything heavy was a challenge for me. It also went against my midwife's advice.

Speaking of midwives, I needed to get this breakfast prep done in short order. Risa Ferguson, our fabulous midwife, was meeting us for a home visit at five. We weren't planning a home birth, but she said it was better to be ready for one, given that the hospital was forty-five minutes away under the best of driving conditions.

I placed a call to Adele after my crew left, but I was disappointed when neither she nor Samuel picked up. I wished they had. I measured milk for the biscuits and stirred it into the other ingredients with a fork. I was grateful Buck's conversation with Carter Kingsley hadn't turned confrontational. Buck had always had a breezy, *Aw Shucks* manner. Underneath it lay a steely resolve to uncover the truth and see justice done for his beloved community.

As I floured the counter and turned out the ragged dough, I thought about Hope. I scraped the bowl clean and began to gently knead it into cohesion. I needed to contact Hope and see what I could find out about how she knew Ivan. I'd never spoken with her about her past.

I couldn't remember who had recommended Hope last summer. I frowned as I divided the mass of dough into four large lumps. My memory was usually better than this. All the pregnancy hormones circulating in me were doing a number on my brain, but I'd better get used to it. Breastfeeding hormones were supposed to have the same effect.

After I'd shaped the four lumps into smooth disks, I wrapped each in plastic wrap to store in the walk-in overnight. We would roll out, cut, and bake the biscuits in the morning.

My phone rang at the same time as I heard a knock on the front door. I dusted off my hands and checked the phone, then groaned to see Juanita McWilliam's name. When I glanced at the glass part of the door, she waved from the other side. I supposed I had to let her in. I didn't mind thinking about murder as I worked, but I didn't want to have a conversation about it at this particular moment.

"The restaurant is closed, Detective," I said after I opened the door.

"Yes, and I don't want food. What I'd like is a few minutes of your time. Is that possible?"

"Come in. It'll have to be while I do prep for tomorrow." I checked the clock. "I need to be cleaned up and out of here in twenty minutes."

"This shouldn't take long. You'll be able to leave when you need to."

"All right." I locked the door after her. "Have a seat. I'll be right back." I grabbed the disks and stashed them in the cooler.

"Can I help at all?" As she had this morning, McWilliam wore detective garb of dark blazer, black pants, and sensible black leather tennies. Under the jacket she wore a deep-rose turtleneck that made her skin glow.

"Thanks, but I have my routine." November being the middle of fall, we were going to offer apple cider muffins at breakfast tomorrow. I measured out the flour, sugar, cinnamon, and other dry ingredients and stirred them together.

The detective sat. "Did you happen to learn any more from your aunt about how she knew the deceased?"

"No. I tried to call her a little while ago, but she didn't pick up." I shifted the dry mix into a big container I had prelabeled. I glanced over at her as I cracked eggs, then measured local cider and oil into the same mixing bowl and set the mixer beating.

"What else do you know, ma'am? You mentioned to your aunt that Sheluk had lunch here yesterday. Did you see him interact adversely with anyone?"

I swallowed. I didn't want to throw Corrine under

the bus, or Hope, either, but I might have to. Carter, I didn't mind, especially since Buck had already gotten involved.

"It wasn't at lunch, but when I first saw Ivan in the bank yesterday morning, he was having words with Carter Kingsley, the manager."

"Do you mean a disagreement? Raised voices and fists, or a polite difference of opinions?"

"Ivan wasn't upset, but Carter was, although not with fists," I said.

"What do you mean?" McWilliam asked.

"His shoulders were tense. He was glaring at Ivan and shaking his head."

"I see. Could you hear what they were saying?"

"Only a little at the end of their conversation. Ivan said something like, 'I think it's something you should do,' but Carter told him he wasn't going to."

"Interesting," she said.

"Then Carter came in for lunch today. The odd thing is, I think he expected to meet Ivan." I told her about telling Buck, and that he'd eaten with Carter. "Buck left before I could find out if he'd learned anything."

"I'll check with Bird. What else?"

I exhaled. "A person named Hope Morris bakes desserts for me. She brought several pans in yesterday. When she caught sight of Ivan, she went pale and rushed out."

"Did he see her?"

"I think he did." I switched off the mixer and snapped a cover onto the bowl. Tomorrow morning we would grate apples to add at the last minute after combining the dry and wet ingredients, so the fruit didn't brown before we baked the muffins. "He looked really sad as she left."

"I'm going to need the baker's contact information."

"Okay." I swallowed. "And, uh, our South Lick mayor might have known Ivan. She saw him as she was coming in."

"Corrine Beedle?"

"Yes. I didn't get the impression she'd interacted with Ivan yesterday, but maybe she can tell you something about his past. She did react negatively to seeing him, but she wouldn't tell me how or when she'd known him."

"I've had dealings with her. I'll pay her a visit." McWilliam laid a business card on the table and stood. "Thank you, Ms. Jordan. I'll let you get on with your day."

"You can call me Robbie. Save the Ms. Jordan bit for Adele."

"Very well." She smiled and pointed at my pod, my ever-larger bun in the oven. "Everything good with that one?"

"As far as I know." I smiled back. "I'm off to see the midwife the minute I leave here."

"Good. I have three of my own, but by now they're in high school. The girl is secretive and the boys are noisy and smelly, and I love them anyway. Don't blink. It'll happen to you before you know it."

I laughed. "I'm sure it will."

"I'll let myself out. My contact info is on my card there. Do keep in touch with whatever you learn."

"I promise."

I doubted I would have anything to get back to her about, but you never knew. At least she seemed like a human being, although I noticed she hadn't reciprocated my offer to use first names.

CHAPTER 14

I showed Risa around the house. We paused in Abe's and my bedroom, where I flipped on the light switch, as night was already falling outside.

"Abe will be here as soon as he can," I said. "He got hung up in a meeting."

"It's okay, Robbie. I've met him before, and I know he'll be there for you during your labor." Possibly over sixty, the midwife had a stocky build and looked physically strong. She was good at her job and had a cheery, caring manner. She wore maroon scrubs and a fleece zip-up emblazoned with the midwifery practice logo, Full Circle Midwifery, which showed two hands cradling a newborn inside a circle.

Birdy jumped up on the bed.

"No, you don't, kitty." I scooped him up. "This is Birdy," I told Risa. "He's not allowed in here at all. None of the pets are."

"Good. If need be, this is likely where you'll give birth. The cleaner the room, the better."

"Wait. What? I am not delivering this kid at home, Risa." *No way.*

"It would only be in case of emergency," she said.

We made our way into the hall. I set down the cat and shut the door.

"Isn't it dangerous to have a baby outside of the hospital?" I asked.

"Not necessarily. Come and sit in your most comfortable chair, and I'll check you and the little one."

I sat and pulled up my shirt. Risa used both hands to palpate the baby's position.

"The head is nicely down." She rubbed the disk of the stethoscope to warm it, then checked the bun's heart. "Want to listen?"

"I'd love to."

She handed me the stethoscope ends to put in my ears, while holding the disk on the taut skin of my belly.

My eyes widened. "It sounds like she's racing around a track."

"Babies have fast heart rates, for sure. She sounds great." Risa took back the stethoscope and fastened a blood pressure cuff around my arm.

My blood pressure had apparently recovered from thinking about giving birth at home, because she said it was fine.

"Now, about the home business," she began. "As I had mentioned, under most circumstances you'll have plenty of time to get to the hospital. But imagine a lightning storm, a tornado, or a baby who's in a big hurry to get out. The end of November should be too early for snow or ice, but you never know. I merely want you and Abe to give a bit of thought about preparations."

"Like what kind of preparations?" Not prepping biscuit dough, for sure.

"I recommend you pick up a rubber sheet. If it comes to that, we'll put it over your regular fitted sheet, then add an old sheet on top of it."

I swallowed. She meant things might get messy. "Okay."

"Have a few old towels around or pick up a half dozen cheap ones and wash them. I saw in the baby's room you already have a sturdy bassinet in the works."

"We do. Abe is almost finished making it," I said.

"And you've acquired little suits, blankets, and diapers, which is great. Make sure you also have a couple of outfits in a larger size than newborn. I've delivered big babies who never wear newborn sizes."

I gaped. "Larger than newborn?"

She laughed. "Robbie, there are infants who are born longer and heavier than others, and some who are tiny creatures. Judging from your recent measurements, this little girl won't need anything smaller than what you already have."

"But if I'm at home, what if I can't stand the pain?" I cringed at the thought. "If I'm not in the hospital—"

Abe hurried in. "I'm sorry I'm late. Hello, Risa."

"Abe." Risa smiled at him. "We were just finishing up. Baby and mom both look fine."

"Did I hear you say something about not being in the hospital, Robbie?" He kissed me and perched on the arm of the upholstered chair where I sat.

"She's going to do well no matter where she gives birth," Risa said. "Robbie, you're a healthy young woman with a healthy baby. Don't forget, your body is made to give birth. Women have been birthing babies since forever, usually at home. It's a normal state, not something pathological."

"Okay. Whatever you say. I guess." Women had died in childbirth, though, and so had babies. I admonished that thought to go get lost. My great-grandmother Rose had been a midwife in New England at a time when all births took place at home, after all, and she'd had five healthy babies of her own the same way. I could do this thing—if I had to.

"And I'll be at her side." Abe beamed at me. "At least you don't have a homicide to investigate, sugar."

Uh-oh. I hadn't had a chance to tell him the news.

"What?" Risa grinned. "You work for the police, Robbie? I had no idea."

"No, no," I protested. "Not at all."

"You've been holding out on me," Risa went on. "I'm the biggest mystery fiction fan around. I love reading them, especially the cozy ones."

"Seriously, Risa. I'm a cook, and I own a restaurant. I don't work for the police."

"But Robbie has helped the authorities in the past," Abe insisted. "In real life."

"Sort of." I gazed into his face. "The thing is, sweetheart, there actually was an unusual death overnight that might turn out to be a homicide. It seems like the authorities think Aunt Adele might have done it."

Risa tilted her head, listening, but she didn't seem shocked.

Abe's big brown eyes grew rounder. "Why her?"

"Because the body was on her farm," I said. "It was near the house but in one of the pastures. Samuel found the guy, and Adele seems to have known him a long time ago."

"Robbie, no." Abe had rarely looked so somber. "You just can't get involved in that."

I knew the news was going to upset him, and I'd planned to tell him later. One of the many things I loved about him was that he'd never told me to back off investigations. He'd never even asked me to, but this was different. I was about to give birth to our child.

He shook his head, then focused on the midwife. "Isn't it bad for the baby for Robbie to be thinking about such a horrible crime?"

"Not necessarily," Risa said. "Certainly you want to stay as calm and relaxed as you can, Robbie. You don't want to put yourself in harm's way. I can understand your concern for your aunt. I'd say puzzling through the facts of the case can't hurt, as long as it's a mental exercise. I bet you're good at that kind of sleuthing."

"Thanks," I said.

Abe frowned, but he stopped objecting.

"Do either of you have any questions for me?" Risa asked.

I appreciated that she never rushed me, or us, through an appointment.

"If weather prohibits us from driving to the hospital, how will you get here?" Abe asked.

"Not to worry. I have a car that can drive in anything, and I live only five miles away, not forty."

"But if you can get here, couldn't an ambulance?" I asked.

"We'll cross that bridge if we get to it." She looked from me to Abe and back. "Your due date is in two weeks. I'll see you in my office next Wednesday."

"The day before Thanksgiving?" Abe asked.

Risa checked her book. "Yes, at ten. Robbie, you downloaded a movement-tracking app, right?"

I nodded.

"Start using it now and call me if you don't feel the baby move in a two-hour period. Don't hesitate to contact me with any other questions you think of. Your daughter is already in what we call the safe zone. Even if she were born tomorrow, her lungs are now mature enough to do well outside the womb. Anyway, the birth won't be tomorrow. I would wager big money on it." She stood and smiled. "You're going to do great, Robbie."

"Sometimes I'm not so sure." I scrunched up my nose.

"I'll see you out," Abe said.

I stayed put. Thoughts of disasters filled my brain. I'd been through an ice storm before, and it was terrifying. A tornado had touched down not far from here one year, which was also terrifying. I'd been confronted and threatened by killers and had rescued myself every time.

The scariest thing I could think of right now was something going wrong with our little girl being born.

CHAPTER 15

The apple cider muffins were a popular item the next morning. A bone-chilling rain had swept in overnight, and everybody came into the store shivering and damp. I did, too. But the smell of bacon frying and the delicious aroma of cinnamon baked into pastry brought a smile to more than one face, including mine.

Abe and I had spent a quiet evening together. He'd put a last coat of paint on the lovely bassinet and stand he and his father had handcrafted. It was a standard size, and we'd found a quilted liner that was ready to fit into it and an inch-thick mattress to go inside. I'd tried again to reach Adele, but with no luck, and had focused on solving a hard crossword puzzle to take my mind off everything else.

I also texted Samuel last night, and he responded that Adele would get in touch with me today. Now that

I was at work, I would have to wait and see if she came in to eat, or if we'd talk later in the day.

Pans 'N Pancakes was busy, but not crazily so. As often happened after a homicide in our area, more than one regular customer stopped me wanting to talk about the body. My store had become a community gathering place, which included being ground zero for gossip. The fact that Ivan's corpse had been found on my aunt's farm only amplified the morbid curiosity from locals who knew her.

"How's Adele doing, hon?" a square-jawed man asked. "She must have had quite the shock."

"She's holding up."

"When you see her, tell her we're all holding her in prayer," his wife added. "Especially the LACs."

I tilted my head. "The lacks?"

"You know, the Ladies Aid Club," she clarified. "Adele's one of our founding members."

"I'll tell her, thank you." I'd never heard of that club and was pretty sure my aunt wasn't active in it these days. I quickly moved on to the next customer, a woman who'd signaled for the check for her and her friends.

"Are you on the case, Robbie?" she asked. "Who do you think murdered that poor man?"

All four women at the table looked eager for any news tidbits I could pass along.

"I don't know anything about a case or a murder." I laid their check face down. "I hope you enjoyed your breakfast." I hurried along. For one thing, I didn't know anything except Ivan's name. And for another, even if I did, the information wouldn't be mine to add to the gossip mill.

I delivered a couple of orders to Turner at the grill.

"Thanks." He didn't glance up, frowning as he folded over an omelet. He slid a stack of pancakes onto a plate, plus three links. "These are for the dude at the two-top."

"Got it." When things slowed down I'd ask him what was going on. Like Adele, Turner was usually even-keeled and quietly good-natured. Frowning and not making eye contact was way out of character.

I carried the breakfast over to a man sitting alone, someone I'd never seen before. "Enjoy your breakfast, sir."

"Thank you, miss." When he smiled, gold sparkled from one of his front teeth, matching the gold stud in his ear. He wore a crew-neck black sweater over a plaid shirt, and both looked new. "You have a nice place here. Has it been open long?"

"Five years this fall, actually. I'm Robbie Jordan, the owner."

"Pleased to make your acquaintance. My name's Oliver Stanganelli."

"Good to meet you, Mr. Stanganelli. Can I get you anything else right now?"

He looked at his plate then back at me. "Not food-wise, no. But I wondered if a man named Ivan Sheluk had been in recently. He told me he was headed this way."

Huh. "Is he a friend of yours?" Ivan Sheluk was a popular guy this week.

"You might say that." He pushed up one sleeve of his sweater and neatly folded the shirtsleeve up his forearm, which was filled with colored tattoo ink.

"I did meet someone by that name a couple of days ago." I glanced at the ink but lifted my gaze before taking time to figure out what the pictures portrayed or what the writing said.

"Did Sheluk happen to say where he was staying?" Oliver asked.

"Sorry, he didn't. I'll let you get to your meal before it gets cold." I turned away. I knew where Ivan was staying now—in the morgue. I headed for my desk, found the business card, and batted out a quick text to Detective McWilliam. She was going to want to know somebody had asked about Ivan.

CHAPTER 16

I kept an eye on the door, but Adele didn't make an appearance. Oliver also watched the entrance for as long as he lingered, then finally hailed me for his check at about ten o'clock.

"I hope you enjoyed your meal, Oliver."

"It was delicious, thank you."

"If I happen to see your friend, would you like me to tell him how to reach you?" I mentally crossed my fingers he would say yes and decided not to plague myself about the untrue suggestion. I would never see Ivan again.

He blinked. "Excellent idea. May I have one of those order slips, please, and borrow your pen?"

"Absolutely." I handed over paper and pen.

He scribbled and handed them back. "Can you make out my writing? I've been out of practice for a while."

"We're all out of practice for handwriting." I read the cell number back to him.

"That's it," he said.

"Do you live locally?"

"No, not at all." A clouded look came into his eyes. "I'm not sure where I . . ." His voice trailed off as he seemed to catch himself. "Never mind."

"I hope you found somewhere comfortable to stay in the area."

"Yes, the Beanblossom Motel. The place is okay. It isn't the fanciest around, but it's clean enough and fits the budget." Oliver stood. "I appreciate your offer to pass along my number to Ivan. I'm much obliged."

"No worries. Thanks for coming in and have a good day."

He made his way out. My brainstorm had paid off, big-time. I quickly texted his number and the name of the motel to Juanita McWilliam. The Beanblossom wasn't fancy at all, but I knew the Mennonite owners. They took pride in making sure it was a clean and safe low-budget lodging for travelers. My B&B rooms upstairs were vacant at the moment, but I charged the going rate for them, probably double of what a small-town motel room cost.

As I cleared Oliver's table, I wondered what his troubled look had been about, and what he'd nearly said about where he lived. I carried the dishes to the kitchen area, where Turner was still at the grill fixing food for one of the unfilled orders.

"Turner, take a break when you can," I told him.

"Okay. These two are the end of the muffins, by the way, in case you want to grab the last one."

"Ooh, thanks."

He slid one onto a small plate for me, then plated up an order of ham, two over easy, and wheat toast. He pointed at a pile of sauteed onions, peppers, and mushrooms on the grill. "Danna, those veggies are for an omelet with sausage and hash browns." He slipped out of his apron and headed for the restroom.

Danna slid over to the grill and poured out a disk of beaten eggs as I bit into the muffin and savored its flavors and mouthfeel.

"Danna, is something up with Turner?" I asked. "He seems preoccupied, worried."

"Yeah, I noticed. He hasn't said anything to me, and I haven't had time to ask."

"Okay. I'll see what I can find out, treading lightly, as I always try to do." I took another bite of muffin.

"You're good about that, boss," she said. "We both know you care about us, and we also appreciate that you're not snoopy about our private lives."

"Thanks. I try." I popped in the last of the muffin, grabbed a rag, and headed out to wipe down cleared tables. I did my best not to pry into my staff's feelings and personal affairs. But if something seemed to be affecting their work, I always asked. It was the in-between ground I found tricky, even though I knew they each regarded me as a friend, which was mutual. Maybe Turner was having girlfriend problems, although I hoped not.

When a text buzzed into my phone, I set down the rag and whipped the device out of my apron pocket. My face lit up to see Adele's name but fell when I read the message.

Can't make it in today, hon. I'm okay, just can't talk yet. XXOO.

I sighed. I couldn't force her to tell me what she knew. But . . . I could bring her food. Maybe I'd whip up another pan of muffins after we closed and take a drive out to the farm. Who could turn down a pan of warm apple-cinnamon heaven?

Having set the empty tables with place mats, silverware rolls, and mugs, I took a minute to sit myself down. One place I wouldn't be going this afternoon was the Beanblossom Motel. I didn't know Oliver's connection to Ivan. In case Oliver was also connected to the murder, the last thing I needed to do was poke around—alone—and ask questions at the place where he was staying. That was the job of the police, and I was happy to leave it to them.

Turner emerged, giving the signal to Danna to take her break. As he tied on a clean apron, I pushed up to standing and made my way to the kitchen. Before I could gently ask what was going on with him, people started flooding in through the door. A few were senior citizens, others were middle-aged or younger.

"Looks like it's tour group time," I said. "Ready?"

"I guess. I'll erase the muffins from the board."

"Thanks. We'll keep Danna at the grill."

He nodded and turned away. I pointed myself at the newcomers to conduct business as usual. The events of the week certainly weren't.

CHAPTER 17

The tour group ran all three of us ragged. Not because they were rude or cranky, but because thirty-eight visitors wanting not only food but information—all at the same time—was a bit much, including for seasoned pros like us.

One of the first newcomers who came through the door said they were members of a historical society from Carmel. They didn't mean the lovely town on the California coast with stress on the second syllable. This one was a small city immediately north of Indianapolis, with emphasis on the first syllable. Being a native Californian, I'd pronounced it wrong a couple of times until Adele corrected me.

Adele. I itched—not literally, thank goodness—to find out what was going on with her. She'd always been an open book with me. Ivan's appearance and subsequent death was really affecting her if she wouldn't open up to me more than twenty-four hours after Samuel had discovered his body.

By eleven I'd gotten the last of the amateur historians seated after the first group had vacated the eight-top. These seven were a group of women who'd been happy to wait in favor of browsing my shelves of vintage pots and pans, tins and utensils, bowls and measuring cups. They wanted to buy on the spot, but I asked them to leave their purchases on the retail counter and I'd ring them up after they were finished eating.

I stood ready with my ordering pad. "We serve breakfast all day, and we usually don't start lunch service this early, but if someone is dying for a burger or a sandwich, I can make it happen."

"Thank you, dear," a white-haired woman said. "I think we're all good with this delightful breakfast menu, right, girls?"

Hearing no objections, I jotted down orders for breakfasts across the menu spectrum. "I'll go put those in for you. I'm afraid it might take a little while." I smiled. "Our customers usually come in gradually."

"Not a problem, hon," a redhead said. "We heard your cute little town has quite a few impressive Art Deco buildings that have been preserved. Am I right?"

"Yes, we do have those buildings downtown just a few blocks away," I said. "They're lovely."

"And a Carnegie Library, too."

"Correct." I nodded. "It has a much-needed modern addition attached to the back, but they were able to preserve the original 1913 building with updates to wiring and plumbing. South Lick has quite a few architectural treasures."

"Is that the original tin ceiling?" The first woman pointed up at the square stamped panels. "It looks like it is."

"Yes," I said. "I was able to save it when I renovated the store."

"That's just super," she said. "It's my favorite kind of ceiling."

"What year was your store built?" Redhead asked.

"In 1870, ma'am."

"Very nice. We always like to see the old places preserved and in continual use."

"So do I. If you'll excuse me, please." I headed to the kitchen with a smile on my face. Unless a place had been severely neglected for many years, there was no reason not to bring it back to life instead of razing the structure and building something modern, which often ended up without any real character. Sure, you had to take the building down to the studs inside, insulate, and replace basic systems like plumbing and wiring. In my view, it was worth it. When features like our ceiling and my beautiful heavy front door with its decorative carvings could be kept, so much the better. I'd had to replace the antique glass in the door a couple of years back, unfortunately, when a bad person intent on hurting me had shattered the pane.

By the time Buck wandered in half an hour later, his favorite two-top had just been vacated. Since nobody else was waiting, I waved him to it with eyes and chin, since my arms were laden with the orders for my eight-top.

White-Hair was frowning at her phone when I set

down her cheese omelet with white toast and bacon, plus a side of biscuits and gravy. She glanced up.

"What's this about a man being killed in South Lick yesterday?"

I groaned inwardly. "I believe a body was found on someone's property, yes."

"This article says it was murder. That's kind of scary, don't you think?"

"It's certainly not something anyone ever wants. But we have an excellent local police force, and I'm sure the county sheriff's homicide division is also working hard to solve it. You have nothing to worry about." I spotted Buck waving to me. "Please excuse me. You ladies enjoy your meals."

I moved away from the questioning and greeted the chief as I sank into the chair opposite him. My feet were getting a beating holding up all this extra weight.

"What a relief it is to sit," I said. "How are you?"

"Morning, Robbie. Welp, I got me a hunger that's more insistent than a starving woodpecker digging for bugs in a hickory post."

"Then it's your lucky day." I ignored his hammering hunger for a moment. "Have there been any developments?"

"Not to speak of. I can't get Corrine to open up about where and when she knew the victim." He kept his voice low. "And it seems McWilliam is running head-on into a cow patty's load of brick walls, too. I'll tell, you, Robbie, I don't know whether to wind my watch or turn to page nine."

I blinked. Non sequitur, much? Or maybe not. "I

know how you feel. Kind of." I smiled. "Full breakfast today, or are you ready for an extra-large lunch?"

He considered for a second. "Let's go with the lunch. And double dessert."

"I'll be back." I set my hands on the table to help me stand.

"Hang on there a little minute. How abouts you? Garnered any intel on our dead fella?"

I settled back into the chair. "A guy came in asking about him. I texted McWilliam the man's name and where he's staying."

"And those would be?"

After I told Buck, I asked, "Does Oliver Stanganelli ring a bell for you?"

"It might could." He drummed his fingers on the table. "It's entirely possible I remember the name. Now I just have to remember from where."

"You work on it while Danna works on your lunch."

Buck did have a deep and wide memory, and he'd lived in South Lick all his adult life. His ability to place a name was right up there with Adele's.

CHAPTER 18

"We're nearly out of brownies and cookies, Robbie," Danna said after I added Buck's order to the carousel. "Despite ordering from the breakfast menu, the women in the tour group also ordered a ton of desserts to finish off their meals."

Hope Morris was scheduled to bring us desserts every other day. That way they were always fresh and we had enough, Tuesday through Sunday. But she hadn't made an appearance today, which concerned me. Most diners wanted their touch of sweet after lunch.

"Hope should have been here by now," I said. "I'll text her as soon as I hit the you-know-where."

"Thanks."

After I emerged from the restroom, I pulled out my phone to send a message. When I saw Hope in the doorway, arms blessedly laden with full trays of sweets, I put the phone away and met her at the kitchen counter.

"Sorry I'm late, Robbie." As she set down the trays, her gaze darted around the room like a trapped animal's. She exhaled and dropped her shoulders. "That guy isn't here, right?"

I pretended I didn't know who she meant. "What guy?"

"The stranger who was in on Tuesday. Older, super-short hair, tattooed?" She didn't meet my eyes.

"The one you said you knew long ago?" Namely, Ivan Sheluk.

"Yes." Her tone and her expression were wary, as if she were afraid I'd say he was here for lunch but momentarily in the restroom. If she knew Ivan was dead, she was a good actress.

"I haven't seen him today," I said.

"That's awesome."

"Yoo-hoo, Ms. Morris," Buck called from across the room, waving as he stood halfway up.

"Oh, for . . ." Hope cast her gaze at the ceiling for a second. "Excuse me, Robbie. Looks like I have to talk to Buck."

"Do you want lunch while you're here?" I asked. "On the house." I wanted to keep my baker happy.

"Actually, that'd be great. Something simple like roast beef on white bread, please. Or do you have tuna melt? I love that."

"Yes, we always have tuna melt. On an English muffin okay?" We'd found English muffins held up better under the combo of tuna salad and cheese.

"That's fine," she said.

"It's yours." I scribbled the order on a slip and stuck it on the wheel for Danna. "Coffee? Soda?"

"Just water is fine." Hope made her way over to Buck's table and sat.

Hope was a mystery. She'd told me she wanted to earn money outside her regular job. If I'd asked what the job was, I'd forgotten. And this was only the present. What did I know about her past, when she knew Ivan? Next to nothing. Maybe Buck would get something out of her.

I waddled about my job, doing all the things. Turner hadn't cheered up one bit and didn't put out a vibe that he wanted to be asked about his mood. At least it wasn't interfering with his work. I let him be how he needed to be.

When I passed by the windows in the front, it looked like the rainstorm had blown through. That was great for the tourists, but it reminded me of Risa's cautions about extreme weather, which could result in a home birth, a path I was terrified to travel. I turned sharply away. I totally didn't need to dwell on thoughts like that.

I turned back when the bell jangled. Seeing Corrine made me smile. Today in a chic red pantsuit with a black silk shell and Louboutin heels to match, right down to the red soles, she was a perfect sight to get my brain away from the idea of not making it to the hospital.

"How's it going?" I asked.

"Not bad. Wish we didn't have another homicide in town, but what can you do?" She glanced around the room. "Mind if I pull up a chair with Buck and his friend?"

"Not at all, although the table's pretty small."

"No prob, hon. I'll grab a bit of their real estate. I'd love me a bowl of coleslaw and a double cheeseburger when you get a little minute."

"Coming right up." I watched her conduct her usual meet and greet with the town on her way to the table. She was up for reelection soon and so far nobody had turned in papers to run against her. Corrine enjoyed widespread support and worked hard for it. Being a natural schmoozer didn't hurt one bit. She waved to Danna before dragging an empty chair over to join Buck and Hope.

Danna and Turner had swapped roles. I added Corrine's request to the ever-rotating lineup.

"Robbie," Turner murmured from the sink, where he rinsed plates.

"Yes?"

"There's something I want to talk with you about after we close."

"Sounds like a plan." I kept my voice casual. "Are you okay to continue until then?"

"Sure." He gave me a look. "Why wouldn't I be?"

"Just checking, my friend." I turned away to the coffee area.

"Hey, the soup's been super popular," he added. "Nice idea."

"Thanks." I took a couple of swigs from the Chumash High School water bottle I'd brought back from my tenth high school reunion in Santa Barbara a couple of years ago. While I was out there, I helped solve the murder of a man my mother knew. I dug up answers to a few important questions about her death, too.

I still missed my mom deeply. Being about to become a mother myself had sharpened the occasional pangs of grief. At those times, I often heard her voice murmuring encouragement and reminding me of how much love and support surrounded me.

Jeanine Jordan had uprooted herself from here and moved to California while she was pregnant with me by an Italian visitor—a lover. Like Corrine with her Charlie, Roberto had gone home without knowing he'd fathered a child, except in my case he was still alive, and my mom had kept me. She raised me with the support she built around her, plus visits from her older sister, Adele. I had a happy, healthy childhood.

If Mommy could parent alone, and do it as well as she did, I could certainly pull off being a mother. I had Abe, his family, Adele, and my close friends to lift me up and make sure our little girl was well loved.

"Boss?" Danna nudged me out of my reverie by dinging the ready bell. "Lunch rush. Customers. Hot food."

"Sorry." I laughed. "I'm on it." I needed to leave the woolgathering to sheep farmer Adele.

CHAPTER 19

Ten minutes after I brought Hope and Corrine their orders, Hope stood and made her way out. Corrine looked well ensconced and in no danger of leaving soon. The next time I made my coffee rounds, I saved their table for last and sat in the chair Hope had vacated. Buck's meal was a thing of the past, and Corrine was nearly finished with hers.

"Hope ate in a hurry," I said.

"She didn't seem none too comfortable acrost the table from me," Buck said. "I plan to dig into the why of her discomfort."

"Let me know if you find out anything."

"You holding up, hon?" Corrine asked. "I remember those last few weeks of pregnancy. It's a load to carry around, and my girl was a big one, too." She pointed toward Danna.

"I'm fine, but it is a load," I said. "How big was she?"

"Near on to ten pounds. One ounce short of that nice even number."

I gaped. "Seriously?"

"Yup. A hundred percent."

Buck gave a whistle. "That's a big one, all right. Bet it felt like you upped and gave birth to a pumpkin. That's what my Melia said way back when she pushed out our second. Why, our boy weighed in at a solid ten pounds three ounces."

Ten-pound babies? OMG. I was suddenly frightened of an entirely new set of circumstances.

"A pumpkin." Corrine snorted. "Thanks for the image, Buck. But, yes, it was pretty much like that." She must have caught sight of my wide eyes and horrified expression. "Now don't you go worrying none, Robbie. By the size of you, you have a healthy, normal-sized cutie in there. Seven and half pounds, maybe nudging eight by time your labor kicks in. You won't have no trouble getting her out the traditional way."

"Can we possibly change the subject?" I asked. "You're both scaring the hoo-hah out of me, as Adele says."

Buck nodded and stopped smiling. "You talk to her today?"

"No," I said. "I wish I had, but she told me she's not ready yet."

"She's going to have to be ready one of these days, or hours, more like." Buck rubbed his head. "We need to know what her connection with the deceased was."

"Corrine," I began. "Have you told Buck what your own connection was? You recognized Ivan on Tuesday."

"What's that, now?" Buck sat up straight. "You knew this Sheluk character? You've been holding out on me, Madam Mayor. No fair."

"Down, boy. I was going to inform you." She took a bite of burger. She swallowed. "And I will do so right this little minute. Buck, you remember Marcus?"

He nodded.

"Well, Ivan was friends with his father," Corrine said.

"The jazz musician," I murmured.

"Yes. Ivan was not a nice person in those days." She traced a circle on the table with her finger, looking lost in thought.

"What kind of not nice?" Buck asked.

"What?" Corrine looked startled.

"I'd like you to tell me in what way was Sheluk not nice." Buck raised his eyebrows.

"Right. He was involved in various petty crimes. Smoked and drank a lot. He wasn't a half-bad pianist, but he was no Oscar Peterson. Plus, he was a whiner. He was the kind of man who'd complain if they hanged him with a brand-new rope. At any rate, I didn't like it when the three of us spent time together."

"Remind me what happened to that boyfriend of yours," Buck said. "He was a deal older than you, as I recall you told me once."

"He was," Corrine said. "By a decade. We weren't married, and my parents didn't approve of Mr. Charles Morton."

I'd met Josephine, an energetic seventy-something who owned her own IT consulting business and still traveled regularly. I didn't know anything about Cor-

rine's father. I could believe neither would have wanted
their teenage daughter to date an older man.

She smiled to herself. "Charlie was so handsome.
You've never seen a smile so pretty, a figure so dashing
when he was in his suit and tie. I fell hard when he
started flirting with me. And he was serious about his
interest."

"What happened to him?" Buck asked.

"He was in a small plane another musician buddy of
his owned. They were headed to a gig in Louisville
when the aircraft crashed, killing both of them." She
shook her head. "Such a loss. I really think my Charlie
would have made it big. And he never knew I was pregnant. I still lived at home, and I couldn't no way imagine how I would go on to college and raise a baby
alone. You know the rest."

The rest included Marcus, who was adopted by a
loving Quaker family in Indianapolis.

"Had you seen Ivan since those days?" I asked.

"Not a once, which is why I felt like I'd seen a ghost
the other day."

Buck gave a slow nod, taking it all in.

I glanced around the restaurant, which was filling
up. I was going to have to get back on the job, ASAP.

"Buck, did you find out how Hope knew Ivan?" I
stood up.

"Kinda sorta." He also stood. "Looks like you're
fixing to return to your customers. I've got to clear out
of here, too. I'll catch you up on Hope later, Robbie.
Suffice it to say the man broke her heart, and that's a
fact." He clapped his hat on his head and made for the
door at a faster amble than his usual.

"Whoa." I gazed after him. "Why did he clear out so quickly?"

"No idea. Never seen the man move so fast, though." Corrine gave a little laugh.

"Me neither. Were you here when he was talking with Hope about the past?"

She shook her head. "He must have grilled her before—" Whatever she'd been about to say was interrupted by the ring of her phone. She pressed it to her ear as she laid a twenty on the table and mouthed, "Bye," to me while striding for the door. "I'll be right there."

It appeared my sleuthing break was over. All kinds of customers were looking for my attention. I was working up until my due date for a reason. I wanted to make sure my livelihood was in good shape when I checked out for a while. I'd better get back to it.

CHAPTER 20

My team and I did what we always did at two thirty. Locked the door after the last customer, then cleaned, prepped, and debriefed. Turner's mood had lightened but he was still quieter than usual, including when Danna teased him about something and hip-bumped him.

"Robbie, what were you talking about with Buck and my mom?" she asked as she scrubbed the now-cool grill. "It looked intense."

I considered. She knew all about Marcus and how his birth father had died. Corrine's history didn't need to be kept secret from Danna. Turner knew about that part of Corrine's past, too.

"During the time Corrine was with Marcus's birth dad, he knew Ivan Sheluk," I said. "Your mom had met him more than once."

"Radical." Danna's light eyebrows shot up. "Truth?"

"Yep." I drew another napkin toward me and grabbed a knife, fork, and spoon from their respective baskets.

"Wow," Turner said. "That's heavy."

"Corrine said she hasn't seen Ivan since then, but she passed him as he was leaving here Tuesday. Although it had been, what, nearly thirty years, she recognized him."

"So, did she like, grab him and give him a big old mayoral hug?" Danna asked.

"It didn't sound like it," I said. "She told us she hadn't liked him at all at the time, and that he was involved in petty crimes. I don't think she spoke to him on Tuesday or that he saw her."

"Robbie, I saw you talking with the dude who came in for breakfast today but kept looking at the door the whole time," Turner said. "What was up with him?"

"It was interesting." I paused my napkin rolling. "He asked about Ivan, said he'd heard he was headed this way."

"So he didn't know the guy was dead?" Danna asked.

"It sure didn't sound like it."

"Could he have been faking it?" Turner brought over the baskets full of condiment caddy supplies.

"Maybe," I said. "He asked if I knew where Ivan was staying."

"Lemme guess. You didn't say the morgue." Danna grinned.

"I sure didn't. But I finagled where he's staying out of him because I'm sneaky that way, and I let the detective know."

"He's not staying upstairs, I guess." Danna began scrubbing the now-empty soup pot.

"Not at all. He said he has a room out at the Bean-blossom Motel."

"The retro joint on Route 135?" Danna asked.

"It is. You both know Martin Dettweiler, our honey man. His brother owns and runs the motel. But I'm not sure it qualifies as retro if it's always looked that way."

Turner laughed. "You might have a point there. Speaking of honey, we're running low in the retail shop."

"Thanks," I said. "I'll give him a call." The jars of local honey were a popular gift item, and Martin always brought an assortment of sizes for us to sell.

"How about a cranberry-spice quick bread for a breakfast special tomorrow?" Danna asked.

"Tasty, easy, and autumnal," I said. "Perfect."

"Along the fall theme, we could do a stuffed squash kind of thing for lunch," Turner suggested. "We have a bunch of winter squash, and it'd be easy to make up a couple of pans with a sausage topping and at least one with the veggie sausage we have in the freezer."

"Sounds like a plan." I smiled at my crew. "Now go home, you two."

Danna was out the door in ten minutes. Turner lingered. He started the dishwasher and wiped down all the tables. He was about to wipe down the counter, an entirely unnecessary move since Danna had done it right before she left.

"Turner, you want to sit down for a minute?"

He approached the table and held onto the back of the chair opposite mine but remained standing.

"You said you had something you wanted to talk with me about," I said softly. "I'm ready to listen."

His shoulders sagged. "I want to, but it's hard. The thing is, Robbie, I have to give you my notice."

Oh. I gave one slow nod. "I'm sorry to hear you're leaving us." At least he hadn't said he had a terrible disease. I waited for more.

"I really hate to do this to you. I got accepted to culinary school for next semester." He finally looked straight at me, his expression a combination of worried and nervous.

"But that's fabulous news, Turner." Smiling, I clapped for a moment. "I'm so happy for you."

"You are?" He pulled out the chair and sat. "Wow."

"I'm beyond happy, Turner. You're a brilliant cook. You deserve it."

"It's something I've wanted to do for a long time."

"I know. Frankly, I'm surprised you didn't go on to bigger and better things before now. Danna, too." I'd been expecting this kind of news for a while from at least one of them.

"You know I love working here, Robbie, and I'll really miss it. I also feel super bad I'm leaving you in the lurch, especially with your baby on the way."

"We'll figure it out. Don't worry." Worrying about staffing was my job, not his. "Now, tell me where you're going."

His face lit up. "I got into the CIA in Hyde Park."

"Culinary Institute of America?"

"That's the one. It's on the Hudson River."

"It's the best school in the country, isn't it?" I asked.

"That's what they say." He didn't quite bounce in his chair, but his excitement was palpable.

"Awesomeness. So I can plan, how long can you stay on the job here?"

"At least until the end of December. I have to check the academic calendar, but colleges usually don't start until the end of January. I'm going to live on campus, at least this spring, so I won't have to go early to find to an apartment."

"Good to know. If you have any foodie friends around here who need a job, send them over, okay?"

"You bet." He reached across and grabbed my hand. "Thanks for being cool about this, boss. I thought you'd hate me for leaving."

"Oh, I do, definitely." I smiled to be sure he knew I was kidding. "But I'm glad you'll be here almost two more months. It'll help."

"I hoped you'd say that," he said. "You should see the campus. It's gorgeous. Students get internships in top New York restaurants." Turner nearly glowed at the prospect.

"We'll be able to say we knew you when."

I was deeply sorry our well-oiled team would lose him. Danna and I would miss him enormously, but Turner totally deserved this experience. I had no doubt he'd take his talent for cooking a long way.

CHAPTER 21

I greased a dozen loaf pans half an hour later. Baking the loaves the day before wouldn't hurt them and it might deepen the flavor. If people thought we were jumping the gun on Thanksgiving a little early with the cranberries, too bad.

The prospect of Turner not being here made me sad, I had to admit. With his father being from India, Turner had often contributed a taste of South Asia to our specials. As I mixed the berries into the quick bread batter, I remembered the Indian-seasoned roasted potatoes he'd made, and the touch of curry he slid into maple syrup biscuits. After he'd started taking culinary classes at IU, one per semester, Turner also suggested an Asian noodle salad for a lunch special and brought in his beloved crepe pan for sweet and savory versions of those delicate French pancakes.

Once I slid the pans full of cranberry bread batter

into the oven, I gave the mixing bowl a quick wash, rinse, and dry and began my daily prep of biscuit dough and the dry ingredients for tomorrow's pancake batter. What I would miss most with Turner's departure was the easy camaraderie he shared with Danna and with me. I couldn't ask for two better employees.

Len was a good fill-in person, but he was still a university student and worked here strictly on a part-time basis. It would be great if Turner could recommend someone he knew from his culinary classes, an experienced cook who was eager to work full-time in a local restaurant. I could only hope.

While I worked, I slid my thoughts over to the death that was a possible homicide. I hoped Adele would open up to me when I headed out there again. A warm cranberry loaf might nudge her into talking.

Speaking of hope, I wanted to talk to Hope about how she knew Ivan. I could call her and ask, but such conversations usually yielded more results when they were in person. She'd brought desserts today, which meant she'd be back on Saturday. If the homicide wasn't solved by then, I would do my best to—gently—corner her and get the scoop. If the cause of death was homicide at all and not from natural causes.

With any luck the mysterious Oliver would come in again tomorrow. Or not. If McWilliam had found him, he might be upset I gave her his cell and location.

I shaped and wrapped the disks of biscuit dough, a job I could do almost without thinking.

The timer dinged. I grabbed pot holders and pulled open the oven door to see a dozen puffy, lightly browned loaves smiling at me. I frowned as my lower abdomen

seized up. I straightened, listening to my body, counting slowly. The sensation was more intense than a
menstrual cramp, but it didn't last more than fifteen
seconds. And then it was gone.

I swallowed. I was in big trouble if this was early
labor, because I didn't feel at all ready. But my due
date was in two weeks, and Risa had said the baby was
now in the safe window for birth, meaning her lungs
and everything else were mature enough to thrive outside of me. I was going to have to be ready, no matter
what happened.

Except the baby had been inside for so long, I found
it hard to remember what not being pregnant felt like.
Not that being the mother of a newborn would resem-
ble anything like the me of nearly nine months ago and
prior.

I sniffed. *Oops.* Better get those loaves out, stat, and
turn off the oven. As they cooled on a rack, I tried to
recall what Risa had told me about monitoring for contractions. She'd mentioned keeping track of the duration and frequency, but those details had slipped my
mind, as so much did these days. I'd either ask Abe or
shoot a text to the midwife.

To be safe, I sent myself a text about today's date,
time, and the duration of the mild pain I'd felt. If I experienced another one, I'd have a record of the first.

While I held my phone, it rang. My eyebrows went
up to see Louise Perlman's ID and photo.

"Lou, it's great to hear from you." I heard the smile
in my voice. My bicycling buddy, Len's older sister,
had finished her doctorate at IU a year and a half ago
and moved to Albuquerque for a teaching job.

"You can hear me in person if you let me in."

What? I hurried to the door to see her grinning face pressed against the glass. In a minute, she was inside and we were hugging.

She stepped back, focusing her gaze on the basketball under my tunic top, which, by now, stuck out so far the shirt was almost too short. Lou was a serious cyclist and hiker and had always moved with an athletic ease. That hadn't changed, and she sported an outdoorsy tan, as she had in years prior, but something about her face looked older, perhaps troubled.

"You look ready to pop," she said.

I rubbed my belly. "I am, in a couple of weeks. I think she's getting ready."

"A daughter? Way to go, Rob. Another Hoosier girl cyclist in the making."

I laughed. "Oops. I forgot we aren't telling anyone her gender. Come sit down and tell me why you're back in town mid-semester. But first, can I get you a beer?"

"I would love one."

"I'll be right back." I grabbed my keys and headed to the apartment in the back of the store where I'd lived before moving in with Abe. I always kept beer in the fridge there, and these days a few non-alcoholic versions, too. It didn't take long until I was clinking a glass with my old friend.

Lou took a long sip, then set down her glass, her expression somber. "I'm back because my dad's sick. I wanted to see him and assess the situation for myself."

"I'm so sorry. Is it serious?" No wonder she looked troubled.

"It looks like it might be. I asked for family leave

until next semester and handed off my classes to a couple of colleagues in the department." She shook her head as she traced her finger through the condensation on the glass. "I just needed to be here, or rather, there."

Her father, a longtime professor, lived farther north in the state in the Lafayette area where Lou and Len had grown up. Their mother had passed away before I'd met Lou.

"I'm so sorry about his illness. That's really hard," I murmured. "Len hasn't said anything about your father being sick."

"He doesn't know. Daddy didn't want to interrupt his studies or have him worry." She shrugged. "It's what comes with being the oldest child. Always having to be responsible."

"I hear you. I was both the oldest and the only." I sipped from my NA beer. "Do you need somewhere to stay in South Lick? Sean's in Italy for the year, so his space in our house is free, and my rooms upstairs are all open right now."

She cocked her head. "I'd love that. One of the B&B rooms, I mean. I don't want to impose on you and Abe, but I'd like to hang out with Len when he's free."

"You wouldn't be imposing. Stay wherever it works for you. And no charge, by the way. That's the nice thing about having the B&B. When the rooms aren't booked, I can host friends and family."

"You're the best, Robbie. I'm heading over to Bloomington soon to have dinner with Len and break the news to him. I'd thought I would rent a hotel room there, but this will be so much nicer."

"I have a bike for you to use, too. I haven't been on it for four months."

"I can see why. I could use a few good Brown County hill workouts to de-stress."

We chatted until our drinks were finished. She fetched her bag from her car, and I made sure she was settled in her room.

"See you at breakfast?" I asked.

"You bet. And thanks again."

I stored eleven of the now-cool loaves for tomorrow but wrapped one in a clean tea towel to take to Adele. How refreshing not to think about the body in the pasture for a few minutes. That was about to change with my visit to my aunt, and I knew Lou would ask tomorrow if I'd been doing any sleuthing lately. Even though the reason for Lou's return to Indiana was a hard one, my outlook on life had lightened by having a good friend around.

CHAPTER 22

I was halfway to Adele's farm and beyond the town's most densely populated areas when I slowed at a derelict two-story brick farmhouse on my right. The west-facing building sat alone next to a field of stubby cut cornstalks. Its four ground-floor windows and center-placed door were boarded up, and I saw no evidence of occupancy, at least not by humans.

I'd driven by the abandoned structure on my way to Adele's plenty of times before. She'd said it was in the Greek Revival style, with its curly supports for the eaves. Each window and the door were topped by what looked like nicely arched eyebrows, a feature I'd seen on other older buildings in the area. Architectural styles weren't my forte, and I'd taken Adele's word for it.

However nice the home had been in its earlier years, these days tall weeds waved in the wind in front of the windows. Volunteer saplings sprouting next to the house would ruin the foundation if they weren't dealt with.

Now at four thirty, with only an hour to go before sunset, the light played around the corners of the building. I frowned at what I saw just past the house and pulled over. The vehicle behind me seemed relieved to pass my tortoise-like rubbernecking.

I'd spotted something hot pink nearly hidden behind the building. I turned off the car and slid out. Two more vehicles and a pickup truck heading into town passed by. I'd vowed not to get into trouble with my investigations, but my curiosity in the face of an unsolved homicide pushed me to check out the colored whatever-it-was. I figured this route had enough traffic I could always hail help, as long as I stayed within sight of the road.

The pink thing might be nothing, but I doubted it was there accidentally. Only humans owned clothing, books, toys, and other objects in hues not found in nature.

I made my way to the left of the house, shivering with the cold. I picked up my feet and watched the ground so I didn't stumble over a root or a hillock concealed by the overgrown grasses.

Pausing and regarding the house from close up, I realized the structure was even more run down than it had appeared from a distance. The upstairs window sashes, with four divided-light panes on the top and bottom, were missing glazing. Row after row of bricks were covered with the white powder known as spalling and were in desperate need of repointing.

The fluorescent pink thing turned out to be one of many cheap plastic toys spilling out of a cardboard box on its side. A sloppy scrawl on the side of the box read, "Free." The sight of it made me sad. Had a family not been able to make their mortgage payments and vacated this home? Or maybe the necessary repairs, not to mention the utility bills, grew too costly. The occupants might have held a yard sale and left these unsold items behind.

Whatever the explanation, I doubted it had anything to do with Ivan Sheluk's death. I left the toys where I'd found them. I glanced around the corner at the back but nothing caught my attention. As on the front and side, the ground-floor windows were boarded up and those upstairs were in poor repair. A back door stood shut and had weeds growing in front of it. Several yards back, a large shed listed to the right, with a sagging roof that was close to caving in.

It was time for me to get out of here. Out front, I climbed back into my driver's seat and started the engine. I gave the forlorn house one more glance. A low ray of light lit up one of the upper windows. I gasped and froze, my heart racing at the sight of a face looking out from behind the glass.

I looked away and tried to breathe through the shock. The person might have watched me the whole time I was checking out the house's perimeter. They might have noted my license plate number. Who could be up there? Not Ivan, for sure. Maybe Oliver had lied about the Beanblossom Motel and was squatting here, instead. I hoped he'd brought a warm sleeping bag.

Or it might be any random unhoused person who'd found a free roof to shelter under. Brown County didn't have a large homeless population, not like a big city or even Bloomington, but sometimes adults and whole families fell on hard times. Unfortunately, the county seat of Nashville didn't have a shelter for the unhoused.

Before I put the car into gear, I glanced up again. The angle of the light had changed, and the wavy antique glass looked like nothing more than old windowpanes.

Except I was sure I'd seen a face. With Ivan's murderer possibly out there—out here—my poking around the house had crossed the line into risky-behavior territory, which I'd promised Abe I'd stay clear of.

I let out a breath and drove away to the safety of my aunt's home.

CHAPTER 23

The sight of a South Lick police cruiser in Adele's driveway did not make me happy, not one bit. I pulled up next to it and hurried inside as fast as my round self could go. In the kitchen, my shoulders relaxed to see Buck sitting at the table across from Adele. His long legs were stretched out and a mug of coffee sat in front of him.

"Roberta?" Adele asked. "What are you doing back here?"

I kissed her cheek and lowered myself onto the chair next to hers. "What, I can't come see my favorite aunt?" I set the fragrant wrapped loaf on the table. Chloe moseyed up and sat on my foot, purring as loudly as she always did.

"Of course you can, hon." She patted my hand. "It's that I didn't know you planned on coming out here."

She looked much recovered from two days ago, nearly back to normal.

"Howdy there, Robbie." Buck raised his hand.

I greeted him as I shrugged out of my oversized orange fleece, the one I could no longer zip. It was a garment that made me feel like a pumpkin, except the word now made me shudder since hearing Buck's comment during our large-newborns discussion. "Adele's not in trouble, I hope."

"Good Lord, no, child," she said. "Buck claims this is a purely social visit." Her stress on "claims" made it sound like she didn't believe him.

He gave us his famous *Aw Shucks* look.

"I brought you a loaf of fresh cranberry bread, Adele." I pointed at Buck. "Hands off. This is for her."

"Don't you worry about a thing, Robbie." He drained his coffee and stood. "I've been dilly-dallying too long and have got to get myself along. Thank you kindly for the coffee, Adele." His expression turned serious. "We'll be in touch, yes?"

"I suppose we will." She didn't meet his gaze.

"Wait." I held up a hand. "Buck, before you go, I wanted to ask you both about a place I passed on my way out here."

"All righty," he said.

I told them about the abandoned brick house. "It's on the right as you drive in this direction from South Lick. I never paid it any attention before today."

"The old Carlsen place." Adele gave a nod. "Samuel, you in there?" she called toward the living room.

Samuel appeared in the doorway.

"Remember the Carlsens, hon?" Adele asked him.

"Certainly. Wasn't he a state senator or some such? I'd say he served fifty odd years ago."

"The son was the last owner of that house, I do believe," Buck said. "Fell on hard times. Business failed. Wife and kids left him."

"He died alone upstairs in the house, didn't he?" Adele asked.

"That was the story I heard, and it's a sad one." Samuel said.

I shivered. Had I seen the son's ghost?

"The death was about ten years ago," Samuel added.

I hauled myself back to reality and stood, my movement making the cat dash away. "That is sad. I'll walk you out, Buck."

"But you're staying a piece, aren't you, Roberta?" Adele asked.

"Sure. I'll be right back."

Outside, Sloopy trotted up, ears and eyes alert. Buck reached down and stroked his head, then dug a dog treat out of his coat pocket and let Sloopy eat it off his open palm.

"Tell me the truth." I folded my arms. "Did you come out here to grill Adele?"

"In a gentle kind of way, yes, except I didn't get a speck of intel out of her. But I s'pose you up and came with the same intention."

"Possibly."

"Welp, I hope you have better luck than me and that you'll be so kind as to share what you learn." He straightened and settled his uniform hat on his head.

"I will if I can. Now, don't think I'm crazy, but I stopped at the abandoned house on my way here, and I saw a face in one of the upstairs windows."

Buck gaped. "For cryin' out loud. You musta been scareder than a sinner in a cyclone."

"Not exactly, although it was kind of chilling. I thought you might want to check it out."

"What, you think it's haunted by the Carlsen fellow? Believing in ghosts ain't like you."

"No, I don't think a ghost is living there." I pushed away the thought. "I only wondered if a homeless person had found a way in. Or maybe Oliver Stanganelli, Ivan's supposed friend. He told me he was staying at the Beanblossom Motel, but that might have been a misdirection. If Oliver killed Ivan, he wouldn't want to be found, would he?"

Buck blinked. "You got yourself a interesting idea, Robbie. We'll see what we can find out about who's squatting in that there house."

"Thanks."

He headed for the cruiser, with Sloopy running circles around him, yipping as he herded his tall human friend. I took a moment to text Abe.

Am out at Adele's, home in maybe an hour.

He wrote right back.

I'm going to banjo practice, remember? See you 8:30 or so. XXOO

I texted back an acknowledgment and returned the abbreviated endearment. He had told me about music practice, and I'd forgotten.

Back inside, Adele had sliced the loaf and laid small

plates on the table. "Grab yourself a cup of tea, hon, and sit with me." She'd also taken out the Four Roses bourbon bottle, no doubt having added a glug or two to her tea. She'd introduced me to the combination, one I enjoyed when I was able to indulge, which was not today.

"I will have tea, thanks, if you have herbal, but let me hit the bathroom first."

"I already set out the boxes of that herby stuff you like."

I smiled to myself as I headed down the hall. Adele didn't believe concoctions like cinnamon-apple or lemon-ginger, not to mention chamomile, were qualified to be labeled tea. Since I'd been avoiding caffeine for almost nine months, tisanes were my only option for a hot drink, and Risa had said chamomile was also off-limits during pregnancy. I'd brought over the two boxes of herby stuff early on and left them in Adele's cabinet.

Once I was back, I dropped a teabag of lemon-ginger into a mug of hot water to steep and brought it to the table.

"You done good with this here loaf, hon," she said. "I love the walnuts."

"Thanks." I took a bite of the slice. "Mmm. It did come out delicious. But you're a baker. You know how easy it is."

"I do." Her face grew shadowed. "Haven't baked one single thing this week, though." She sipped her doctored tea. Or maybe it was straight bourbon.

Samuel ambled in and grabbed his jacket from the

coat-tree by the back door. "I'm off, my sweet." He kissed Adele's forehead, murmuring, "You know what I think you should do."

"Yes, dear." Her shoulders slumped. "I do."

"Go with God, Robbie," he said.

"You too, Samuel."

After he left, Adele said, "He's off on his prayer visits. He and young Justin go around and call on the infirm and the 'elderly.'" She surrounded the word with finger quotes. "What does Samuel think he is, a spring chicken? Why, the man is eighty-five next month." She shook her head but the expression on her face was a fond one.

"It's good of him to do that. He can still drive safely at night?"

"No, not at all. Justin was out there to pick him up."

"Good." Was the time right to ask her what I wanted to know? Samuel's comment to her made me think he wanted her to open up. I had one way to find out. "Adele, won't you tell me how you knew Ivan?"

"I figured getting info out of me is why you come out here with this tasty bribe." She spoke slowly, her voice low, staring at her mug. She glanced up. "How long you got?"

CHAPTER 24

"This is a sad tale, Roberta," she began, "which happened long ago and not so far away. I was in my thirties, single, and feeling frisky. Ivan Sheluk had the allure of being a bad boy. You know the type?"

I nodded. "Good-looking with risky behavior?"

"You got it on the nose, hon. All of that. Smoking, drinking, driving too fast, the works. When he started coming after me, I knew he was the worst kind of news—and I didn't care. He called me his sexy older woman."

"How much older than him were you?" Chloe wandered in and arched her back as she rubbed along my leg, purring like a loud little machine.

"About eight or nine years," she said. "It doesn't matter much at that age, really, but he'd dropped a younger girlfriend in favor of me."

Sloopy pushed in through the flap on his personal

door. He lapped up water and came over to Adele and to me for a scritch. He circled three times on his bed in the corner before lying with his head on his front paws.

"So what happened?" I fished out my teabag with a spoon and took a sip.

My aunt let out a noisy breath. "What didn't happen? The first clue I got was when he showed me the pistol in his glove box. He was so proud to have it, but listen to this, Roberta. It was loaded."

I frowned. "Which is dangerous."

"You think? I mean, I got nothing against owning a gun for hunting or self-protection. You're well aware I have a rifle and a pistol up in the cupboard there." She gestured with her chin. "And I use them."

She did, to scare off critters threatening her livestock as well as for murderers who came to call, as had happened a few years ago. Between the rifle and her cast-iron skillet, Adele and her friend Vera had subdued a couple of truly bad people.

"But you can't up and load the thing and then leave it in nearly plain view," she went on. "In the glove box of a junker he couldn't even lock, for Pete's sake. I mean, it's dumber than a sack of hair. His friends and them, they all thought it was groovy."

"That's the definition of risky behavior."

"So is enjoying a roll in the hay without protection." She grimaced. "Before long, I found myself in the family way."

My frown gave way to a dropped jaw. "You did?" I knew she hadn't raised a child. I waited for the next scene in this astonishing story.

"Yes. On top of that, well, Ivan got it in his misguided head to rob a Quick Pick at gunpoint. He wasn't caught, and he bragged to me and his buddies about it."

A mild swear word slipped out. "Sorry." I knew Adele didn't approve of any kind of swearing. "That's terrible. What did you do?"

She again traced a heart on the table with her finger. "I couldn't raise a child with a criminal, with someone who was so crazy and had such disregard for human life. Roberta, I took and turned him in."

"Wow." The father of her baby.

"It was one of the hardest things I ever done. They convicted Ivan and sent him to prison for quite some while."

Aha. "That must be why he looked like he'd had a hard life. Maybe he'd recently gotten out and wanted to apologize to you." Having spent years in prison was also probably why he'd winced when I'd said the word "cell."

"Yes. He had actually up and sent me a note last week saying he wanted to pay me a visit."

That explained Adele seeming distracted at the baby shower and since.

"He'd had a long time to think about it," I said.

"Indeedy, he had."

"And the baby?" I asked softly. She could have had a dangerous abortion, since that era would have been before the procedure was legal, or she might have given the child up for adoption.

"I lost it. The whole thing caused me so much worry, I miscarried the little bit of a thing." Her eyes welled with tears.

I reached for her hand. "I'm so sorry." Adele's reaction to something I'd said last spring started to make sense. At the Memorial Day cookout she'd hosted, I had asked her if she'd ever wanted children. My question had seemed to distress her. Now I knew why.

Adele swiped at her eyes. "I didn't want to tell you about my loss for fear of upsetting you and that sweet bun you're carrying."

"I'm fine, truly." I rubbed my belly and got a kick for my efforts. "We're fine."

"Well, I wouldn't have told you now, but you're so dang pushy." She laughed through her tears. "And I love you for it."

I smiled at her. "You've been carrying this memory for a long time. No wonder it shook you up to hear Ivan was in town."

"It disturbed me a good measure, in fact. But I was looking forward to seeing that bad boy. I did love him back then, in my youthful, misguided way."

"And why wouldn't you? You know, a long stay in prison has to be hard, but it hadn't hardened Ivan. His voice and manner were gentle." I thought of Oliver. "Did he have a friend at the time called Oliver?"

"No, not that I know of."

"A man named Oliver was in the restaurant today asking about Ivan. He had the same kind of appearance as Ivan, like life had treated him roughly. Maybe he was a friend who'd also just gotten out of prison. His clothes looked brand-new."

"Roberta, maybe he wasn't a friend." It was Adele's turn to gape. "He might be my Ivan's murderer."

"The detective knows all about him, and so does Buck. I wouldn't worry about Oliver. That's the police's job." I cleared my throat. "But I think it's time you filled them in on how you knew Ivan."

"I know." She dragged out the words. "Past time, I'd say. Thing is, hon, it's personal and not a period in my life I'm particularly proud of."

"It'll be hard, but you need to tell Buck. He admires you and knows you'd never kill anyone." I popped in my last bite of cranberry bread.

"He sure don't act like it sometimes." She snorted, apparently recovered from her attack of sadness. "Asking me questions like I'm some kind of homicidal maniac."

"He has to cover his bases. I really think the sooner you fill him in on your past, the sooner he and McWilliam will stop considering you as a person of interest."

"I s'pose you're right, Roberta. You usually are."

"I don't know about that, but in this case, I might be." I finished my tea. "Are you going to be okay if I leave? If you want, I can stay until Samuel gets home."

"For crying out loud, sugar, I'm seventy-five, not seven. Get along home with you. Put your feet up and stop thinking about murder. It's bad for my great-niece." She stood and extended a hand to help me up.

As I drove home, I wondered if thinking about homicide would hurt our girl. I hoped not. This was the third case I'd been involved in during the pregnancy. Adele was right about one thing. Getting home and putting my feet up was exactly what I needed.

CHAPTER 25

Once home, I showered and dressed in pajamas and an extra-large fleece hoodie, plus fuzzy slippers. I didn't bother to dry my thick curly hair, a legacy from my father. I heated a frozen—but homemade—chicken burrito for my solo supper and topped it with my favorite medium salsa, then took plate and napkin to the sofa so I could follow Dr. Adele's orders.

My large belly made the perfect tabletop to rest my dinner on. Birdy jumped up and nestled next to me, while Maceo perched on the back of the sofa. The two cats were friendly playmates, but they didn't curl up together. Cocoa snoozed on his bed. Abe had let me know he'd already walked and fed the dog.

I flipped on a mainstream news channel but turned it off after only a few minutes. I didn't need to hear or see so much bad news, whether local, national, or international. Plus, I had things to think about.

I'd driven home in the twilight but I hadn't seen any lights inside the abandoned house. Could I have been mistaken about the face in the window? Maybe, but I didn't think so.

And then there was Adele and her history with Ivan. Last spring, when I'd asked her whether she'd ever wanted babies of her own, she'd first looked stricken, but she'd recovered and brushed it off, saying life didn't always turn out as we expected it to. Her pregnancy with her beloved bad boy was that, in spades.

I hoped she called Buck after I left. Rather than being angry with Ivan after all these years, she'd seemed eager to see him again and devastated she didn't get the chance.

Oliver Stanganelli, on the other hand, presented a murkier, more mysterious story. Hope had been acquainted with Ivan, but how? And what about Carter Kingsley? When and where had he known Ivan, and why had Ivan's appearance made him angry? The last few days' profit needed depositing. I would head to the bank tomorrow and try to ask Carter about Ivan, in the safety of a well-populated bank, that is.

I swiped a dribble of salsa off of my chin and popped in the last bite of burrito, with its delicious combination of textures and flavors. Spicy shredded chicken, smooth refried beans, creamy melted cheese, a few chopped jalapenos, all wrapped in the comfort of a flour tortilla and moistened by the tomato-based salsa. Perfection in a mostly neat package. Maybe we should consider offering burritos for a lunch special soon.

The ring of my phone was muffled by the pocket of

my fleece, but I fished it out in time and connected with none other than Lou.

I swallowed my bite. "Hey, my friend. How was your dinner with Len?"

"That's what I want to talk about. Can I come by? I don't want to interrupt you and Abe."

I laughed. "Don't worry. He's not here. I'm in my jammies but I'd love to see you. I'll unlock the side door."

"Thanks. See you in five."

Within ten minutes I had her settled with a glass of red wine and me with a mug of apple-spice tea. She sipped. I blew on my tea and set it down. She sipped again.

"Lou? You said you wanted to talk about Len." I kept my tone soft.

She let out a heavy sigh. "I do. The poor kid took the news really hard, Robbie. He insisted on driving up there tonight to see Dad."

"I'm so sorry."

"He was angry with me for not telling him earlier. I didn't know myself how bad Dad's health was until I got out here. He's had congestive heart failure for a while, but it's getting worse fast, and now his kidneys are starting to fail."

I shook my head in sympathy. "Is Len going to be all right driving so far at night, being upset like he is?" I asked. "It's what, two hours north of here?"

"Yes, pretty much. He's going to have to be okay. Neither of us had anything to drink at dinner, and he's twenty-one. He'll be fine." Lou took another sip then set down her glass. "The thing is, Robbie, Daddy and

Len had a big falling-out when he told him he was a trans male. I thought Daddy would have been more understanding, but it was hard for him to accept that his younger child was transgender."

Len had transitioned a year or two ago, right before I'd hired him as a part-timer in the restaurant.

"I'm sure it's hard for a lot of parents," I said.

Lou nodded. "But recently they'd patched things up. I know how much Len loves our father, and after Mom died, well, Daddy's the only parent we have."

My business owner's brain kicked in. "Let me guess. He's staying through the weekend."

"He'd like to, and he realizes he's on the schedule for shifts in your restaurant both Saturday and Sunday. If you're willing, I'll work in his place. I know the ropes since I helped out before I moved away."

"I remember. If you're serious, I gladly accept the offer. But don't you want to be at your dad's side, too?"

"I don't need to be." She made a sad but resigned face. "He's on his way out, but his doctor says he still has an unspecified amount of time, and I'm sticking around until January."

"As long as you're sure, the answer is yes, and thank you. We can use the extra hand."

"To change the subject, what's this I hear about a new murder in town?" Lou straightened her shoulders. "Can I assume you're involved somehow?"

"You know me too well. It's true that a body was found. In fact, Samuel discovered the corpse in one of Adele's pastures."

"Yowza. And the dude was murdered? I mean, the person."

"The body was a man, in fact." I went on to give her the high-speed thumbnail about Ivan and the possible persons of interest—Hope, Carter, and Oliver. I left out Adele's personal history with Ivan, saying only she'd known him when she was much younger. "Actually, Corrine knew him a long time ago, too. As far as I know, I don't think the death has been confirmed as a homicide yet."

"You mean the guy might have decided a sheep farm was a good place to die of a heart attack?"

"I don't mean anything except what I said."

"You mentioned an Oliver Stanganelli, right?" She tilted her head.

"Yes. Why, do you know him?"

"Not personally, but he might have lived in the town where I grew up. It's an unusual name, and I went to school with an Olly Stanganelli."

"He could be Oliver Junior. What kind of boy was he?" I asked.

"He was a couple of years younger than me, but not as young as Len. Olly was a troublemaker, as I recall. He got into fights even in elementary school."

"Maybe something he learned from his father?"

"Exactly what I was thinking." Lou picked up her wineglass. "I'll ask around. My aunt has always lived near us. She might know more."

"Thanks." Any additional details about Oliver Senior would be more than I knew now.

"You don't think the detective is seriously considering Adele being guilty, do you?" Lou asked.

"I certainly hope not."

"But Adele might be on her list."

I nodded. "Juanita McWilliam seems sharp. Adele might well be on her list."

"You know and I know Adele would never ever take someone's life except maybe in dire self-defense. To think she's a murderer is beyond ridiculous."

"No kidding."

"Listen, my friend." Lou pointed at me. "I am here to help you way beyond taking shifts in Pans 'N Pancakes, okay?"

"Deal." I smiled. "I missed you."

"Same here. I'm finding it a lot harder to make friends in New Mexico than I expected." She stood. "I plan to get out on the road for a good cycling session early tomorrow. I'll see you in the restaurant after my ride."

Cocoa jumped to his feet at hearing her say "out."

"Awesome." I let both her and the dog out the side door. "Make sure the gate latches after you, okay?"

She gave me a thumbs-up. Cocoa would do his thing and let me know when he wanted back in. I was still smiling. Not at her news. Not at her father's illness or her brother's distress. Definitely not at Adele being possibly connected with murder.

But having a girlfriend nearby again? That deserved a happy expression, and then some.

CHAPTER 26

My feet already hurt the next morning at nine thirty, and I'd only been working for an hour and a half. My lower back ached, too. I tried to practice the tailbone-forward standing position the midwife had recommended, but a pelvic tilt wasn't easy to accomplish with the load I had to tilt.

The restaurant being super busy didn't help. Why were all these people here on a Friday morning? Had they jumped the gun on their Thanksgiving break by a week? Or maybe they'd decided the weekend started a day early.

I gave myself a little virtual head slap. Being annoyed at my business thriving was no way to operate. Maybe I should start my maternity leave early if I was going to have that kind of attitude. I wanted to stay on as long as I could. I would have Sunday off, and we were always closed on Mondays. Lying around with my feet up for two days sounded dreamy.

Who was I kidding? I was terrible at sitting still. Either way, I was in no danger of doing that now.

Abe's mom Freddy bustled in, beaming. There are people who move through life scowling. Freddy was the opposite type of person, one who smiled even when she was by herself. I'd seen her through a window more than once, smiling as she climbed out of her car, and I loved her for it. I made my way over to where she shrugged out of her coat.

She held out her arms. "How's it going, Robbie? And how's my grandbaby?"

"We're both fine." I leaned in for a hug. "Feeling large and slow, but it won't be for forever."

"It certainly won't."

"How is Howard's brother doing?"

"Much better. He rallied and Howard came home." She glanced around and lowered her voice. "I understand you're working on a new case."

"I'm not sure it's a case, exactly. But, yes, I have been doing the tiniest bit of poking around."

"Because of Adele, right?"

"Exactly." I had no idea how she knew that, but whatever. Freddy was nothing if not tuned into local happenings. "Did you come in to eat?"

"You bet. I just left water aerobics, and I'm positively starving."

I glanced around the restaurant. Lou had come downstairs a few minutes earlier, and I'd given her the last open two-top. "You remember Lou Perlman, right?"

"Your friend? She earned her doctorate in sociology

a couple years back, if I'm not mistaken. Of course I remember her."

"She's staying upstairs for a few days. Let me check if she wants company." I headed over to Lou, whose breakfast hadn't been delivered yet.

She was busy composing something on her phone, but she glanced up. "Hey, Robbie."

"Lou, my mother-in-law is here, and all the tables are full. I wondered—"

"If I would share with Freddy O'Neill? I'd love to." She waved at the person in question, gesturing for her to come to the table. "I adore that woman."

"Perfect, and thank you. Listen, if you can be back here at two thirty or three today, we can do a little training with Danna and Turner to get you up to speed."

"Will do." She greeted Freddy when she arrived.

I took Freddy's order and waded back into the fray of orders, payments, and coffee pouring.

Both her and Lou's meals were ready before too long. I delivered oatmeal, fruit, and a slice of cranberry bread to Lou, and a Southwestern omelet with a side of biscuit and gravy to Freddy.

"You got the last serving of the special," I told Lou.

"I would have fought her for it, but you know me and nuts," Freddy said.

I slapped my forehead. "I'm sorry, Freddy. I know about your allergies, and those of so many others. I should have made a nut-free version. Or made all the loaves without walnuts."

"No worries, Robbie," Freddy said. "I have plenty of yummy food right here."

My brain had really deserted me. Maybe I would be

better off staying home. What worse kinds of over-sights would I make? I cleared a couple of tables. It was harder to make a mistake when cleaning up.

Lou beckoned me over. I glanced around the restaurant. The place had grown quieter since Freddy's entrance, with people having eaten and not been replaced by a flood of new customers. I pulled over a chair and sat at the corner of the table.

Lou swallowed a bite of oatmeal. "Freddy and I were talking about Oliver."

"As one does," I murmured.

"I know the name, hon." Freddy said.

"Have you been talking to your younger son?" I asked. I'd filled in Abe about the day's happenings after he came home last evening.

"Not for a couple of days, no." Freddy tapped her temple with her index finger. "You might not know this, but I never forget a name. Stanganelli isn't common in these parts." She forked in a sloppy bite of biscuit and gravy. Unlike Buck, she didn't let it drip down her chin, instead grabbing her napkin to mop up the mess.

"But you don't need a steel-trap memory to run an internet search on somebody." Lou smiled at Freddy, then took a bite of cranberry-nut bread.

Freddy, in turn, filled her mouth with omelet.

I looked from one to the other. "Are you two ganging up on me?" The ready bell dinged, twice. I pushed up to standing. "I need to get back to work. Now, dish. What did you learn about our friend Oliver?"

"He tried to rob a bank at gunpoint, got caught, and went to prison," Freddy announced, albeit in a low voice. "That's what."

CHAPTER 27

By ten thirty the restaurant was nearly deserted. I'd gotten over my shock at Lou and Freddy having researched Oliver Stanganelli better than I had, but I wasn't bothered by their delight at scooping me. All information was—or could be—useful information. Both women had finished eating and conspiring and each went off to the rest of their day half an hour ago.

"I'm headed for the bank, gang," I said to Danna and Turner after all three of us had taken much-needed breaks. "You guys okay?"

"Go for it, boss," Turner said. "The stuffed squash is nearly ready to bake."

"You'll make sure we also have a nut-free version?" I asked.

"The veggie pans are void of gluten, nuts, meat, or dairy. It tastes good, too," he said with a note of pride.

"You rock, Turner." I suited up for chilly air and grabbed the zippered cash bag. Turner did rock, and he was going to be hard to replace. Actually, hard didn't begin to describe it.

When I stepped onto the wide covered porch of Pans 'N Pancakes, I was surprised by the sunshine. When I arrived earlier, it had been barely light out, with clouds blocking the sun. Now I dragged my sunglasses out of my bag and loosened the scarf at my neck. I didn't aim for any speed records as I strolled into downtown South Lick, thinking all the way.

Oliver, apparently an acquaintance of Ivan's, used a gun to rob a bank and hadn't gotten away with it. I didn't have a chance to query Lou and Freddy about details. Had the robbed bank been South Lick's First Savings Bank, my destination this morning? Had Oliver been released from prison early for good behavior or served his full term? He must not have killed anyone with the gun or he would likely still be incarcerated. Perhaps most important, were he and Ivan imprisoned together, or had they known each other before their convictions?

A South Lick PD cruiser approached and slowed, with Buck at the wheel. He lowered the passenger window and leaned toward me.

"Need a lift, Robbie?"

"No, thanks. Just moseying to the bank." I smiled at him.

"All righty, then. Catch you later." He drove off.

I was lucky to have a good relationship with local law enforcement. When I'd first started looking into murders, I myself had been a person of interest, having publicly argued with the victim. The police finding one of my restaurant's cheese biscuits stuffed in the corpse's mouth hadn't helped.

Buck, then a lieutenant, had been adamant about me staying well away from doing any investigation on my own behalf. Our relationship had now evolved to a point where we genuinely cared about each other. He still didn't like it when I poked my curious nose where it didn't belong, but he welcomed pertinent information when I—safely—came across any.

If Buck came in to eat later, as was his habit, I would inquire about the long-ago bank robbery attempt. His memory was every bit as good as Freddy's, and he'd said he might remember something about Oliver. Tonight I'd do my own internet searching on the Stanganelli father and son. I could also pair Oliver's and Ivan's names.

In my musings, I nearly crashed into the door of Buddy's Bread, the artisanal bakery, when it opened outward. I staggered a little but caught myself.

"I'm so sorry," a woman exclaimed. "Robbie?"

"Hi, Hope."

"Are you all right?" In the crook of her left arm, Hope Morris held three baguettes in paper sleeves.

"Thank you, yes." I pointed to the bread, which smelled heavenly. "You're a baker. What are you doing buying bread?"

"I bake sweet things. Bread, especially chewy crusty sourdough, is a step beyond."

"Buddy is definitely a master." It was all I could do not to grab one of those baguettes, tear off an end, and chow down on it.

"You look, um, hungry," Hope said. "Want one?"

I laughed. "Yes, but I'll go in and buy my own."

"Enjoy. I'll be in tomorrow with desserts." She strode away.

Was that an extra-fast exit, as if she didn't want to linger talking with me? Possibly. It felt like Hope was hiding something, and I wanted to know what.

I decided to pick up my warm baguette on my way back from the bank. I knew I wouldn't be able to resist breaking off a chunk and eating it as I walked. Being covered with breadcrumbs while I did my banking wasn't a good look.

I groaned to see the long line of customers waiting inside the bank. Both tellers seemed to be doing complicated transactions, and one kept getting called away to service the drive-up window. Maybe I should have walked up to the window outside. Standing and waiting was growing more uncomfortable by the day.

When Carter Kingsley popped his head out of his office, one of the tellers gave him a desperate look as she flipped open both hands in a "what gives?" kind of gesture.

He looked up at the ceiling for a moment, then made his reluctant way behind the counter. "I can help the next person in line."

A part of me wished he'd taken the excessively pregnant woman at the end of the line first, but that wouldn't be fair. I could wait. More people came in behind me, so Carter had no chance to escape back to his office.

When my turn came, both regular tellers were busy. Carter caught sight of me and waved me forward with his lips pressed into an unpleasant line. I hoped he didn't treat other customers to such a dour expression.

I smiled and greeted him as I slid the zipped envelope onto the counter. "The deposit slip is in the bag."

He didn't smile back. He drew out the slip and the cash and began to do whatever tellers do at the computer. "I understand you're a private investigator, and I hear you're involved in solving the murder out at your aunt's farm," he muttered.

My jaw dropped, but I rescued it before it hit the floor. "Carter, I'm a cook and I own a business. That's it."

He snorted. "Right. So you haven't been asking questions about who knew Sheluk and when?" His raised eyebrows creased his forehead and made his severely receding hairline move farther back on his head.

How did I respond? With a non-response, that's how. "Could you please focus on counting my deposit? I need to get back to my place of business."

His nostrils flared, but he did as I asked. After the receipt printed out, he slid it into the now-empty bag. "I'd advise you to stay out of affairs not concerning you."

"And if I don't?"

The icicles in his smile dug right into my gut.

"Who knows what could happen?" He turned away.

Yeah, you have a nice day, too. I headed for the door. He hadn't specifically threatened me, but it felt that way, and I didn't like it. A threat against me was also a threat against my baby girl, and I already felt like Fierce Mama Bear.

CHAPTER 28

I greeted Corrine at the door of Pans 'N Pancakes after she blew in at about eleven thirty.

"I stopped by to see you at Town Hall on my way back from the bank a little while ago, but they said you were in a meeting." Elbows out, I pressed my palms into my lower back.

"And what a awful meeting it was." She slid out of her red trench coat. "Robbie, I'll tell you, even my teeth were bored. I took and skipped breakfast at home because they were supposed to offer a spread, but alls they had were measly little sweet rolls. I couldn't wait to get out of there and hightail it over here to get a plate of real food into me, ASAP."

I smiled at her customary exaggerations. "You've come to the right place."

She peered at me. "You doing okay, Robbie? You're looking a little pale."

"I'm fine, as far as I know. I'm pretty tired of hauling this weight around, but she'll . . ." I clapped my hand over my mouth.

Corrine's face lit up. "It's a she?"

"Ssh. Yes, but please don't tell anyone."

"How's come you don't want folks to know?"

"It's just something Abe and I agreed on," I murmured. "Partly so people wouldn't start giving us everything in shades of pink with ruffles."

She guffawed. "I hear you on that. Lucky for me, I didn't know if I was having a girl or a boy when I was pregnant with her." She pointed her chin at Danna. "When friends asked what I was having, I told them I expected I'd be giving birth to a human. That stopped 'em in their tracks but good. I always said, nothing wrong with a girl wearing blue and a boy wearing pink, anyhoo."

"Nothing at all. Anyway, our baby will be here soon and my burden will shift to my arms, which is fine with me." I glanced around. "You have your choice of tables. Is anyone joining you?"

The bell on the door jangled. Oliver Stanganelli came through wearing a tentative air.

"Why, I'd know that face anywhere." Corrine stepped toward him. "If it isn't Oliver Stanganelli in the flesh. Howdy, there." She extended her hand to a confused-looking Oliver.

"Do I know you, ma'am?" he asked.

"Hey now, none of this ma'am business." She beamed, pumping his hand. "I'm the current mayor of this sweet town, but I used to babysit your kiddos, remember? Corrine Beedle? You know, before y'all moved away."

His eyebrows lifted, and he swallowed. "You mean before I committed the stupidest act anyone could have imagined, and my wife took the kids and ran back to her parents? Yes, I remember you, Corrine."

Huh. So much to process in those two short exchanges.

"Robbie, we'll take that four-top, if you don't mind. Oliver here's going to join me for lunch so we can catch up on old times, and I won't take no for an answer."

He had no choice but to follow in Corrine's wake. I watched them go, with her keeping up both ends of the conversation, as she was so good at doing.

For Oliver's part, his hair looked clean and he was freshly shaved. It didn't appear he was sleeping rough, as the Brits say. That is, in a sleeping bag in an abandoned brick house on a country lane. So, whose face had I seen? Not a ghost's. Please, not a ghost's.

Five more hungry people came in, kicking off the lunch rush and leaving me no time to think about what Oliver had said. It took me a few minutes to get back to his and Corrine's table.

"What can I get you both for lunch?" I put pen to order pad.

Corrine pointed at Oliver. "You first, my friend."

"I'd like a cheeseburger, please, a green salad, and a glass of chocolate milk, if you have it."

"Sounds healthy," Corrine said. "Bet the salad in prison wasn't none too fresh."

He winced but acknowledged her with a nod. "No, it wasn't, and I dreamed of tasting chocolate milk, if you can imagine."

"I can," I said. Ivan had also ordered chocolate milk, possibly for the same reason. "Ours comes from a small local dairy. It's creamy and chocolaty and the best I've ever had. You'll love it. Corrine, what can I get for you?"

"Robbie, I'll have the squash special, the one with meat, plus a hamburger, and a side of fries." She rubbed her stomach. "I'm as hungry as Buck Bird today. Oliver here made chocolate milk sound so good, gimme a glass of it too, please."

"Got it." I scribbled both orders on the pad. "Oliver, are you finding your Beanblossom lodgings comfortable?"

He seemed to give his answer a measure of thought, finally settling for, "Yes."

"What?" Corrine said. "Only place to stay in little old Beanblossom is the motel."

"It's been clean and comfortable." Oliver shifted in his seat and focused anywhere but at his children's former babysitter.

"Let me go put your orders in." I headed for the grill. Why was he nervous? He'd said, "It's been . . ." Maybe he checked out this morning—after showering—because he ran out of money, or maybe he was headed out of town after lunch. I knew one thing. If anybody could get the story out of him, it would be Corrine.

CHAPTER 29

Unfortunately, we were so swamped I never found a free minute to sit down with Corrine and Oliver—not that I had an invitation—to have a friendly chat. Turner had delivered their food while I was busy with a big group of Australian tourists, and Oliver was gone by the time things quieted down.

Quiet was a relative term, but after Buck replaced Oliver at Corrine's table, I took the liberty of asking Danna to fix him one of his usual giant lunch platters.

Then I carved out a couple of minutes to sit down with the chief and the mayor, invited or not. I needed to get off my feet, and I wanted to let Buck know about Carter's veiled threat to me.

"Before you up your hyperbole quotient by telling me how hungry you are, Buck, you should know your lunch order is already in process." I smiled.

"You're a peach, Robbie, no two ways about it," he said.

"She is, for sure," Corrine agreed. "If peaches were sized in a triple-X."

"That's definitely how it feels." I cradled my belly with my hands. "Except this is an extra-large volleyball, not a peach."

Buck chuckled. "Did you get your banking done earlier?"

"I did." I wrinkled my nose. "But that's one thing I wanted to talk to you about."

"Oh?" he asked. "First Savings is giving you a hard time about something?"

"Not the whole bank, but one of the managers."

"Lemme guess. It was Kingsley," Corrine said.

"How did you know?" I cocked my head.

"He's a big pain in the behind, that's how." She gave her head a shake. "What'd he do this time?"

I told them about his waiting on me at the bank and what he'd said about staying out of affairs that didn't concern me. "He was referring to Ivan Sheluk."

"And how did you respond?" Buck asked.

"When I wondered out loud what would happen if I didn't, he said, 'Who knows what could happen?' But it was his expression that frankly scared me. Only for a second, then I got mad."

"You have to be careful, Robbie," Corrine said.

"Don't worry," I said. "I know I do. I didn't respond, and I left. But a threat to me is also a threat to this one." I patted my bulge. "And that's not going to fly. Not at all."

"I'll keep an eye on him, hon," Buck said. "Now, you think my lunch'll be ready anytime soon?"

I smiled. "Danna's working on it."

"Bless your heart." He stretched out his legs halfway to Kentucky. "I'm as hollow as a big old dead redwood."

I cringed a little. "My mom and I used to go camping in Sequoia National Park. There's a giant sequoia named General Sherman. It's a hundred feet around at the base and is more than two thousand years old. Luckily, it's still alive and not a bit hollow."

"I went out there to Sequoia once during my checkered youth," Buck said.

"You had a checkered youth?" I asked.

"Didn't we all?" Corrine asked.

"Not me." I shook my head. Yes, I'd fallen in love with and married the wrong man, but I'd been a too-serious college student at the time. I now realized his leaving me for a sexy female pilot was exactly what I needed. I never would have met Abe if I hadn't left California to become a chef in Indiana, living near Aunt Adele and connecting with my mom's Midwestern roots.

"Welp, I loved me them redwoods," Buck said. "The air's so clear at night up there in them Sierras you can see all the stars and the Milky Way, too."

"I know." I nodded. "It's amazing what you can see at seven thousand feet."

"Sounds like I'm going to have to make a trip west one of these years," Corrine said.

"You should," Buck agreed. "I need to take the missus out there sometime. Show her around Frisco, too."

I cleared my throat. "Buck, nobody calls it Frisco."

"What do I know?" He laughed. "I'm nothin' but a hick Hoosier."

Which was a role he loved to play.

"Corrine," I began, "did you learn anything more from Oliver?"

"What, was Stanganelli in here?" Buck asked.

"He certainly was," Corrine said. "Sat right there in your very chair."

"The man's elusive, and that's a fact," Buck said. "I'd appreciate you filling me in on what you up and learned from him."

Corrine told Buck about having babysat Oliver's kids.

"You don't say." Buck wagged his head.

"I do."

"He admitted trying to rob the bank was the stupidest thing he'd ever done," I said. "But I had to get back to work, so I didn't hear anything else."

"I got the man to fess up he'd been in prison alongside the Sheluk fellow," Corrine went on. "He made it sound like the two were friends, but I wasn't entirely convinced."

Turner arrived, both arms toting Buck's lunch.

"Thank you, son," Buck said.

"Enjoy your meal, sir. Can I get you or Madam Mayor anything else?"

Corrine snorted. "You don't have to be all formal with me, sugar pie. Corrine will do just fine. But no, thanks, I'm good."

"Me too," Buck mumbled around a mouthful of burger.

"Robbie, I hate to bother you," Turner said. "But we're getting busy." He gestured toward the door, where a dozen would-be diners milled about, waiting to be seated.

"Of course. Thanks, Turner." I hoisted myself to my feet. "Enjoy your lunch, Buck."

He blessedly held his hand in front of his mouth before speaking. "I'll be in touch."

Good. As I resumed my rounds, I thought about two things Buck had said. He'd promised to keep an eye on Carter. I knew if he personally couldn't, he would assign an officer the task.

He'd also mentioned Oliver was being elusive. The visitor wasn't exactly in hiding if he came to an entirely public restaurant like mine for lunch. Maybe he wasn't returning calls from the authorities or had failed to show up for a scheduled interview.

What I hadn't remembered to ask Buck was if anyone knew yet how Ivan had died. I hoped I would get a chance to inquire. All this wondering and investigating was moot if he'd expired from natural causes. It wouldn't explain what in the world he'd been doing in Adele's pasture, but it would certainly lift the dark cloud of suspicion from everyone's heads.

CHAPTER 30

Lou came back at a little before three o'clock as my team and I were cleaning up. After they all greeted each other and Lou joined me at the table, I asked Danna and Turner to pause what they were doing for the moment.

"Come sit down for a quick meeting," I said. "But first, beers all around?"

At three nods, I stood up.

"You sit, boss. I'll get them." Danna held out her hand for the keys to my apartment.

"Thanks," I said, then pointed at my bulge. "This one is plenty big enough for me to probably indulge in a few sips, but any alcohol right now would knock me on my keester. I'm pretty sure there are still a few NAs in the fridge back there."

Once everyone had a libation, I began. "First of all,

we need to celebrate Turner being accepted to the Culinary Institute of America for next term. That's huge, and I couldn't be happier." I'd heard him telling Danna earlier.

We clinked bottles as the two women congratulated him. Turner blushed and grinned at the same time.

"Next, Lou here is going to take Len's shifts this weekend." I glanced at her. The reason wasn't my story to tell.

She gave the slightest of headshakes.

"He had something urgent come up," I went on. "So his sister came all the way from Albuquerque to fill in."

"This one exaggerates, as usual." Lou smiled. "But yeah, since I was already out here visiting family, I said I'd be happy to sub in."

"I really appreciate it," I said. "I've been staying home every Sunday, but it's so much less hectic to have three people on the job. Danna and Turner alternate who gets Saturday off."

"It's Danna's free day tomorrow," Turner said.

"Yeah." She took a swig from her bottle. "Isaac's taking me on a surprise excursion, or so he says. I have no idea what that even means." She gave a little head-shake but looked happy about the mystery.

"Are you also having a non-beer, Danna?" I asked.

She shrugged. "Yep."

"Happy to have you on board, Lou," Turner added. "Anybody can bus and take orders, but do you have experience on the grill? Short-order cooking?"

"It's been a while, but I did help out cooking at my uncle's diner when I was in high school."

"Did you? I had no idea," I said. "I'm sure it'll come back. I think we can forgo specials for the weekend. Yes, team?"

"Absolutely." Danna nodded. "Our regular menu is delicious enough."

Turner took a swig of beer. "Have you learned anything new about that dude's death, Robbie?"

"Unfortunately, not really." I gazed at Danna. "There's a guy who has been in here today and yesterday. At first he was asking about Ivan Sheluk. It turns out your mom babysat for his kids when he and his family lived here."

"Man, is he the one who robbed the bank?" Danna asked.

"The same," I said. "You knew that story?"

"Mom used to tell me about it but without naming names."

I pointed at Lou. "And you knew his son later."

"Right," she said. "Olly, the troublemaker. I'm still waiting to hear back from my aunt about the family. I'll let you know when I do."

"Thanks." I took a sip of my drink.

"Who else are the police looking at?" Turner asked.

"I'm not sure if they're looking closely at him," I began, "but one of the bank managers in town seems to have had a history with Ivan."

"What's the manager's name?" Turner frowned.

"Carter Kingsley."

"Thought so," he said. "You can't believe how rude he's been to my dad."

"Because he's from India?" Danna's voice rose.

"Maybe," Turner said.

"That's unacceptable." She rapped the table. "What's with these people?"

"Carter was sort of rude to me this morning, too," I said. "Maybe he's simply that kind of person."

Lou snorted. "Then he shouldn't be in a customer-facing job."

"Ya think?" Danna picked up her bottle and stood. "I'm going to get back to my scrubbing. My secret get-away starts tonight, according to the big guy. For all I know, we're going on a tour of Hoosier iron sculptures."

"Not exactly romantic," Turner said.

"Nah." Danna made her way to the grill. "But if he's happy, I'm happy." She smiled to herself.

Isaac was, in fact, a big man. Tall, broad, and strong, his build was perfect for a welder and an iron artist, and for Danna.

I decided not to bring Hope's possible past with Ivan into the discussion. Nobody wanted a murderer baking their desserts. Until I had more information, I didn't want my staff to worry.

"Turner, would you mind bringing over the napkins and silverware?" I asked. "Lou and I can roll while we're sitting."

He delivered the items and began loading the dishwasher.

"Let me show you how we do this." I gave Lou a quick lesson, and the two of us got to work.

"They still don't know what this Ivan guy was doing in Adele's pasture?" Lou finished a roll and set it aside.

"Not exactly." I glanced up.

Danna and Turner were working, but I could tell

they were also listening. I could launder this story. They didn't need to know the details.

"Adele knew Ivan a long time ago," I said. "I don't think it's a secret he was recently released from prison. She thinks he came to apologize to her for something that happened."

"He didn't get a chance to?" Turner asked.

"No." I paused my busy hands.

"That's so sad." Danna also stopped scrubbing.

"The saddest," Lou agreed.

The four of us worked in silence for a minute or two. My eyes widened as my belly contracted. A little groan escaped my lips.

Lou peered at me. "Are you okay?"

"OMG, Robbie, is your labor starting?" Danna looked alarmed. "Should I put water on to boil?"

I breathed in, as deeply as I could, and out through my lips. I did it again, listening to my body, counting the seconds, checking the wall clock, until the pain passed.

"I'm fine," I said when I could speak again. "It's gone. I've been having these practice contractions, or at least that's what the midwife calls them."

This one hadn't lasted a minute. As long as the pains didn't start coming at regular intervals, Risa had said to ignore them. I hoped she was right. I didn't feel the least bit ready to give birth.

CHAPTER 31

After we finished at Pans 'N Pancakes, Lou agreed to accompany me on a sleuthing jaunt to Bean-blossom. We dropped my car at home, and I climbed into her late model sedan. It felt like the lap of luxury after my only-the-basics little hybrid. This car was pristine and clean, too. No dust on the dashboard, no grit on the floor mats, and not a single fast-food bag or gum wrapper anywhere.

"Is this a rental vehicle?" I asked Lou as I clicked my seat belt closed.

"A Volvo rental? Not a chance. No, this is Daddy's car." She stared straight ahead instead of starting the engine.

"And your father isn't driving any longer." I kept my voice soft.

"No, he's not."

"I'm so sorry, my friend."

She had seemed her centered, upbeat self earlier. Now I saw it was probably a front she'd mustered to get through the hours.

"Thanks, Rob." She squared her shoulders. "But we have to keep going, don't we? Me dissolving isn't going to help anyone." She pushed the Start button. "Now, where to?"

"Beanblossom Road."

"I'm rusty on my South Lick geography," she said. "I've been gone too long. You'll have to direct me."

"Not a problem."

It was true, Lou had lived in Bloomington, not South Lick. She'd come here to go cycling and eat at Pans 'N Pancakes. She'd helped me do a bit of investigation a couple of times, but that had been several years ago now.

Today's earlier sunshine had disappeared behind clouds. I'd pulled on my beret with my coat and scarf before we left the store. The Volvo seemed to heat up quickly, and I dragged off the hat. Then I realized the vehicle provided another source of warmth.

"This car has heated seats?" I asked.

"Yes. Aren't they nice?"

"I'm not actually sure. I have this thing about not liking to sit in a chair someone else's tush has pre-warmed. You know? It feels icky."

Lou glanced over at me with a laugh. "You're weird. Turn off the heat on your side, if you want." She pointed to the controls. "But it'll stop automatically once the seat reaches whatever temperature it's set to."

"It's okay. I'm getting used to it." I checked our surroundings. "Darn. We missed our turnoff."

"Should I reverse direction?"

"No, we can get there another way." I directed her to a state route that passed near the small unincorporated town that was our destination. "Thanks for coming with me, by the way. I'm a lot more cautious than I used to be, and I really didn't want to be out asking questions in public away from people who know me."

"You have the best reason in the universe to be cautious. You have to take care of a tiny helpless human as well as yourself. I fully expect to be named honorary auntie, you know."

"I'm already thinking of you as Auntie Lou."

Ten minutes later we passed the white Beanblossom Mennonite Church with its delightful invitation. "Strangers Expected" was painted in large letters above the double doors. I pointed a block ahead to a sign with rounded corners and stylized letters à la the Art Deco style from a century ago. A Vacancy sign hung down from the sign by two short chains. No fancy digital signage for this place.

"There's the motel," I said.

"Do you have a plan?" she asked.

"I do, but it's only three minutes old. If I ask straight out about Oliver, I'm sure they won't tell me if he's a guest. I thought I'd mention that he was an old friend and he told me he's staying here but I forgot the room number."

"And then they'll call the room. If he's there, they'll give him your name, and he'll know you're poking around. Let me handle it."

"You have a better idea?" I asked.

"Definitely." She pulled into a parking space in

front of the door labeled "Office" at the end of the long row of rooms.

The place had seen better days. The outside areas were swept and tidy, all the doors had fresh paint, and the window glass sparkled. But overall it looked tired with faded clapboards and a sagging awning. A fir tree behind the rooms had dead needles at the bottom, and the ghostly parking lines could use renewing. In front of one of the rooms a dingy white plastic chair was parked next to a bucket of sand filled with cigarette butts.

Inside the office, no one stood behind the reception counter. At least it didn't smell like stale cigarette smoke in here. I tapped the little bell. A man appeared in a doorway in the back holding a cloth napkin to his lips.

"Robbie?" Martin Dettweiler's voice rose along with his eyebrows.

I blinked to see my honey supplier working at the motel. "Martin. I'm surprised to see you here."

"Likewise." He wore his usual collarless shirt buttoned all the way up to his neck. Suspenders clipped onto black trousers completed the outfit. "Surely you or your friend do not need a motel room."

"No, sir, we don't." Lou smiled and extended her hand. "We've met before, Mr. Dettweiler. Lou Perlman, remember? We shut down traffic together in a protest a few years ago."

"Yes, yes." He shook her hand and smiled above his chinstrap beard. "Please forgive me for not recognizing you."

"No worries. It's been a while."

"Martin, do you own the motel now?" I asked.

"Not at all. But my brother does, and he has been called away to emergency grandchild-sitting while his daughter undergoes surgery."

"That's good of him," I said.

"He is a good man and would do the same for me. Regardless, late fall is a slow time in the beekeeping business, as you can imagine. I have time." He smiled at my vastness. "It looks like Adele is going to become a great-aunt any day now."

"She is." I patted my baby and the fluid she swam in. "Hopefully not for another week or two."

"God willing. Now, how can I help you ladies?" His keen brown eyes didn't miss a trick.

Martin was an honest, trustworthy person, and he knew about my bent toward justice. We weren't going to need our trumped-up stories after all.

"We were wondering about a man who said he's staying here," I began.

Martin glanced out the window behind us and spoke softly. "Would you mean Mr. Stanganelli?"

Lou whirled. I kept my focus on Martin.

"No, he is not out there," he said. "But you are not the first ones to ask about him."

"Let me guess," I said. "Were the police here?"

"The county sheriff's detective was." Martin stroked his salt-and-pepper beard. "The word 'homicide' was mentioned, may the good Lord keep the soul of the deceased."

I nodded slowly.

"Would you be able to give us Oliver's room number?" Lou asked. "I knew his son in high school up in Lafayette, and I wanted to say hello."

I looked at her. She didn't need to use her ruse. Too late now.

"I'm afraid I cannot give you his number," Martin said.

"Because it's against policy?" I asked.

"Well, there is that. But it is more because Oliver Stanganelli is not currently a guest here. In fact, he checked out this morning."

"Did he say where he was headed?" Lou asked Martin.

"No, and I did not ask. He was polite and paid his full bill in cash. He also left the room in good condition."

"Did he mention an Ivan Sheluk at all?" I asked.

"He did not, although he did say he was in the area to connect with a friend."

"Thank you, Martin," I said. "If he happens to come back, will you please let me know?"

"I will." He gave us a somber look. "If what I hear is true, some poor misguided soul has committed the sin of murder. You ladies stay safe now, promise?"

"Girl Scout's honor, Mr. Dettweiler," Lou said. "It was good to see you again."

"We promise to be careful," I added.

A woman wearing a green John Deere cap trudged in. "I'd like a room for the night, please."

"Certainly," Martin said.

"Okay if I park the rig out back, sir? I don't like to sleep in them big truck stops."

"You are welcome to, ma'am."

"We'll leave you to it, Martin." I smiled. "Be in touch."

He smiled in return. I followed Lou out the door. A semi idled at the edge of the parking lot, but the driver hadn't blocked Lou's car.

"That's got to be a hard job, a woman driving such a big truck all over the country," she murmured.

"Sounds like she's keeping herself safe by staying here."

We were going to keep ourselves safe, too. No question about it.

CHAPTER 32

The sky was already dimming at five as we headed back toward South Lick. The days would keep growing shorter from now until nearly Christmas. That was as it should be and always had been. Still, it made fall seem a lot more melancholy than it had when I was growing up in Santa Barbara at a lower latitude amid plentiful sunshine on a sparkling Pacific Ocean.

I wished I'd asked Buck when I'd seen him earlier if Adele had gotten in touch with him. There were several ways I could learn that, and one was directly on our way back to my house.

"Do you mind if we stop in at Adele's for a couple minutes?" I asked Lou. "We'll pass right by her place."

"I'd love to see her again. I'll need you to remind me which house it is when we get close."

I didn't usually come at my aunt's house from this

direction. I peered closely at the road until I saw her farm sign ahead.

"There." I pointed. "Where it says Ovinia Farm."

"Got it." Lou turned up the long drive after the sheep-shaped sign of a big-eyed, smiling sheep wearing a blue-and-green knitted sweater.

The house was lit from within only by the one lamp Adele always left on, and her old red truck was gone.

"Darn," I said. "Looks like she's out. Hover here for a sec and let me call her, okay?" I pressed the number for her landline phone, but neither she nor Samuel picked up.

"No answer?" Lou asked.

"No. If Adele doesn't answer the landline, she's either out or sound asleep. It's okay. I'll connect with her later."

"Onward?"

"Homeward ho."

I had sent Abe a message about my plans before we'd left South Lick. I didn't want him to worry about why my car was home but I wasn't. A text from him dinged on my phone.

Strom and Pete's pizza and salad takeout for dinner?

I wrote back.

OK if Lou joins us?

He immediately replied it was fine.

I glanced at Lou. "Want to stay for dinner? Abe is picking up pizza and salad for dinner."

"If I'm not intruding, eating with you both sounds lovely."

"You're not," I told Lou. "He'll be happy to see you."

I sent another message saying she was a yes.

"Rats," I said. "We need more of Martin's honey in the store and I forgot to ask him to bring a box of jars over."

"Can't you text him?"

"He doesn't text. I'll give him a quick call."

When he didn't pick up—which of course he didn't, since he was in the motel and his landline was in his house—I left a voicemail message with my request, then gazed out at the approaching dusk as we drove. We approached the abandoned brick house on the left, and again I pointed.

"Do you mind pulling in there?" I asked.

"Not at all." She crossed over the center line and parked in front, idling the engine. "Is this the Bean-blossom Road Homes Beautiful Tour?"

I laughed. "How about the Derelict Buildings Tour?" I leaned forward and peered through the windshield at all the upstairs windows.

"What are you looking for?" Lou asked.

"I'm not sure." I explained about thinking I'd seen a face on the second floor.

"And you think this face might be connected to the dead body."

"'Might' is the right word. Maybe I didn't actually see anyone."

"Do you want to do a walk-around? With me, I mean."

"Would you?" I asked. "I made my way down one side of the place yesterday, but it was earlier in the day. I didn't exactly investigate. Staying safe and so on."

"Staying safe is good, and you know what they say. There's power in numbers, even if the number is only two." She switched off the car and opened her door. "Let's do it."

I smiled to myself. It was so much better to do this kind of thing—snooping, that is—with a partner in crime, as it were. I boosted my large self out of my seat and lumbered after her.

Lou stood at the front door. "This entrance looks pretty well secured."

The heavy wooden door with its carved border was, in fact, secured by a padlock in a thick hasp. The narrow strips of plywood screwed onto each side had to be protecting what were probably glass sidelights.

"Nobody's going in that way," I agreed.

"So, which way, Miss Marple?"

I gave her a look. "I don't think Miss Marple ever went sleuthing carrying a nearly at-term baby inside her."

"You would be correct," Lou said. "Christie wrote her as a widow or a spinster, I think. Either way, she was well past baby-making age."

"But still plenty sharp enough to ask questions and solve crimes." I glanced toward the right and then the left. "I headed along the left side yesterday. Let's do it again and make a circuit."

"After you, ma'am."

I tugged my phone out of my coat pocket and turned on the flashlight app. "This is in lieu of either a magnifying glass or a torch, as Jane Marple called it."

Lou did the same and followed me along the side.

Nothing appeared different, except . . . where was the box of toys? I came to a stop at the corner of the house.

"Yesterday a cardboard box of plastic toys was here," I said in a low voice. "It was labeled *Free* and looked like it had been there a while." Today the air smelled mustier here, maybe because the weather was damper. The dim light made the bricks look in worse shape, too. "It might have been sitting there for weeks, months, or years. I couldn't tell."

"Probably not years, right? The box would have dis-integrated." Lou swept her light over the area. She stooped, picked up a small object, and held it out. "Toys like this one?"

In her gloved hand was a yellow plastic duckie. Probably originally a bath toy, it was now faded and dinged with spots of mold, its perky, upturned orange beak and bright black eyes garish instead of cute.

"Yes." I nodded. "I wonder where the rest of the toys went, along with the box holding them. Let's keep moving." I'd gone an hour without relieving my poor compressed bladder, and I wanted to get home to do exactly that.

I rounded the corner and halted so abruptly Lou al-most bumped into me. My breath rushed in at the sight of a car, a boxy sedan decades old with rust patches near the wheel wells. Its red paint had faded, especially on the roof. The driver's-side door had either been re-painted blue or was a junkyard replacement.

"Do I gather that car wasn't here yesterday?" Lou asked in a whisper.

"It was not," I murmured as I peered into the gloaming at the back door of the house. "And weeds were growing in front of the door. They're gone now."

Lou moved ahead of me and snapped a picture of the license plate on the back of the car. I didn't budge. Was that a noise from inside the house?

"Lou." My voiced rasped. "We need to go."

She straightened and took a photo of the whole car.

"Lou!" My uterus contracted again, like it had this afternoon.

I couldn't help letting out a groan, which finally got her attention. She hurried toward me. I wanted to stay here and monitor whatever was happening to my body, but we couldn't. She took my arm. As we retraced our steps, the Braxton-Hicks thing ended. I let out a noisy exhale.

"Are you all right, Robbie?" she asked.

"I'm fine. Did you hear a noise from inside?"

"Car first. Talk later."

Good plan. This felt dangerous, and that was a place I did not want to be.

Lou waited to speak until she'd driven us well away from the house. "You heard a noise from inside the house?"

"I think so." How had we thought two would be safe enough in the face of danger? At twilight, no less.

"My heart was beating so hard back there, I couldn't hear anything else," Lou said. "I got a good shot of the plate and of the whole car. I haven't seen a seventy-seven Volvo in a long time."

"The one out back was the same make of car as the one we're in?" I asked.

"You bet. My uncle had a blue one he nursed along for years, but when it got rust holes in the floorboards, it was curtains for the car." She smiled. "In fact, the door on the one we saw could have come from whatever junkyard my uncle's Volvo ended up in."

CHAPTER 33

Lou and I continued back to South Lick along the hilly country lane. If we passed any more abandoned homes possibly occupied by possible murderers, I didn't notice.

I fell silent as we drove, thinking about the car behind the house.

"After we get to my house," I began, "will you text me those pictures you took?"

"Sure. You want to forward them to the police?"

"I think it's information Buck will want to have. I mean, it could be any squatter's car. But if it's Oliver's, and if the authorities want to talk with him, they're going to need to find his car to find him."

"He does have ties to where I grew up," Lou said. "Seriously, the blue door on the seventy-seven we saw could well have come off my uncle's car."

"Right. I wonder where the box of toys went. Maybe

he got rid of them because the box was visible from the road. Others besides me could have gone snooping around the back and seen his car."

"That sounds like a good explanation."

After about ten minutes, the road straightened as we reached the more populated part of town. Lights from living rooms and kitchens warmed the darkness. I'd always loved this time of the evening, when people were home with their lamps lit but hadn't yet closed blinds and drapes. Every window afforded a momentary and fascinating peek into an entire life, from people doing dinner prep in kitchens to seniors in easy chairs perusing the newspaper to children clustered around video games.

"Have you heard from Len today?" I asked.

"I did. He says he's pretty broken up about Dad, but he's trying to hold it together." She smiled. "They've been watching a lot of videos of women's basketball. Pro, college, and our former high school's championship team."

"The one Len played on," I murmured.

"Yeah. Dad was always his biggest supporter."

"It's sweet they can share basketball again."

"I know. I can't tell you how happy it makes me they're spending this time together, Robbie."

I touched her knee. "It's so great your dad accepts Len now."

Lou swallowed a sob. "It's all the time they'll have." She sniffled and fell silent, focusing on the drive.

I kept quiet, as well.

When we approached my house, Lou shot me a glance. "Do you want to tell Abe about our excursion?"

"Ugh." I scrunched up my nose. "I'd rather not, but I don't want to keep secrets from him."

"Not keeping secrets from each other sounds like a good practice for a married couple about to have a child." She pulled up to the curb.

"Excuse me for dashing in, but I have something urgent to do."

Lou laughed. "I'll be right behind you."

Abe pulled into the driveway as I was unlocking the front door. I raised my hand in a wave and did my dashing. By the time I came out, much refreshed and with clean face and hands, Lou was setting the table, while Abe poured drinks. Fragrant flat boxes from Strom and Pete's sat on the counter, and Abe had already transferred the green salad to our wide bowl. Lou excused herself to wash up.

After delivering a kiss and a hug to Abe, I sank onto a chair.

"Thank you for bringing food, darling husband." My stomach gurgled.

He laughed. "Hungry much?"

"Very."

It wasn't long before we three sat devouring hot, cheesy, delicious slices. Abe dug into the pepperoni on his piece. I savored the Kalamata olives and caramelized onions on mine, and Lou looked happy with a slice of the Mexican-flavored chicken version. Abe and Lou sipped beer, but I stuck with water.

Abe and I came up for air at the same time.

"How was your day?" he asked, preempting my asking him the same.

"Full, as always," I said. "Yours?" I didn't mean to practice avoidance, but I also didn't want the focus on me.

"Had an entire preschool come for a visit, or that was what it felt like." He winked.

"Wait. What's your job these days?" Lou asked.

"I'm in charge of wildlife education at the state park here in Brown County. Sometimes the job includes educating toddlers."

"I bet you love it," Lou said. "When I moved away, you were an electric company lineperson."

"I was," he said. "This is much safer and a lot more fun."

"And when little kids show up, it's good practice, right?" Lou grinned.

"You bet." Abe sipped his beer. "Hey, I'm sorry about your father, Lou. Robbie told me he's not doing well."

Her eyes filled. "Thank you. No, he's not doing well at all, but my brother is with him right now, and I'm back in Indiana for as long as I need to be."

"She's filling in for Len in the restaurant while he's up north," I told him. I decided to take the plunge on explaining my own day to Abe, but where to start? At the beginning, surely. "Your mom came in for breakfast this morning."

"She told me." Abe frowned. "She also said she found out this Stanganelli guy robbed a bank. You are being careful, sweetheart, aren't you?"

"Always, my dear." I opened my mouth to go on when the trifecta hit. My phone started playing "All You Need is Love" by the Beatles, which was my ring tone for Adele. The doorbell rang. And my gigantic belly contracted.

Abe stood. "I'll get the door." He disappeared into the hall.

Unlike him, Lou noticed my grimace. "Another one, Rob? How can I help?"

"Answer Adele." I swiped the call open and handed her the phone.

"Robbie's phone." Lou shot me a worried look. "Lou Perlman speaking."

I cradled my giant cramp and hoped this was a practice contraction and not the real thing. I inhaled, slowly and deeply. I sent my breath to my uterus, as Risa had recommended, and then let it out.

"Yes, she's here," Lou said. "Hang on a minute, okay?" She raised her eyebrows.

The pain passed. I held out my hand for the phone. "Hi, Adele."

"Hey there, sugar pie. How are you making out?"

"I'm pretty good. Lou and I stopped by your house an hour or so ago, but you didn't seem to be home."

"Just got back. I wanted to let you know I stopped by the station and spoke to Buck. Took and told him everything I know, leastwise about me and Ivan."

"I'm glad." I was, very. "Thank you for letting me know."

"Sure thing, sweetheart." Away from the phone she said, "What, sugar love?"

As I waited, Abe ushered Buck into the room. I held up my index finger.

"Roberta, I gotta skedaddle," Adele said. "My honey-bun's got dinner on the table."

"Enjoy." I smiled at the thought of my aunt having a "honeybun" and Samuel cooking for his beloved. Mostly I smiled at her coming clean about her past. "Love you."

"You take care, now. Love you, too." Adele disconnected.

Still smiling, I gazed up at Buck. "Welcome to the pizza party, Buck. We have plenty. Have a seat."

He did not return my smile. He did not sit. Abe looked serious, too. *Uh-oh.* Something was up, and it wasn't a good something.

CHAPTER 34

Buck finally agreed to sit at the table with us. With his usual congeniality being AWOL, my bad-news radar was way up.

Abe let Cocoa in from the backyard. He preferred to walk the dog, but sometimes having a fenced-in yard was more than convenient.

"Buck, do you remember Lou Perlman?" I asked.

"Evening, sir." She smiled at him.

"Yes, of course." He drummed his fingers on the table.

"So, give," I said. "What's up?"

Maceo strolled up and wove his body around Buck's legs. Buck reached down to pet him. Cocoa yipped and trotted over to join the black-pets-being-petted party.

This was all lovely, but I was getting antsy about why Buck had showed up here on a Friday night looking either like somebody had died, which I desperately

hoped wasn't someone I was close to, or as if somebody was about to be arrested. Arrest better not happen
to anybody in this house or to Adele. Not tonight, not
ever.

"Cocoa, bed." Abe used his no-nonsense voice and
pointed at the dog's bed in the corner.

Cocoa went. Maceo trotted over and curled up next
to him, a sight that always amazed me. Maybe they
both missed Sean and took comfort in each other. I
didn't know where Birdy was, but he never took part in
the love fests.

Buck straightened. He cleared his throat. "It seems
our esteemed mayor has come under suspicion in the
possible homicide of Mr. Sheluk."

"What?" My voice rose. My jaw felt like it dropped
to the floor. I scooped it up, because I needed it to object. "Corrine? You can't think, I mean . . ." My voice
trailed off. I am not usually struck speechless, but this
time I was.

"Believe me, I'm not happy about it," Buck said.
"Seems McWilliam uncovered information about Corrine's past. I mean in the wayback kind of past."

"Like when she was a teen and briefly knew Ivan." I
frowned, thinking back on what she'd told me.

Buck nodded. Abe looked confused. Lou gave me
an intense gaze.

"It must have been, what, thirty years ago?" she asked.

"About that," I said. "What exactly did McWilliam
find out?"

"All's I know is it's something incriminating and
worthy of more investigation." He shifted in his seat.
"Our fine detective asked Corrine to temporarily step

down from her job. The mayor—rightly, in my opinion—refused."

"I agree," Abe said. "She hasn't been officially accused of anything, has she? She's not in jail, not arrested, I assume."

"You would be correct," Buck said.

"Buck, why does McWilliam think Corrine would have murdered Ivan?" I asked. "She told me she hadn't liked him when she briefly knew him through Charles Morton."

"The daddy of her birth son," Buck said.

"Right," I said. "But that doesn't mean she killed Ivan."

Lou snorted. "There would be a lot fewer men alive today if I'd killed all the ones I didn't like as a teenager." She looked at Buck's somber expression. "Sorry, sir, didn't mean to joke, but seriously. You don't murder someone you haven't seen in thirty years because he was rude to you years ago. Many years ago."

A thought hit me. "Does Danna know?"

"I don't know," Buck said.

"This must have just happened, right?" I asked Buck. "You and Corrine ate lunch together today."

"I learned about it an hour ago. Adele came in to share her own past with the deceased, but she'd gone home. I was on my way to dine with my sainted wife when McWilliam asked me to come back to the station."

"Isn't Danna off on a getaway with her boyfriend?" Lou cocked her head at me. "She said this afternoon they were leaving tonight."

"She is," I said. "That's a good thing." *Whew*. I was

quite fond of Danna, and I felt protective of her, not that she'd ever shown any need for protection. "I'm sure Corrine wouldn't call and disturb her with un-founded bad news like this. It's the kind of information you want to deliver in person, and only if you ab-solutely have to."

Buck nodded, but his attention had wandered. He cast a hungry eye at the Strom and Pete's boxes.

"Buck." Abe gestured at all the uneaten pizza. "You'll help us out with these pies, won't you?"

Leave it to my gentle husband to couch the invita-tion as a favor Buck would be doing us.

"I have to acknowledge I am a mite hungry," Buck said. "I already told Melia our dinner would have to be a rain check."

"Let me get you a plate." Abe stood. "And a beer, a soda, coffee?"

"I'd best not accept a beer, although one would wet the whistle quite nicely. Do you happen to have any root beer in the house? Or any other cocola would be dandy."

"I'll check." Abe headed off to the kitchen.

"This must mean Corrine doesn't have an alibi for the night of the murder," I said.

"She don't," Buck said. "And that's a fact. But no-body does, nobody who might could have had a reason to kill the man."

"Adele must," Lou chimed in. "Wasn't she with Samuel all night?"

"Go on, now," Buck said. "We ain't looking at Adele for real."

"A court probably wouldn't give a person's domestic

partner much credence as a witness, anyway, would they?" I asked.

"Nope, they would not."

Abe brought a plate, napkin, fork and knife, and a cold bottle of Dr Pepper to Buck. "This close enough to root beer for you, Chief?"

"It surely is, and I thank you, O'Neill." Buck tucked his napkin into his collar.

"Help yourself to all you want," I said.

He loaded three slices onto his plate, which left enough for each of us to have one more. It was a good thing Abe had ordered three large pizzas. He was still used to feeding a lanky growing teenage boy along with the two of us.

As I took a bite, I couldn't stop wondering what Juanita McWilliam thought she had on Corrine. I found it hard to believe it was anything of substance. Maybe the detective needed something else to work on.

"Lou, when you're done, send me those shots of the car, okay?" I asked.

"I already did."

I wiped my mouth and checked my phone. "Sorry, I hadn't noticed." I explained to Buck and Abe what we'd seen behind the brick house. "Before either of you gets upset, we were only driving by after stopping in to see Adele. All we did was take a peek—together—behind the building. I'm quite sure a car wasn't back there the first time I looked. I'm going to forward Lou's photos to you now, Buck, and to McWilliam."

"All righty," Buck said. "Trying to distract her from looking too close at Corrine?" He grinned.

"How'd you know?" I wrote a quick message to

Buck and the detective and tapped Send. "I don't know whether it'll work or not, but it's worth a try."

"I'll have one of my people run the plate," Buck added.

Lou shot me a glance, raising her eyebrows. I had the feeling she wanted to know if we should talk about our little visit to the motel. I tried to shake my head slowly, subtly. I'd already told the detective where Oliver had been staying. She would find out soon enough that he'd checked out.

Abe knit his brow. "What else did you two get up to?"

Oops. He knew me too well. "We paid a visit to my friend Martin Dettweiler over in Beanblossom. You know, the guy who brings honey for sale at the store?"

"You've spoken of him," Abe said, "but I haven't met the man."

"Robbie was taking me on a driving tour of our old cycling routes," Lou said. "When she saw Martin outside the motel, we had to stop to say hello."

Way to pull off a little white lie, I thought. "Yes, he's managing the place for his brother right now."

"Such a lovely man," Lou added. "We had a nice chat with him."

I mustered my most angelic face. I was quite sure Abe hadn't fallen for any of it, but it didn't matter. Both Lou and I had stayed safe while poking around, which was what counted in the end.

CHAPTER 35

L ast night had blessedly passed with not a single
contraction. Buck and Lou left before eight o'clock,
leaving Abe and me to snuggle, read, and go to bed
early. He had to work this morning, despite it being
Saturday, but he said he'd try to get to the restaurant for
lunch.

Before I drove to work, I took a minute to call
Corrine, except she didn't pick up. I didn't blame her. I
sent a text, instead.

**Buck told me about false accusation. Wanted to
offer my support. Hugs.**

Sure, she was the mayor, but she'd also become a
friend and had been supportive to me in hard times in
the past. Plus, she was Danna's mom. I felt close to
both of them. At the moment I also felt rather fierce
about anyone thinking Corrine might be a murderer.

I arrived at Pans 'N Pancakes on time, and by now

I'd been trudging through my job for forty-five minutes. My body seemed heavier today—physically, not psychically—which made my movements slower and more difficult. I hadn't eaten that much pizza. It was almost as if something had shifted inside, or maybe Baby Girl had a growth spurt overnight.

Lou was doing a great job as Danna's substitute. When she needed to know something, she asked. I was making fresh coffee when she bustled up with a table's worth of dirty dishes.

"Any fallout with Abe after we left?" she asked in a low voice.

"No. He was cool. I assured him we stayed safe and that was that."

"I'm glad. I didn't want to get you in trouble."

"It's all good." I smiled.

The bell jangled. My happy expression slid away to see Detective McWilliam stride in. She halted and looked around, appearing as serious as Buck had last night.

"Who's she?" Lou asked.

"The detective on the case, Juanita McWilliam."

"She doesn't look happy."

"No, she doesn't, and I'm going to find out why."

Turner hit the Ready bell. Lou dried her hands.

"Let me know when you need a break, Turner," I said.

"I can swap in when you're ready," Lou added.

"I'm good for now, thanks." He flipped an omelet and reached for the pitcher of pancake batter. "But this is running low, boss."

"I'll mix up more in a minute." I headed for McWilliam. "Good morning," I said when I reached her.

She surveyed the room. "I need to speak with Danna Beedle." Her turtleneck today was an aqua that matched her readers, which were again atop her head.

"You can't."

She had a finely shaped nose, but even a pretty nose looks worse with flared nostrils.

"It's official police business." The detective folded her arms on her chest. "Why can't I speak to her?"

"Because A, if she were here, she'd be working. And B, because she's not here."

"Where did she go?"

I turned my face away for a moment so I didn't blow up at her. I returned my focus to the detective. "I have no idea. She has the day off. Her personal life is private, as it should be." I let out a breath. "Will you be eating here this morning?"

"No." She seemed to catch her own rudeness. "No, thank you."

Adele pushed through the door. She began to smile at me, then the detective's presence apparently registered. I thought my aunt might turn around and leave. Instead, she made her way toward us. I pulled her in for a side hug.

"Howdy, sugar," she said to me. "Morning, Detective."

"Ms. Jordan." McWilliam bobbed her head.

"Robbie, can I get me somewheres to eat a bite of breakfast?"

"Certainly." I made my own survey. "We have a four-top free. Is that okay?"

"It's perfect, hon."

"May I have a word, Ms. Jordan?" McWilliam asked her.

"You may, long's you call me Adele and come set a spell while I have my breakfast."

"Thank you." The detective checked her watch. "I guess I will eat after all, Robbie."

Adele lifted her chin. "I sure as heck hope you're ready to explain what in tarnation you were thinking to call our mayor a murderer. I've never heard of a more lame-brained idea."

McWilliam opened her mouth. And closed it. Smart move. It wasn't a good idea to argue with Adele when she'd made up her mind about something.

"You ladies can seat yourselves," I said. "I'll be over in a few minutes to take your orders."

The detective followed Adele to the table. I used my few minutes for a quick restroom break and a swig of water. By the time I slid into a clean apron, Buck had joined the women.

I jotted down their orders. "I'd love to hear any news, but right now I have a couple of things to do."

"We ain't going nowheres," Buck drawled.

Back in the kitchen area, Lou and Turner had switched roles. I stuck the order slip on the carousel and read it out loud to her.

"Grits with sausage gravy, plus two sunny-side-up with bacon and white toast, and a side of pancakes. All of that is for Buck. Adele asked for a cheese omelet and a biscuit with gravy. Oatmeal, fruit, and nonfat milk for the detective."

"Got it."

I quickly mixed together the dry ingredients for our signature whole wheat pancakes, a recipe I knew by heart, having made it almost daily for years. I beat in the eggs, oil, and milk, and decanted some of it into a clean straight-sided pitcher.

Frowning, Turner unloaded a table's worth of dirty dishes. "Robbie, the customers at that four-top are asking about Mayor Beedle. They said something about her being arrested for murder. They can't be right, can they?"

It never took long for South Lick's gossip mill to crank into high gear. I looked around the restaurant and knew exactly who he meant. Those men were regulars in here for breakfast and usually seemed like they were playing a game of telephone, with each embellishing a story worse than the next.

"The table nearest the door?" I asked.

"Yes." He nodded.

"They have a shred of truth in their story, but, no," I said. "Corrine hasn't been arrested for anything."

"Good. Danna would be beside herself, you know? Devastated and mad all at once."

"She would." She might still be after she heard the news. "Buck stopped by last night and said Detective McWilliam seems to have something on Corrine. Lou was with us. What did you think, Lou? I felt like Buck didn't think it was a credible accusation."

"That was my impression, too." She slid scrambled eggs, two links, and a pile of hash browns onto a plate and set it under the warmer. "These need wheat toast. The order of pancakes and bacon is for the other person at table six."

"Got it," I said.

Turner finished rinsing. He slid the dishes into the dishwasher, still frowning.

"Don't worry, Turner," I told him. "Corrine didn't kill anybody. Danna has nothing to worry about."

I crossed my fingers as I spoke, as if that would make it true.

CHAPTER 36

By the time I had a minute free, it was nine thirty. Adele had eaten and left. McWilliam lingered at the table with Buck, the two of them with their heads together over a tablet. With customers and food under control, at least for the moment, I aimed for the law enforcement table.

"Set yourself down, Robbie." Buck jumped up to pull out a chair for me.

"Thanks, Buck." A creaky breath escaped me as I sat. Despite how good it felt to be off my feet, I knew I might not have much time to relax. I got straight to my long list of questions. "Were you able to track down the owner of the car Lou and I saw?"

McWilliam glanced at me over the top of her reading glasses. She grimaced and pointed to Buck.

"Seems it was reported stolen," he said. "We've impounded the vehicle and are dusting for fingerprints and such."

"That's disappointing," I said.

"It sure enough is," Buck agreed.

"Where was it stolen from?" I asked.

"Up Lafayette way." Buck held up his hand. "Yep, I know up north there is where the Stanganelli man lived."

Maybe the car behind the house hadn't been his after all. Maybe he'd never gone near the abandoned building. Or maybe they would match fingerprints in the car to his. He'd been incarcerated. His prints surely were in an official database.

"Where were he and Ivan in prison?" I realized I had no idea.

"FCI Terre Haute," Buck said. "It's a medium security federal corrections institution. Apparently they both, while not model prisoners, mostly behaved theirselves and kept their noses clean."

"Do either of you know yet how Ivan died?" I asked.

"More's the pity, no," the detective said. "I thought I could pull a few strings with the coroner. So far I haven't been able to."

"Which means you don't know for sure if his death was a homicide," I said.

"Correct," she said.

"Any idea how long it will take?" I pressed. I knew I was being intrusive, but either of them could stop responding any time they wanted.

The detective shook her head.

I glanced around. Still quiet. "What about Carter

Kingsley? Have you found out how he and Ivan knew each other?"

"The man's being singularly unhelpful along those lines," Buck said. "Kingsley don't seem to have a record, so we know they didn't meet in the lockup."

"Huh." I gazed at McWilliam. Maybe a lighter touch would work. "Detective, Buck mentioned you have an idea Corrine Beedle might.be involved in Ivan's death. I'd love it if you'd share the reason." It was worth a try.

"I'm sure you would, Robbie." She stuck her reading glasses on top of her head and folded her hands on the table. "By virtue of the fact you are close to both the mayor and her daughter, your employee, that's not going to happen."

Darn.

She rose, laid cash on the table, and stashed her tablet in her shoulder bag. "Thank you for the meal, Robbie. See you in an hour, Buck." And she was gone.

Buck stood. "Give you a hoist, my friend?"

I laughed. "No, thanks. I can manage." I did feel like a personal crane would be helpful at times, but I could still lay my palms flat on a table and use my cyclist's thighs and strong core to get myself on my feet. "What do you and the fine detective have in an hour?"

He wrinkled his nose. "Some kind of meeting about the case with her boss. Don't know why they want to up and rope me into these shenanigans."

"Maybe because you're the chief of police for our lovely town?" I smiled.

"I s'pose. You take care now, hon." He set his hat on his head and peered down at me. "You know who to call if you happen to need emergency transport—on my personal cell, mind you."

"Thank you. Let's hope I won't be part of any emergencies."

He laid money on the table, too much as always, and moseyed for the door.

I'd stopped protesting at the amount. I slid his bills and McWilliam's cash into my apron pocket. I glanced at the jangling door and took in a deep breath. Hungry diners in hiking clothes poured in, one after another. A group of women followed. By the look of them, they were tourists out for a day of shopping and eating.

The Saturday mid-morning rush was upon us. I quickly cleared the four-top as Turner arrived with a rag and spray bottle.

I made my way to the kitchen. "Ready for your first rush?" I asked Lou.

"I guess I'd better be." She flipped three pancakes in a row.

"Do you want to take a break real quick?"

"I should, right?" She slid out of her apron. "Did you learn anything from those two?" she whispered.

"As a matter of fact, not really."

She hurried off to the restroom. I used the spatula to carefully mix around a pile of peppers and mushrooms. I rescued an omelet and flipped two eggs without breaking their yolks.

The lack of a cause of death disturbed me the most. How could they pursue an investigation without that information? I wished I could have learned more about what the detective thought she had on Corrine.

A rasher of bacon popped hot oil, which hit the back

of my hand. I jumped back, dropping the spatula on the grill. My unwieldy bulk bumped backwards into Turner. His armful of dishes crashed to the floor, and not quietly.

I swore. Quietly, but out loud. I slid past him to the sink, crunching shards of broken china underfoot, and ran my hand under cold water.

"Are you all right, boss?" Turner asked.

"Hot oil. Burned my hand, but only a little. I'm so sorry about the dishes." I sniffed. "Can you fill in at the grill? Something's burning, and Lou's on a quick break."

"Got it." He carefully slid the spatula off the hot surface with another one and went to work. It looked like the pancakes were a lost cause, and possibly a sausage or two, but we had plenty.

I vowed to make this the last time I tried to multitask thinking and cooking. My rational brain seemed to be on a sabbatical, which was dangerous around a hot grill.

I grabbed the aloe gel out of our first aid kit. I applied it to my burn, added a rectangular adhesive bandage, and slid a latex glove over my hand. I moved our trash receptacle closer to the detritus, then squatted and began picking up the biggest pieces of broken dishes.

"You shouldn't oughta be down on the floor, now, Robbie."

I glanced up, way up, at Corrine in her weekend outfit of red sneakers, pressed blue jeans, and a black and white sweater.

"I'm supposed to be practicing my squatting for labor," I said.

"Don't be ridiculous. Here, let me help you up." She extended her hand. "I'll finish this mess."

With a smile, I accepted the assist. "Thank you. I'm the one who caused it by backing into Turner."

"No worries, hon." She knelt but glanced up. "When you get a minute free, I'd like to have a quick chat."

"Absolutely."

I would like to have a chat, too. What I hadn't dug out of Buck and McWilliam might come freely from Corrine herself.

CHAPTER 37

It took more than half an hour to seat and serve the influx of diners. Corrine sat in our waiting area, patiently working on her phone when she wasn't smiling at and schmoozing with locals. She was an extrovert through and through. Doing her mayoral thing came naturally to her.

I finally got her seated at a two-top. By the time her food was ready, my feet and I were ready for a break. Business was at a manageable dull roar, and my curiosity about what Danna's mom wanted to tell me was peaking.

"I'm going to sit with Corrine for a few, okay?" I asked Lou at the grill and Turner, who'd just stuck a couple of order slips on the carousel.

"Go for it," Lou said.

Turner nodded his agreement. I picked up Corrine's plate of cheese omelet with ham, hash browns, and toasted English muffin, plus a side of biscuit and gravy. It smelled heavenly as I made my way to her table.

"Take a load off, Robbie." Corrine pointed to the other chair.

"Thanks. Sitting was my plan." A happy groan slipped out as I sat. "I'm glad I'm due soon. For lots of reasons, primary being that I'll get to meet my baby in person. But carrying around this weight is getting old." At least I hadn't had any Braxton-Hicks contractions today— so far.

"I hear ya, hon." She tucked into a bite of omelet. When she came up for air, she sighed. "As a girl who grew up with nothing but American cheese, I'm kind of deliriously glad to have discovered the world of real cheese. Whatever kind y'all put in these omelets, it sure is tasty."

I smiled. "We combine sharp cheddar and gouda, with a little mild goat cheese thrown in for creaminess. I'm glad you like it."

"I do. Makes the other stuff taste like plastic."

I waited to speak until she'd swallowed another bite of real cheese in her omelet. "Buck told me Detective McWilliam seems to have connected you in some way with Ivan Sheluk's death, or maybe it's with his past."

Corrine nodded but took a bite of ham with hash browns instead of speaking.

"You said he was a friend of Danna's birth father," I prompted.

"Yep, he was, and that's all my connection was." She picked up her napkin and patted her mouth without making eye contact. "McWilliam doesn't seem to be-lieve me."

I sat waiting for more. And waited longer. She'd been the one to say she wanted to talk. So why wasn't she talking?

Around me the restaurant hummed with clinks of flatware on dishes, conversations soft and loud punctuated with laughter, meat sizzling on the grill, the jangle of the cow bell.

I glanced at the entrance. Hope once again backed in, arms full of dessert-laden trays. I wanted to speak with her, as well as with Corrine. Turner hurried over to help Hope. She probably had more cookies and brownies in her car, but she might not. If Corrine was going to share something with me, now was the time.

"Corrine? You said you wanted to talk, but I need to check in with Hope." I pointed with my chin. "Are you going to be here a little longer?"

As if startled out of a reverie, Corrine looked up from her nearly empty plate. "Perfect. Bring her on over. She's part of it, you know, this whole mess."

I blinked. *Part of it?* "Will do." I stood. I assumed the mess she referred to was Ivan's death, and I had the promise of finding out more soon. "Back in a flash."

I intercepted Hope at the door. "Thanks for bringing those in, Hope. Are you heading out to your car to grab more?"

"No. You asked for a reduced order because you're closed Mondays, didn't you?"

"Right." I shrugged off my forgetfulness, which I hoped was due to pregnancy brain. "Can you join Corrine and me for a bite to eat? On the house, of course." I gestured in the mayor's direction.

Hope's eyes narrowed and her brow furrowed. As

she glanced at Corrine, a tic began to beat next to her upper lip. She pressed a finger on it. She breathed in, deeply, and let it out. "Okay, sure. Thanks." She followed me to the table.

"Hey there, Hope," Corrine said. "Long time, no see. You gonna take a seat and join us?"

"Apparently." She laid her hand on her cheek and chin, as if thinking, but she still pressed on the tic.

"You can have this chair," I urged. "I'll pull up another one." I slid a chair from a nearby empty four-top but stayed on my feet. "What can I get you to eat? It can be breakfast or lunch."

"I'd like a turkey and cheddar on rye, if I can." Her voice was flat. Was she not hungry or not eager to chat with the Queen of Schmooze?

"Grilled?" I asked. "Fries?"

"Both, please, and a ginger ale."

"You got it." I scribbled the order on my pad. "Be right back." I hurried so I didn't miss anything. As it turned out, I didn't have to go far. I handed the order to Turner as he passed by, then reversed course and joined Corrine and Hope.

Except Hope had her phone out, apparently avoiding speaking with Corrine, who used her English muffin to mop up every morsel on her plate and on the small one that had held the gravy-laden biscuit.

"I'm back." I mustered my cheeriest voice. "So, how did you two know each other in the past?"

Corrine popped in a last bite of biscuit and pointed at Hope, who looked reluctant as she stashed her phone.

"Ivan was a kind of magnet," she began.

Corrine nodded and swallowed. "He was that sort of man, for sure."

"I was young when I met him," Hope said. "Not as young as you were at the time, Corrine, but nearly. I completely fell for the guy."

"And it was mutual?" I asked in a soft voice.

"It seemed to be." Hope folded her hands on the table, staring at them.

"You two were a number," Corrine murmured. "Remember that time the four of us went dancing? You and Ivan could have been glued together, you were dancing so close. I remember my Charlie joking that you should get a room. I was a little jealous. Charlie was crazy about me, but he didn't like showing it in public."

"We were close—until Ivan decided we weren't. I got dropped faster than a potato boiled in hot pepper oil."

"I could never figure that out," Corrine said. "You were devoted and gorgeous and sultry. Why would he leave?"

Gorgeous? Hope was now thirty years older. She was still attractive, but the look was spoiled by the permanent frown lines between her brows and her always-turned-down mouth, which made her look like she was displeased with life instead of happy with it.

"Who did he leave you for?" I asked.

"Some older chick," Hope said. "Older than me, but she was also older than him." Her gaze bore into mine.

My heart sank. The older woman had to have been

Adele. "I'm sorry to hear it." I glanced around the room, as if surveying the customers. What I was doing was avoiding what felt like Hope's unspoken accusation.

"I heard the same story," Corrine said. "Did you know Ivan was back in town, Hope?"

"Not until I saw him in here that day."

"You probably hadn't laid eyes on him since those long-ago days," Corrine went on. Her tone was casual, but it made me wonder if she was trying to get information out of Hope.

"I hadn't," Hope said.

"Musta been kinda like catching sight of a ghost," Corrine added.

"A ghost I frankly never wanted to see again." Hope's nostrils flared.

"And now you never will." Corrine clapped her hands once. "What's done is done."

It was my turn to frown. Her reaction seemed over the top. Corrine was usually both more respectful and more caring than that.

"What did Ivan ever do to you?" Hope asked.

I'd been about to ask the same question.

"He lied to me." Corrine gave her big hair a shake. "He told me my man was having a piece on the side." Her expression drooped. "Charlie and I argued. He swore he wasn't being unfaithful, and that he loved only me. But I was hurt and turned away. I still curse the day Ivan Sheluk was born."

"Did you and your Charlie fix it up?" I asked.

"We didn't get a chance. He was killed in that awful plane crash the next day."

My breath rushed in. Corrine also had a long-standing grudge against Ivan. No wonder McWilliam wanted to question her. But how had the detective found out? Still, being upset about somebody interfering in a relationship many years in the past wasn't grounds for murder. Was it?

CHAPTER 38

"Hey, beautiful," Abe's voice said from behind me as I worked at the coffee station at about one o'clock.

I turned, smiling. "Hey, yourself." I pulled him in for a quick kiss. We were married. A momentary public display of affection wasn't a crime. "Here for lunch?"

"I am, and Mom is going to join me."

"Awesome." I checked the door. "And there she is. We have a few open tables. Take whichever one you want."

"We will."

"I'll be over in a minute after I finish setting up this coffee."

He laid his hand on my shoulder. "How are you feeling today?"

"I'm fine. Tired of standing, but closing time isn't too far away."

"Good. You're still taking tomorrow off, right?" Concern etched his face.

"Yes, dear, I am." I reached up and smoothed the wrinkles from his brow. "Don't worry."

He lifted my hand and kissed it. "As if." He headed over to greet his mom.

Abe and I were both going to be worrying about our daughter for the rest of our lives, I expected. How does a parent not worry, no matter how old their child is?

When I lumbered up to their four-top, Freddy jumped to her feet to hug me.

"How's my favorite mother-to-be?" Her eyes sparkled.

"I'm good, thanks. How are you?"

"Couldn't be better." She sat again.

"What can I get you each for lunch?" I asked. "I'm afraid we didn't prepare any specials today."

"I have Thanksgiving on my mind," Freddy said. "I'd love a turkey burger and fries."

"You got it," I said. "Something to drink?"

"Water is all I need."

"Abe?" I asked.

"I'd like cheese and tomato on sourdough with potato salad, please, and a Coke."

"Coming right up." I smiled at the two.

"When you bring the food, see if you can stay a minute." Freddy lowered her voice to a raspy whisper. "I might have a little something to share. You know, about the you-know-what." She waggled her eyebrows in a Groucho Marx imitation.

Abe didn't hold back from snorting. I almost burst out laughing at his mom's dramatic gesture, but I turned away in time not to.

Lou was on the grill. I added the O'Neill order slip to the carousel.

"For Abe and Freddy?" Lou asked.

"It is." I pressed my palms against my lower back and tried to ease the pressure there, rotating my hips in a circle.

Lou glanced over. "I read that belly dancing is great for pregnancy."

"You did?" I stopped and peered at her.

"Absolutely." She flipped three meat patties and laid a slice of cheese on each. "Part of its origin was for women in labor. Makes sense, doesn't it? Moving the pelvis in circles and figure eights might help the baby out."

"You're a treasure trove of information, my friend." I tried moving in a figure eight. "It does feel good."

"I assume shimmying isn't part of the recommendation." Lou grinned.

I laughed. "I hope my midwife doesn't ask me to start twerking."

She snorted. "Definitely not. But it's interesting that something good for women in labor ended up being performed for men."

"Right. That's all we ever hear or see about belly dancing. Anyway, I'm going to ask Risa about doing belly dancing moves, although I know what she'll say. She's been telling me if something feels good during labor, I should do it." I felt the familiar pressure. "I'm going to take a quick break, Lou."

"Go," she said.

And I went, straight to the loo. As I came out, drying my hands, the sounds and smells of my restaurant washed over me.

I loved this place, even when a pancake or burger patty got too crispy, even when a customer argued about the amount of a check, even when I struggled to compensate myself after my employees and the bills were paid. Blessedly, none of the first two ever happened with any frequency, and I hadn't had trouble with payroll or creditors in years.

Pans 'N Pancakes was my first baby. I had envisioned it, built it, and made it successful. I'd had plenty of help, and I had stretched and grown enormously in the process. Still, the business was my only big success in life so far, and I cherished it.

Right now? Food was ready to be delivered. Customers still pushed through the door like clockwork. My husband and mother-in-law awaited their lunch. I hurried to the kitchen area to make a dent in all the work.

Turner had subbed in for Lou while I was on my break. I glanced around and finally saw her leaning a hip on the desk in the office nook. She frowned at her phone.

"Is Lou okay?" I asked Turner.

"I don't know." He plated a double cheeseburger with coleslaw, plus two brownies on a small plate. "She got a text. She tried to ignore it, but three more came in, one after the other. Whatever's going on seemed to be serious, and she asked me to swap jobs."

"Thanks. I'll check with her when I can. For now, I'm back. What do we have?"

"Abe and Freddy's orders are ready." He pointed at the array of plates under the warming lights. "This is for Buck, plus a root beer."

"Buck's here?" My voice rose.

"He joined your family a couple of minutes ago."

I checked Abe's table. Sure enough, there sat our perpetually hungry chief of police. "It seems like only an hour ago Buck was chowing down breakfast."

"Make that four hours," Turner said. "And we both know he's a bottomless pit."

"True enough." I started loading a tray with the three lunch orders.

"Until Lou gets back on the job, Robbie, we have diners asking for their checks and wanting drink refills, if you can get to them."

"I'll do my best." I lifted the tray and made my way to the threesome, as I sneaked in a look at Lou. She'd turned her back and was speaking on the phone. The text must have been something about her father. I only hoped he hadn't died suddenly. It would devastate her not to have been at his side during his final hours.

In case Lou had to rush back to Lafayette, I knew I could count on both Abe and Freddy to help out for the rest of the day if we needed them. It wouldn't be the first time, nor the last.

I set down the three orders and greeted Buck.

"Thanks, Robbie," Buck said. "I was about to eat my hat, I'm that hungry."

"Go on with you, Buck," Freddy said. "You like food too much to chow down on a piece of police-issue felt."

"Mom, I'm sure his hat isn't made of felt," Abe said in a gentle tone.

"Whatever. I don't know what they make official hats out of." She smiled, then took a bite of her turkey burger.

"Freddy, you said you had something to tell me," I said. "But Lou is occupied and I have to get moving. Can we talk before you leave? Or later, if that works better."

"Any time, sweetheart." She held her hand in front of her mouth to hide the food within.

"Thanks," I said. "Enjoy your meals."

I waded back into the busyness of the day. Freddy wouldn't fail to tell me whatever it was she knew. I only hoped I wouldn't have to wait too long.

CHAPTER 39

A few minutes later, I brought a load of dishes to the kitchen area and found Lou off the phone and washing her hands.

"Sorry about going AWOL," she said.

"Is everything okay?" I set down my dishes on the counter next to the sink.

Turner glanced over from the grill.

"Not really." She grabbed a length of paper towels to dry her hands. "Len called, saying our father wanted to talk, and he handed the phone to Dad. He asked when I was coming back, but he sounded confused."

"If you need to head up there today, we'll make it work." I peered into her face. "Seriously. He's your priority."

"I'm with Robbie," Turner said. "We've made do with only two on staff plenty of times. You should totally get out of here, dude."

"Thanks, but it's not urgent." Lou shook her head. "I told him I'd be home Sunday night. I'll drive back after we close the store tomorrow."

"Are you sure?" I asked.

"Yes." She checked the wall clock. "It's almost two. You want me back on the grill, Turner, or working the floor?"

"I'm cool here until closing."

Lou grabbed both coffeepots and aimed herself at the customers.

"Tough stuff," Turner murmured. "It's no fun to worry about your father."

"We've both been there, haven't we?"

"We sure have."

In his case and mine, it hadn't been a fatal illness we were concerned about. Having the person who fathered you being looked at for murder was a different kind of worry altogether.

As I scraped and rinsed the dishes I'd brought over and loaded them into the machine, I listened to the familiar soundtrack of a successful restaurant. Voices murmured and laughed. Spoons clinked stirring sugar into coffee. Chairs clunked on the antique wooden floor. Combined with the smell of peppers and onions frying next to beef patties and the whiff of chocolate from a brownie, it was pretty much heaven.

"These are ready for the four-top of men." Turner slid a fourth full plate under the warmer.

"Got it." I loaded a tray with two of the orders and headed out. With my center of gravity so off-kilter, I wasn't sure I could balance four full plates.

As I passed the table where Abe, Freddy, and Buck sat, Abe stood. He blew me a kiss.

"See you at home later, my sweet," he said.

"You bet." I smiled. "Freddy, are you going to be here a little longer?"

"I will, hon," she said.

"Same," Buck added. "We should talk."

Ooh. "Sounds good. I'll stop by soon." Buck also thought we should talk. What did he know?

Customers were finishing and leaving, and the place was gradually emptying. Lou was back on the job. As long as we didn't get an influx of new diners in the next half hour, I should have time to sit and find out what Freddy wanted to tell me, and Buck, too.

"I'm locking the door," I told Lou and Turner, "and I need to sit down with Freddy and Buck. You guys all right if I do?"

"It's all good," Lou said.

"No worries, boss," Turner agreed. "We got this."

"Thanks." I headed to the door and locked it against anyone new entering. As always, anybody could exit out that door. Freddy and Buck seemed to be having a serious conversation as I sank onto the third chair.

"You look relieved," Buck said.

"To be off my feet? Absolutely."

"It's almost closing time," Freddy said.

"It is." I looked from her to Buck and back. "Here I am, all ears. Who wants to go first?"

Neither spoke.

I folded my hands on the table. "I might need to get back to the job at any moment, so . . ." I let my voice trail off instead of asking these two to get to the point, already.

"It's this way, hon," Freddy said. "Buck was asking me about Carter Kingsley. Carter and I go way back."

"You do?" I shouldn't be surprised. Freddy was a local through and through.

"We do," she said. "I told the chief here, but I thought you should know. Carter and I served on the board of the youth symphony together. It was quite a while ago. I'm frankly surprised he now has a job in banking after what happened." She folded her hands and examined them.

I waited.

Freddy glanced up. "You see, Carter was doing the accounting for the organization. He said he was happy to. You might know that in an all-volunteer group, someone who actually wants to do one of the hard jobs is never turned down. It eventually transpired that he was, as they say, cooking the books."

"What, like stealing from the youth symphony?" I asked.

"Yes." Freddy bobbed her head.

"That's embezzling, isn't it?" I stared at Buck. "That's a crime."

"Indeed it is," he said.

"We always operated on a tight margin," Freddy went on. "It became clear one reason things were tight was because part of the money went into Carter's personal pocket."

"Did he serve time for it?" I asked.

"No, which was probably a mistake," she said. "He

did have to step down and make restitution to the group. In other words, pay back what he took."

"So he doesn't have a criminal record," I said.

"He does not," Buck chimed in. "We checked."

"I can't believe the bank hired him." I tapped the table. "Wouldn't you think they would do a background check or something?"

"That's the board's fault." Freddy shrugged. "I'm sure the bank did check Carter's past, but there was nothing official about what he'd done. What's done is done."

"Either way, he knew Ivan from somewhere," I said. "Apparently not from prison, though."

"How old was Ivan?" Freddy asked.

"Somewhere in his sixties, I think," I said.

Buck nodded. "Yup."

"Then they were close in age." Freddy gave a little laugh. "One I share. Anyway, the two men might have known each other when they were younger."

"Buck, what do you think about that?" I asked him.

"I think it's going to be worth having another little yak session with old Carter," he drawled.

"To change the subject, Robbie." Freddy swallowed as her smile fell away. "I don't want to butt in or be a pushy kind of mother-in-law."

What was this about? Freddy wasn't a bossy in-law. She didn't intrude on our lives, and I appreciated her being a nearby and loving presence.

"I wanted to let you know that, if you want another woman around for your labor and birth, just say the word," she said. "I know your mom is gone, and I would be happy to fill in for her in a small way."

My throat thickened with emotion. I tried to swallow as I listened. Freddy didn't seem to notice my eyes welling up.

"Lou is kind of occupied with her dad," Freddy went on, "and Adele doesn't quite seem like the doula type, especially not if the labor goes on overnight, which happens quite often. So I wanted to offer. And"—she held up her palm—"my feelings won't be hurt if you only want to be with Abe and your midwife, okay?"

I sat back. "Freddy, thank you." So many thoughts raced through my mind, but she looked nervous, and I didn't want her to be. I smiled at her. "I love your offer. Can I think about it for a little while? I'll need to check with Abe, too."

"Absolutely." Her expression brightened back to the usual. "Either way, Howard and I can't wait to meet our new grandbaby, and you know we'll always be there to help with babysitting or whatever else you need."

I reached for her hand. "I appreciate it. We both do."

"You should oughta take her up on the babysitting offer," Buck said. "Not all new parents are lucky enough to have family in the same town or even near to hand in the area. When our kiddos were little tykes, me and Melia sure as heck weren't."

"We both want Freddy and Howard to be close to our baby," I said. "I know how lucky we are, for so many reasons."

We totally were. Still, what she'd said about Carter kept trying to bump into the happy vibe of family.

CHAPTER 40

"What about specials for tomorrow?" I asked at three thirty as Lou, Turner, and I readied the place for the next day. The latecomers hadn't finished until a few minutes ago, despite our polite hints about closing time and Turner moving around spraying and wiping down all the other tables. We were running late on clearing out of here.

"I thought we decided not to have any specials for the weekend," Turner said from the half-scrubbed grill.

Oops. "Right." My brain really was AWOL.

"No specials simplifies things, doesn't it?" Lou asked.

"Kind of, yes," I said. "Except our regular customers have come to expect a couple of entries on the specials board. They like the variety, and it lets us keep things fresh for them."

"Then let's plan for next week," Turner said. "You

SCONE COLD DEAD 205

can put in an order for whatever we'll need ahead of time."

"Sounds good." I wrinkled my nose. "Have I set you and Danna up with the ordering app and the store password?"

"Not me." He shook his head. "Maybe you told Danna?"

"I can't remember," I said. "Let's do it before you leave today, okay? Plus, I'll write down the information and leave it in the desk."

"Perfect." He resumed his scrubbing.

"I think I'll still be here for another week or two, but you never know." It was entirely possible I could go into labor at any minute.

We sat planning, jotting, and ordering. I texted Turner and Danna the promised app details and password, and wrote them down, too. I finished the napkin rolls and Lou vacuumed the floor, while Turner started the dishwasher.

After they left, I busied myself with my usual breakfast prep. I would be snug in bed at home tomorrow morning, not here baking biscuits and plating pancakes. I was always tired after a full day being a restaurateur, but this was still a favorite time for me. I usually streamed a favorite opera from my phone to the speaker. Nobody talked to me, asking for this or demanding that. My mind could wander idly through the garden of my thoughts, sniffing an idea here or plucking a plan there.

When a homicide investigation was active, that was the garden path my brain took. After I was home with hands clean and a pen and graph paper in front of me, I often devised a crossword puzzle to lay everything out in black and white.

I realized that, after Freddy had talked about Carter, Buck hadn't shared whatever he'd meant to. I'd gotten busy and forgot to ask him. Oh, well. I'd see him again.

For now, being elbow-deep in flour let my brain loose on the problem. Or it would have if I hadn't heard knocking at the door. I twisted to see Martin Dettweiler's cheerful face pressed against the glass. I grabbed a dishtowel to cover my flour-dusted hand and hurried over to let him in. He carried a cardboard box in his arms.

"I received your message, Robbie, and brought you more honey."

"Great, thanks. Can you please bring it in?" I held out my messy hands. "As you can see, I'm in the middle of breakfast prep."

"I am happy to oblige." He followed me back to the kitchen area.

"Set the box on any table, if you don't mind."

"They are already priced, and you're busy. Would you like me to add them to the display?"

I glanced over at him. "Please and thank you."

Martin busied himself in the retail area as I mixed and kneaded and shaped disks of biscuit dough. He came back, laying his neatly written invoice on the table and his flat-brimmed Mennonite hat next to it. He kept on his woolen square-cut shirt, which was heavy enough to double as a jacket.

"How has business been?" he asked.

"Busy, which is good." I glanced over at him. "Did

you find someone to take your place at the motel this afternoon?"

"Yes." He cleared his throat and stroked his salt-and-pepper chinstrap beard. "I was thinking about the guest you mentioned, Mr. Stanganelli."

My radar went on high alert, but I kept silent, measuring flour, sugar, baking powder, and salt for the pancake mix.

"After we spoke yesterday, I went back into his room. My brother does the cleaning himself, you see, and I had not had a chance to get into the room yet that day. It did not matter, since this is not a time of year when the motel is much in demand. A number of other rooms were unoccupied and had been readied for guests."

I bobbed my head to show I was listening. Martin was typically a man of few words. I didn't want to interrupt whatever he wanted to share with me in this uncharacteristic flow of information.

"My brother insists on a thorough cleaning after a guest has checked out. When I pulled the desk out from the wall to vacuum behind it, I discovered a photograph." He fished a plastic sleeve out of his shirt's chest pocket and held it near me so I could see it.

The black-and-white picture was a police mug shot with the name Ivan Stanley Sheluk printed below it. Ivan was much younger but was clearly the same man I'd met, despite the way the photo had been altered. Where the eyes had been, the paper was gouged out. Red devil's horns now sprouted from the head. The word "Stanley" had a wide X through it with "Satan" scrawled above it.

"How disturbing," I said.

"I find it so, as well."

"Is there anything on the back?"

Martin turned it over. "*NEVER AGAIN*" was scrawled in the same handwriting as the word on the other side.

"Wow," I murmured. "I guess the back matches the front."

"I am sure you are also wondering if Mr. Stanganelli came here with the intent of ending Mr. Sheluk's life."

"Absolutely. I hope you'll hand over the picture to the South Lick police, Martin."

"I planned a visit to the local authorities as my next step," he said. "I shall drive there directly from here."

I cocked my head. "What kind of car did Oliver park at the motel?"

"I believe it was an older model Volvo in disrepair."

Bingo. "Thank you for showing me the photograph, and for being willing to relinquish it."

"I strive to avoid negative people and situations in my life, Robbie. Nothing will make me happier than getting this particular example out of my hands. I will pray for Mr. Stanganelli. May he do the right thing and find peace."

I smiled at him. "Your brother isn't the only good man in the family, my friend."

He didn't return the smile as he tucked the sleeve back into his pocket and donned his hat.

"I'll mail you a check," I added.

"There is no hurry." His keen brown eyes gazed into mine. "May your impending birth be easy and joyful."

"Thank you. From your mouth to God's ears," I said, and then hoped I hadn't offended him.

He finally smiled. "I shall pray for you and your child. Please send news when you are able."

"I will. Thank you."

"Go with God, Robbie." He made his way out.

I finished the pancake mix and put away my supplies. The photo Martin had brought was a stunner. I wished I'd snapped a picture of it with my phone, but it was too late. He'd taken the defaced photo with him. He said he would take it straight to the South Lick PD, and I trusted that he would. The beekeeper was nothing if not a man of honor.

More important was why Oliver had the ruined mug shot in his possession. Had he done the altering and kept it on his person, waiting until this week to accomplish the "never again" part? But what did "never again" mean? If Oliver had made those changes to the photo decades earlier, maybe he'd kept it to remind himself to find Ivan and apologize. If the reminder was that important, I doubted he would have been so careless to let it drop behind a piece of furniture. Unless . . . he'd realized the detective was coming after him and cleared out of the motel room in a hurry.

So many questions. So few answers.

CHAPTER 41

After Martin left, I did my best to let go of what he'd told me about Oliver. I wasn't going to solve the question of Ivan's death this afternoon, or ever, most likely. I had to trust kind, worshipful Martin to turn over the photo to the authorities as promised.

I brought a cutting board, knife, and basket full of peppers and mushrooms to a table, then sat to prep omelet ingredients for tomorrow. I sliced the peppers in half and scraped the seeds and pith into a bowl for compost, then began dicing.

The more I thought about Freddy's offer to help at the birth, the more I liked the idea. She'd been ultra-cautious the way she phrased it, which I appreciated. I knew she didn't want to be a pushy, intrusive mother-in-law. If my mom had been alive, I would have loved for her to be either nearby or in the room while I birthed her grandchild, and I teared up again thinking about it.

Grief was an odd thing. Right now the pain of losing Mommy was almost as sharp as it had been five years ago. The missing reared its head when you least expected it. Jeanine Jordan had been my entire family, plus Adele halfway across the country, for the rest of my mother's life. We'd been the world's smallest nuclear family, and it had been a happy one.

Family still meant everything to me. And I was about to create a slightly larger one with Abe. More correctly, we already had, but I didn't want to jinx anything. Until the baby was out, alive and healthy, he and Sean and I were a family of three.

Abe would be my primary support as I labored, with Risa's expertise to guide us. But I realized another woman's presence, especially one as warm and generous as Freddy, would be important. I sniffed and swiped away my tears, appreciating marrying into such a wonderful family. Then I laughed. Freddy was right about Adele. I adored my aunt and I knew she'd be a strong support for our new little family. But as a labor companion? I couldn't see it.

I gave the whole mushrooms a quick rinse, gently dried them in a clean towel, then wrapped them in the towel and set them aside to slice in the morning. I barely saw my hands as I did this routine task. Apparently, labor often went on all night, as Freddy mentioned. She wasn't young, but she was energetic and lively. Adele had been showing her age more and more lately. No way was I going to ask my aunt to do that kind of marathon.

It might be nice to have Lou around, as a good friend and a much younger labor support person. But the situation with her father was fraught and unpredictable. I wouldn't dream of asking her to make the commitment, even though I loved having her back in town. I'd missed her since she moved, a lot.

Funny, she and I had rarely talked about how we shared the state of being motherless. Now that I was about to become a mother myself, I realized Lou and I also hadn't discussed her own plans for a family. She was a few years older than me. Was she waiting to meet the right man? If she didn't, would she take any steps to adopt a child or find a male donor so she could birth her own child and be a single mom? None of us women had all the time in the world to make pregnancy happen. Maybe she was satisfied with her career as a professor and her other interests and decided she didn't want or need a husband or children to complete her life.

Lou and I clearly needed to sit down and have a girl-to-girl. Although, if we didn't before this baby came, it might be a while before it could happen. We'd see how things went with Lou's dad and with my baby's idea about when she felt like leaving her warm, cozy cocoon to confront the outside world.

I finished all the vegetables and sat back. I really should put them away in the walk-in. It'd be good to prep the melons for fruit salad and accomplish a couple of other tasks. At this exact minute, resting and not thinking about evil deeds seemed like a better goal.

My brain refused to obey orders. What Freddy said about Carter popped up. Why hadn't the board of the symphony turned him in to the police for financial wrongdoings? Surely the bank—my bank—didn't know about Carter's past or he wouldn't be working there, much less as a manager. Was he still up to his old tricks, or had he reformed his behavior?

Ivan might have known about Carter's embezzlement, if embezzlement was what it was, and urged him to come clean about it. Or maybe Carter had had other hidden crimes in his past Ivan was aware of.

My racing brain had another matter it was wiggling like a loose tooth. Martin had sat on the defaced photo for nearly twenty-four hours. The time lag concerned me. I hoped his delay was because he'd been busy with the motel work. Today he'd found someone to sub in for him at the desk. He hadn't said if it had been his wife or someone else. Couldn't he have asked them to help last night or this morning and turn in the picture much earlier? It seemed to provide clear evidence of conflict between Oliver and Ivan.

I reminded myself, it wasn't my job to figure out what the conflict had been. I was an enormously pregnant woman with loose ends to wrap up in her business and her life, and it was after five thirty. I pushed up to my feet. The crew tomorrow could cut the fruit.

CHAPTER 42

I put away everything and swiped down the surfaces, then suited up in coat, knit cap, and gloves. I'd set my hand on the exit bar on the service door at the side of the building when my phone rang.

I groaned. All I wanted to do was drive home and start my delayed weekend, which beckoned with husband, dog, cats, comfy clothes, lots of sitting, and no work.

Instead, I put on my Responsible Person hat, pulled off a glove, and checked the display, which showed Turner's name.

"Hey, Turner," I said. "Did you miss me already?" He'd left less than two hours ago.

"Robbie, I'm so sorry." His words rushed out, ending on a sob. "My mom's been in an accident. Dad's in India, and I have to be with her. I can't work tomorrow."

"Of course you have to be at your mother's side. How is she, and where is she?"

"Bloomington." His voice shook. "I don't know how she is, except she's alive and awake. A car ran a red light and hit hers."

"Listen, don't worry about here. We'll be fine. You go. We'll all be pulling for her."

"Thanks. I'll let you know more after I get there." He disconnected.

I stared at the phone. Poor Turner. I'd met Mona a few times and really liked her. Her last name was Turner, now Turner-Rao, thus my employee's first name. I couldn't remember if Turner's sister was around these days. She'd been in medical school, but if she was already out, she could be doing a residency anywhere in the country.

My shoulders slumped. The news also meant I'd be working tomorrow after all. I'd better get home, ASAP, and rest as much as I could. Letting Danna and Lou know Turner's—and our—news could wait until then. I slipped my glove on again and leaned against the bar. I refused to call it a crash bar or, worse, a panic bar, but it was designed to allow an easy exit from the inside of public places at any time but especially in an emergency. I headed toward my car, first making sure the door clicked shut behind me.

The motion-detecting light over the door flared on when I exited, which was good, since the sun had already set. It was a clear and frosty night, and the moon was in a waning phase. It wouldn't rise for hours. A bat flew erratically over my head. It was probably looking for a few last bugs before the impending hard frost killed them and the bats hibernated or migrated or whatever bats do in the winter.

My little hybrid car was parked down the drive toward the barn out back. By the time I got halfway there, the store's outside light switched off. On the other side of the driveway began the woods skirting the rear of the property, and the only streetlight was around the corner in front of Pans 'N Pancakes. It was dark back here, and quiet. An owl's wavering cry from behind the barn was the only sound.

I brought out my phone to use its light, but my gloved hand made me fumble and drop it. Not being in the company of anyone but nocturnal creatures whom I was pretty sure didn't speak English, I swore out loud. Luckily, I always used a heavy-duty phone case, which so far had survived all my frequent drops. I bent my knees a little and, in the most awkward stance possible, leaned over to retrieve the phone.

When I straightened, my breath rushed in. My heart met it halfway. A dark figure stood next to the driver's door. A human figure.

No. My heart pounded in my ears. I could hardly swallow. My hands were numb inside my gloves. I'd been so careful, shielding my baby from danger. A murderer wouldn't care I was pregnant.

Who stood there, silent, menacing? I had to move. Do something. Protect myself and my child. But do what? I was paralyzed, frozen.

Maybe I should run and try to get into the street where someone passing could see me. Except I couldn't move fast enough to escape someone who wasn't almost nine months pregnant. There was no way I could use any self-defense moves. I tugged off my glove with my teeth, ready to press the phone's emergency button that was always there.

The person took a step toward me.

My fear turned to anger. Or maybe it was Mom fierceness. This was my property. Nobody had a right to loiter back here, to invade my territory without permission.

"Stop right there," I demanded. "Who are you?" I tapped the screen to at least provide a little light, if not the flashlight app, and held it up aimed at the person.

"I'm sorry for startling you, ma'am." Oliver Stanganelli held up both palms. "I wanted to talk, and I saw through the front window you were leaving through the side door."

Sure. He wanted to talk, but he hadn't waited near the door where there was light, instead staying back there in the dark. He must have circled the building while I was talking with Turner. At least Oliver hadn't moved any closer to me, and he sounded polite, respectful. Not threatening. I made my decision.

I switched on the actual phone flashlight, then began to stride as fast as I could toward the front. "If you want to talk, we're doing it in public where I can see you," I called over my shoulder.

Would he follow? I turned when I reached the front corner of the building. He'd come halfway down the drive but stopped near the service door. My movement had triggered the light to come on as I neared it, and he winced in the illumination.

"I apologize," he said. "Thing is, right now me being seen by people passing by isn't a great idea."

"Why?"

He cleared his throat. "It's complicated."

"Try me." I switched off the flashlight and set my fists on my hips.

"You might have heard I was recently released from being incarcerated."

"I did."

"Life can be hard, ma'am. I have made serious mistakes, which are difficult to explain. Recently, Ivan and I had both been in a pre-release program. It stressed making amends, and I had a few to make with him. He was released shortly before me, but he'd told me he was headed this way. When I got out, I followed."

Aha. One thing explained.

"As I believe you well know, I arrived too late," he added.

"Were you squatting in a brick house outside of town?"

His shoulders slumped. "Yes. I saw you stop by there."

"Did you steal a car?" I was so ready to call Buck and be done with this conversation.

"No!" He stuck his hands in his coat pocket. "I mean, I borrowed it from a friend back home. It turns out he had stolen it. Robbie, I can't seem to get a break."

I was almost believing this story, but a seasoned felon might also be an expert at telling lies.

"Did you kill Ivan?" I asked, not demanding, but curious about his answer.

"I did not. I never would. He and I had had our share of conflict, but both of us had finally gained our freedom. I wanted to finish resolving our differences. I wouldn't take his future away from him."

"Listen, Oliver. Why don't you tell the police all this?"

"You think they're going to take my word for it?" He had stood still long enough for the motion detector to deactivate. He now stood in the dark. "In my considerable experience, the cops are famous for not listening."

"It's worth a try." I flipped open my palms. My nostrils flared as my womb squeezed. I reached one hand toward the edge of the building to stabilize myself, trying to keep calm and breathe and pay attention to what was happening.

"Hey, are you all right?" he asked. "Can I do something?"

And then all heck broke loose.

CHAPTER 43

A police officer, weapon ready in two hands, appeared behind Oliver. The motion detector kicked in again, flooding them with bright light. Red and blue lights strobed in the street. Two South Lick PD officers in bulky vests hurried past me.

Oliver's face went the color of bleached linen, and his expression was the same as a trapped animal's.

"Police," one officer said. "Hands on your head, Mr. Stanganelli."

Oliver gave a fast glance toward the back, his body half turned.

"Face front and hands up," the woman behind him ordered.

He twisted toward me and seemed to shrink as his hands drifted slowly to the top of his head. He stared at the ground. Juanita McWilliam strode up, moving past me to Oliver's side.

I, meanwhile, couldn't hold back a creaky groan.

"Robbie, are you all right?" Buck materialized next to me. He touched my shoulder, keeping his voice low. "Did he hurt you? Is your baby coming?"

I shook my head. As the contraction passed, I blew out a breath. "Oliver didn't harm me in any way. I'm fine." I hoped I spoke the truth. Let this be another Braxton-Hicks that had hit me instead of the real thing.

"Oliver Stanganelli," McWilliam began, "you are under arrest for suspicion of automobile theft and for violating the terms of your parole."

He kept his mouth shut. Probably a wise move. McWilliam nodded at the officer behind Oliver, who fastened a handcuff to one of his hands then brought both down behind his back and clicked shut the other cuff.

"We've been looking for you, sir," the detective said.

"I know," he murmured as he raised his chin. "I'm innocent, ma'am."

"We'll be doing a lot of talking about that real soon." She signaled to the handcuffing officer, who took Oliver's arm and escorted him toward the street.

McWilliam clasped her hands behind her back and turned to me. "Did he accost you?"

"Not at all," I said. "I'm happy to tell you about what happened, but I need to get off my feet. I'd like to go home, which is where I was headed, or we can talk inside for a few minutes."

She thought for a moment. "I have to get to the station. Bird, can you take a statement?"

"Surely."

She thanked him and left, along with the other two officers.

Buck peered into my face. "You name the place."

By now I needed to use the restroom again. "Let's go inside, but only for a few minutes, okay? I really do want to get home."

"It's a deal."

It didn't take long to let him in, turn on a light, do what I had to do, and sink gratefully into a chair at the two-top where he waited. I couldn't be happier to be in my safe, fragrant, comforting business.

"I need to text Abe first." I thumbed a quick message that I'd been delayed but was fine and would be home soon.

"You sure you're okay, Robbie?" With a wrinkled forehead, Buck clasped his hands and leaned forward.

"Yes. But let me blurt out this story straight through."

He nodded.

"It was time to go home, and I let myself out the side door," I began. "I'd parked down near the barn, as I usually do. Halfway there the outside light switched off, and it was super dark. I dropped my phone, and when I stood up, I saw someone standing near my car. In silence."

"And you were more freaked out than a little child in a haunted house."

"Correct. In this state"—I pointed to my midsection—"I knew I wouldn't be able to get away with any speed or strength. I couldn't see who it was. I fumbled with my phone again but finally saw Oliver." A shudder ran through me.

"And you were terrified for the wee one you're carrying. Rightly so."

"Absolutely. Then I got mad." I spoke about how polite Oliver had been. "He didn't threaten me at all, but I told him I wasn't talking unless we were visible from the street. Off I marched." I pictured the scene again.

"Good for you. Always best to be in a place where others can see you." Buck made a rolling motion with his hand. "You did say you wanted to get on home, Robbie."

"I do. So, as you saw, he stopped near the side door. Unlike me, he didn't want people to catch sight of him. He said he'd known Ivan in prison, and that they'd both been part of a program encouraging the inmates to make amends when they got out. Oliver came here to fix things up with Ivan. He said he wanted to resolve his differences with him, but he arrived too late."

"Seems fixing things is what Ivan himself was trying to do, what with his message to Adele."

"Exactly," I said. "Oliver admitted to squatting in the brick house. He also said he hadn't stolen the car. He told me he'd borrowed it from a friend and then learned the friend had stolen it. When I asked Oliver if he killed Ivan, he said he never would have done such a thing. Oliver knew how it felt to have his freedom back. He said he wouldn't have robbed Ivan of his future."

Buck smiled, shaking his head. "You've never been short on guts, my friend."

"It's gotten me into hot water a few times, too." And could have this time.

"Did you find out why Stanganelli didn't want to be seen talking with you?" he asked.

"Not really. He mentioned something about life being difficult for someone recently released from incarceration. He was a convicted felon, right?"

"He was," Buck said. "And he'd be right about life being hard for someone in his circumstances. Nobody wants to hire them. They been inside for years, and all of a sudden they gots to pay their own way. Family often doesn't want nothing to do with them. If they go back to their old friends, plenty of these guys fall right back into a life of crime. I'll tell you, it's a situation best never fallen into in the first place."

"I hope Oliver's current detention isn't serious," I said.

"The photograph Mr. Dettweiler dropped off won't help Stanganelli's case none."

"It looked really old. Maybe he was carrying it around so he could apologize to Ivan for it," I mused. "At least McWilliam didn't arrest Oliver for murder."

"Can't very well arrest anyone when we don't have a cause of death yet, can she?"

A text pinged in from Abe. All it held was a string of emojis—hearts, roses, hugging arms, and kissing lips—which made me smile. I glanced up. "Buck, how did you and the detective know Oliver was here?"

"It was a kind of convergence. McWilliam had been tracking him, or at least trying to. I had an extra person keeping watch on the store. You showing up at the front when you did helped us put it all together. We mobilized our forces real quick-like and quietly, too. You got anything else to tell me?"

"I don't think so."

"Let's get you out of here." He stood and extended a hand to me.

"Best idea I've heard all day." I accepted his help.

"I'll see you to your car with my trusty police-issue flashlight." He pulled a tiny flashlight no more than three inches long out of his jacket pocket and chuckled.

"Cutest weapon I've ever seen." I smiled at him, knowing how fortunate I was to have him as a friend and not an enemy or an antagonist.

As I made my way with Buck to the back, I reflected on how Oliver could use a friend. Over the course of the last hour I'd come to feel less suspicious of him and more sympathetic. I could only hope he'd spoken the truth and hadn't been trying to dupe me.

CHAPTER 44

Over the dinner he had waiting for me, Abe was rightly concerned when I told him about my confrontation with Oliver.

"Sugar, I don't ever want to see you in danger. Either of you." He reached for my hand.

"Believe me, I don't want to be there, either." I squeezed his strong, warm hand before taking mine back. "As it turned out, I don't think I was at any risk of being hurt. But the adrenaline rush at not being certain was no fun. I promise to not go out alone in the dark until this case is buttoned up."

I took another bite of creamy, cheesy scalloped potato, the perfect comfort food. Abe had roasted a whole chicken with a delicious salty dry rub of herbs and made sauteed baby spinach with olive oil and garlic. The whole dinner was comforting and perfect for tonight.

"Good." He frowned. "But you said the detective arrested Stanganelli. Doesn't that end the case?"

"No." I explained about the authorities still not knowing Ivan's cause of death. "Unfortunately, it's still open."

"Why don't they know yet how he died?" Abe sipped from his glass of beer. "That seems crazy in this day and age."

"I guess they have a long line of autopsies ahead of Ivan's. But I don't want to talk about corpses while we're eating." I smiled. "How was your day?"

"A little too busy for a Saturday, with having to work this morning. But it was an interesting group of teachers who took my workshop. They have plenty of lessons they seemed eager to take back to their students."

"Lucky teachers, lucky students." I slid in another forkful of potatoes. "Mmm. This meal is exactly what I needed, Abe. Thank you."

"You are so welcome. I love taking care of you, Robbie." He gave me a fond smile. "I plan to pamper you all day tomorrow."

Oops. I cringed a little as I cleared my throat. "Pampering sounds delightful. Except Turner called right before I left the store. He's had an emergency and can't be there. I'm going to have to go in to Pans 'N Pancakes tomorrow to back up Danna and Lou."

Abe stared at me. "You're kidding me."

"Sorry." I shook my head. "I'm not."

"You should be resting, Robbie. Letting me coddle you. Getting ready to give birth. Keeping your blood pressure down and nourishing our little girl, not using up calories being on your feet all day and then getting into trouble with criminals." He drained his beer and stood.

"Abe?" I held out my hand. "I have to go in. Len's away. Turner's mom was in an accident and is in the hospital. Only two on shift at the store is too hard. The baby's going to be fine."

"I . . . I just can't deal with this." He ignored my outstretched hand and exhaled with a noisy breath. "Cocoa? Come here, buddy. Let's go for a walk."

Cocoa jumped up and trotted to the side door. Abe threw on a jacket. He grabbed the dog's leash and disappeared through the door without a backwards glance.

I swore out loud. I hated making him unhappy, and I knew his reaction stemmed from worry. This was a stressful, fraught time for both of us. Risa had told me an interesting analogy once while we were chatting during an appointment.

"It's like you're getting ready to run a marathon, except you can't train for it," she'd said. "And you don't know when it's going to happen."

If that wasn't the definition of stressful, I didn't know what was. For now, all I could do was finish my dinner and let Danna and Lou know what the plan for tomorrow was. Abe and I would make up when he got back. I hoped. I was glad I hadn't told him about the contraction I'd had during the driveway scene. At least it hadn't recurred.

I'd cleared the table and was about to rinse the dishes when Adele called.

"What's this I hear about a man being apprehended at your store?" she asked without preamble.

She'd no doubt learned about it from her police scanner.

"And hello to you, favorite aunt," I replied.

"Tell me you weren't involved, weren't putting our little girlie in peril."

"I was there, Adele." I squared my shoulders, even though she couldn't see me. "But don't worry, I wasn't in danger."

"The gent was Stanganelli?"

"Yes." *Wait.* "Did you know him, back when you knew Ivan?" Had she? I couldn't remember.

"You asked me if I did a couple few days ago, remember?"

"That's right. I guess I'm having not a senior moment but a pregnancy moment."

"You take care there, hon," Adele said. "You don't work Sundays, am I right?"

"Not usually, but I'll be there tomorrow helping out," I said.

"Let me know if you need me."

"Will do. Love you."

"Likewise." She disconnected. For someone who'd claimed to be concerned about me, she'd kept her call to a near-record brief duration.

I finished cleaning up and putting the food away, it being the least I could do, and carried a cup of peppermint tea to our cozy couch. The image of Abe pampering me for a day was a huge allure, making me regret how responsible I was. I would do my best to make tomorrow as short a day as I could. Maybe I should ask Adele for help. Freddy might be willing if she was free.

I was pretty sure Abe's anger would have burned off during his walk. No, not anger. It was more that he was upset with me and had left so he didn't say something he'd regret. Right now I'd better get the rest of tonight's business out of the way so I'd be relaxed and welcoming when he returned.

"Danna," I began after she picked up my call, "Turner won't be in tomorrow, so I'll be filling in for him."

"Aren't you supposed to be resting on Sundays?"

"Yes, and I'll keep my hours as short as I can. Which two of you three were going to be opening?" I had let them work Sunday schedules out among themselves.

"Lou and me."

"Perfect. I'll give her a heads-up."

"What's Turner slacking off to do?" she asked.

"He's not slacking off, not at all." I explained about his mom's accident and how the rest of the family was out of town. "He called about it a few hours ago right before I left the store. I asked him to let me know how she was, but I haven't heard back. I'm sure he's completely absorbed at the hospital."

"Man, the poor dude. Coping with an injured mom by himself has gotta be hard."

"For sure. I'll text you if he gets in touch. Hey, did you and Isaac have a good getaway?"

"It was optimal." Her smile came through in her voice. "I'll tell you about it tomorrow."

"Glad to hear it." Should I let her know about the incident with Oliver? *Nah.* If customers happened to have seen the police presence at the store this evening and asked her about it before I got in tomorrow morning, she could profess honest ignorance. "I'd better call Lou before it gets any later. I'll see you at nine."

We said our goodbyes, and I tapped Lou's number, but she didn't pick up. That was okay. I didn't really need to talk with her about the situation with Turner. She was already set to come in early and start the day with Danna, who would fill her in on his news.

I settled in with my tea, a pen, and the most recent Sunday puzzle. Nothing relaxed me more than conquering a word challenge.

CHAPTER 45

Sure enough, last night Abe and I had talked—and embraced—through our differences and his worries after he and Cocoa had returned from an extra-long walk. I hoped we never, ever went to bed angry with each other for as long as we lived.

This morning I let him pamper me right up until when I left for the store at a few minutes before nine. He fixed me a delicious breakfast of eggs Benedict, California style. In my opinion, avocado added to anything gave it a taste of my home state. The glass of fresh-squeezed orange juice was the cherry on top.

"Please let me drive you to work," he pleaded.

"No, my dear. I can drive myself." That level of coddling went too far. "I promise, I'll leave for home before dark, and I'll let you know when I do. Girls Scout's honor."

"All right. Promise me you'll park in front?"

"I will, for sure." I kissed him and waddled out to my car. What I hadn't told him was about the several practice contractions yesterday. They hadn't been actual labor, and I didn't see any need to add to his worries.

I found a spot near the front steps of Pans 'N Pancakes. Normally my team and I left the closest spaces for customers. By law and by inclination we also had two well-labeled official handicapped parking spots next to the ramp I'd installed at the end of the porch. I called owner's privilege today and snagged the nearest regular spot.

When I eased myself out of the car, I shivered. The sky was a glowering sheet metal, and the air felt cold and damp. I sniffed. Were we going to get snow today? *Brr.* The third week in November was too early for white stuff to fall.

Once I stashed my bag, aproned up, and washed my hands, I greeted Lou, who was on a griddle shift.

"Danna told me about Turner." Her brow furrowed. "The poor guy. No more word from him?"

"Only a quick text last night."

Danna approached holding three order slips.

"Hey, Danna," I said. "I was about to tell Lou I heard from Turner last night. He messaged me that his mom's leg is broken. She's otherwise okay, and his sister is on her way to help out."

"Thanks. No fun, but I'm glad it wasn't worse," Danna said.

"Which it could have been," Lou added. "A lot worse."

I watched as Danna stuck the orders on the carousel with her left hand. *Wait a second.*

"Danna," I began. "Do you have something to tell us?"

She blushed. "Lou already wondered." Danna extended her left hand, revealing a gold filigree ring with a cluster of petals surrounding a small diamond. "I told him yes."

Isaac, who was a bit older than Danna, had wanted to marry her a couple of years ago. When she said she wasn't ready, he said he would wait. It seemed she was ready now.

"You go, girl." I beamed and held out my arms for a hug. "It was an engagement getaway?"

A smile split her glowing face. "So it seems."

"Don't you love the vintage ring, Robbie?" Lou flipped pancakes and an omelet, smiling as she did.

"It's beautiful." I pulled Danna's hand closer. "Look at the detail."

"It was Isaac's grandma's," Danna said.

"I do love it. Congratulations." My smile slid away as a contraction started. I gripped the counter.

"Robbie?" Danna asked. "Is this labor?"

I waved away her concern. The pain passed. "It's only a rehearsal. Don't mind me."

"You should not be here working, girlfriend," Lou said. "We can totally manage."

"It's fine. I probably won't have another one all day." Fingers crossed on that intention.

"Okay." Lou added bacon and sausages to two plated omelets and slid them in next to the others under the warming lights. "Danna, these four plates are for those two couples at the four-top next to the back wall."

"I'm on it." Danna loaded up her arms.

"Miss?" a customer called.

"You'll do coffee and orders, Robbie?" Danna asked.

"Yes, ma'am. You have to tell me everything later. You know, if you've set a date, how he popped the question, your mom's reaction. The entire story." I smiled. "Every single thing."

"I promise." She headed toward the tables full of diners.

I grabbed the coffee carafes and made my awkward way after her. As usual, we had the early-bird outdoorsy types—hikers, cyclists, and hunters—plus the before-church crowd, all dressed according to their activities. Our customers later would be those who liked a more relaxed Sunday and sometimes brought the thick Sunday newspaper to peruse over a late breakfast.

After noon we got the BYO bubbly crowd, customers who wanted to indulge in an adult beverage while they enjoyed a brunch they didn't have to cook. I didn't hold a liquor license, but in Indiana it was legal for customers to bring their own as long as we poured it. If we were open for dinner, I would have endured the application process to serve alcohol. The profit margin was high for a restaurant serving spirits of any kind.

I liked my business model as it was. I saw no need to shift our hours to later in the day and serve different kinds of meals. Pans 'N Pancakes was both popular and profitable.

Adele came in about an hour later. The worshipful ones were off to their services. Most of the first wave of outdoorsy folks had finished and headed out, which meant a few tables were free. I greeted my aunt at the door.

"Are you by yourself this morning?" I asked.

"Always on a Sunday. Samuel's off with his pious parishioners."

"The Faithful Fellows?"

"Yeah, and the rest of them religious types, too." She surveyed the restaurant. "I was hoping to find Buck or maybe that lady detective here."

My attention perked up. "Do you have news?"

"Might could have."

I waited but I couldn't hang out here too long. We were still nearly at capacity.

"What did you learn?" I finally asked. "Or what happened?"

The door opened to let in none other than Juanita McWilliam, with Buck right behind her.

Perfect. "Good morning," I said to them both. "Adele was about to tell me news she wanted to share with you both."

My aunt gave me the side eye, but then nodded. "That's correct."

"Robbie." McWilliam acknowledged me without smiling.

Uh-oh. Something was up, but I had no idea what.

The door opened behind Buck. A crowd of women clustered on the porch began filing in.

I lowered my voice. "Let me seat you three quickly, while we still have open tables." I glanced around the restaurant.

"Appreciate it, Robbie," Buck said.

"Take that four-top." I pointed, then added to Adele, "But only if you promise to share what you know."

She gave an affectionate eyeroll. "Yes, Robbie, I surely will."

I turned to the newcomers. "Welcome to Pans 'N Pancakes."

I mustered my cheeriest business owner's expression. Except all I wanted to do was grab Adele by the shoulders and find out what her news was.

CHAPTER 46

Seating the tour group took me a few minutes, and several of the twenty had to wait for tables. I slid over to where Adele sat as soon as I could. Buck's appetite would be gnawing a hole in his stomach as surely as my curiosity about Adele's news was gnawing at my brain.

"We already gave Danna our orders," Buck said. "Thank goodness, because right now I could eat my weight in grits and grub."

"I only have a second to talk," I said. "What's your news, Adele?"

McWilliam folded her hands on the table, still not smiling. Come to think of it, looking dead serious wasn't out of character for her. Buck stretched his legs out, but his gaze was intent on Adele's face. He didn't smile, either.

"I was out there checking on Aries III." She looked

at Buck and the detective. "He's the ram in the pasture where poor Ivan died."

"Got it," Buck said. "Please go on."

"Welp, all these goings-on have been disturbing for the fella," Adele said. "He's been pawing up the ground and huffing and puffing something serious. I wandered out there with a treat and calmed him down some. I know a few tricks on how to talk to the boys."

"She's the ram whisperer," I told Buck and McWilliam.

"Anyhoo, I was taking a close look at his horns," Adele continued. "I do believe there's dried blood on one of them. Thought you official types should oughta know."

"That's interesting, all right," Buck said. "McWilliam, I don't s'pose your crime scene team checked the animal himself."

"I'm quite sure they didn't. You and Mr. MacDonald moved the fence before we arrived, didn't you?" she asked Adele.

"Well, sure," my aunt said. "Wouldn't want the big guy disturbing a body, you know."

"Did you happen to take a picture of the horn?" the detective asked.

"I didn't think to."

"Could it have been blood from another animal?" I asked.

"Nope. Aries III is by himself in the pasture, and I haven't seen any coyote corpses or other vagrant wildlife dead inside the fence. Nobody else the dried blood could have come from but Ivan, and that's a fact."

"Detective." I pressed my palms into my lower back

as I spoke. "When I saw you out at Adele's, didn't you say blunt trauma might have been involved?"

"I did. I'll get somebody out there to take a look."

"Wait a chicken-picking minute," Adele said. "You're not going to shoot him up with a sedative, are you?"

"I am not an animal forensics specialist, ma'am," McWilliam said. "If you can give us a time when you'll keep the animal calm while we sample the substance, that should be fine, but at this moment I can't promise anything."

"You know they've got to check the evidence, Adele." Buck used his own calming voice. "I'm sure y'all can work something out."

"All righty," Adele said. "I'll help your person do the examination."

"Ma'am?" a customer called to me.

"Can we get more coffee over here, please?" another asked.

"I have to go," I said. "Thanks for sharing, Adele."

I needed to get back to the job at hand, stat. I wasn't helping Lou and Danna at all by schmoozing at one table, important conversation or not. As I went about my tasks, I couldn't stop seeing the image of a big, assertive ram butting hard into a man who had no business being inside the fence instead of outside.

Buck and McWilliam left at a few minutes past eleven. I hadn't gotten back to their table once, but Adele still sat there. My feet hurt, and I used a free minute to take a fluids break. When I emerged, Corrine had joined my aunt.

"I'm going to go sit for a few," I told Danna, who was currently flipping pancakes and omelets with gusto.

"Do it. Me and Lou got this, at least until the brunch crowd swamps us."

"I'll be over there when you need me." I pointed at Adele's table, then moseyed over to join her and the mayor.

"You look ready to pop there, Robbie," Corrine said. "Did that baby of yours put on five pounds this week?"

"Sure feels like it." I smiled at her. "Congratulations on the engagement."

"What?" Adele asked. "You tying the knot with that fellow of yours, Corrine?"

"No, but my baby girl is." She beamed. "Isaac gave her the prettiest ring yesterday."

"I'm glad she finally said yes to that big handsome ironworker." Adele smiled, too.

"Did you know, Corrine?" I asked.

"Isaac actually came to me in my office beforehand and asked my permission to marry her. Can you believe it? I didn't think nobody did that these days."

"What did you say?" Adele asked.

"Told him it was up to her, naturally. I also said he had my blessing, and I'd surely be happy to have him in the family."

The bell on the door started jangling nonstop. I didn't have long here.

"Adele, did you pick up anything new from Buck or McWilliam?" I set my palms on the table, ready to stand.

"What, did I miss them two?" Corrine asked.

"You did." Adele raised her eyebrows. "Just."

"I'd say that's a good thing. I always like a schmooze-fest with Buck, but I don't much care if I see Detective McWilliam right at this particular minute."

"To answer your question, Robbie, I didn't learn nothing from them two," Adele added. "The detective was keen on pinning me down about Aries III, although she didn't reveal a thing in return."

"She wants to interview your sheep," Corrine said. "Why in the world?"

Adele explained about the blood on his horn. Corrine wrinkled her nose. I got to my feet.

"I need to get back to the job at hand," I said. "Corrine, has McWilliam stopped bothering you about whatever she thinks you did?"

"Not entirely, but I'm doing my best to avoid her."

"Did you want to order food?" I asked.

"Gosh, yes, hon. I'm more peckish right now than a starving hen." She grinned. "To mix a metaphor or whatever. You can hit me with all the breakfast, please. Grits, a couple eggs sunny side up, ham, potatoes, toast. You know, like Buck eats."

"You got it." I left the pair talking.

Corrine trying to avoid the detective ultimately wouldn't be successful, but interviewing her was McWilliam's business, not mine. Anyway, if Ivan died from being butted by the ram, it wasn't homicide, it was sheepicide, or maybe it would be called ovinicide. The label only mattered if a human had ended Ivan's life.

CHAPTER 47

By one thirty, I was beat. Things were at a dull roar, customer-wise, and I was hungry again after my big breakfast.

Lou, busy at the grill, glanced at me. "You look toasted, Robbie. Can I make you something to eat?"

"You're an angel, my friend, and you're right. I'm tired."

"Go sit down. I'll bring you a plate of lunch."

"Thank you. I think you should give up your professor gig and come to work for me."

She tilted her head. "I might just consider it."

A couple of minutes later she slid a plate holding a grilled ham, tomato, and cheese sandwich on whole wheat along with a glass of chocolate milk onto the table where I sat.

"This is awesome. Thanks, Lou."

Propping my feet on another chair, I took a bite and

checked my phone. Abe had written a text full of love emojis, so I sent a few hearts and flowers back to him, plus a row of Xs and Os. No news from Adele, although she'd promised before she left here to send me an update after the police checked for evidence on Aries III's horn.

As I ate, I tried to push away thoughts of murder and past intrigues. I failed. Ivan had tangled with so many lives. Oliver now resided—again—behind bars, at least for the moment. Corrine was avoiding a state police detective. Adele had endured sorrow and angst at having missed Ivan's apparent apology. Hope was Ivan's jilted lover, thrown over in favor of my aunt, who had eventually turned him in. Carter had history with the dead man. At least the banker hadn't been around lately.

Lou made her way over to my table.

"Hey." I took another look at her worried expression. "Uh-oh."

"Robbie, I know we have almost two hours until closing, and then there's cleanup, but I have to go. I mean, back to Lafayette."

"Your dad's condition is worsening?"

"Sounds like it. Len called a minute ago and said Dad is asking for me. My bag's already in the car. I really want to hit the road, and Danna said she'll cover for me. Do you mind?"

"Of course I don't mind." I set my feet on the floor and stood. "Being with your father is first priority, always. Anyway, I was thinking we would close early today. I am the boss, after all." I held out my arms for a hug.

"Thanks, my friend." She choked back a tear. "Thanks for the room upstairs, too. It was lovely and quiet. Peaceful. Exactly what I needed."

"Anytime it isn't booked, it's yours."

She sniffed, then laid her palm on my pregnant belly. "You better call me with breaking news."

"Deal," I said. "Drive safely. And ping me when you get there."

"Yes, Mom." She shot me a wan smile.

After she left, I chowed down on my ham and cheese and drank every drop of the chocolate milk at a record pace. My relaxed break was over.

When Hope Morris pushed through the door at two o'clock, her dark brimmed hat was covered with snow. After a record-hot summer, during which we all had sweltered through life, particularly working over a toasty grill, now we were getting early snow? The world's weather had gone bonkers, or at least it had in my neck of the woods.

I was busy pouring coffee and settling checks, and all the tables were full. When I had a minute to look Hope's way, she still stood near the door. With her arms folded and one ankle crossed over the other, she leaned against the wall.

She didn't owe us desserts, because we were closed tomorrow. She hadn't come in to pick up a check, because I paid her with direct deposit. I didn't think I'd done anything to offend her. Somehow her expression wasn't the look of a hungry diner. *Huh*. I made my way over and said hello.

"Looks like it's snowing out," I said.

"It is." She removed the hat and shook the snow onto the mat.

"Are you here to warm up with a late lunch?"

"No." She straightened her spine. "I'm resigning, Robbie. I can't bake for you any longer."

Yikes. My jaw dropped. "Um. Okay, I guess. Can I ask why?"

"Sure." She closed her mouth and uncrossed her ankle, lifting her chin in a defiant expression.

She wanted me to pull teeth? I could do that. "Why do you want to stop baking for my restaurant?"

"I don't want to, but I have to. I'm leaving town."

"I'm sorry to hear it." I took a moment to absorb her news. Was it something I said? "What's the reason you're moving?"

"It's not a good place for me any longer." She squinted, but not at me. Into the past, perhaps. "Too many bad memories."

"I hope the bad memories aren't because you've been baking for my restaurant."

She blinked. "What? No. How could they be?"

"Because I've really appreciated your quality product and regular deliveries. I'll miss you."

"Thanks. Sorry, but I'm leaving tonight." She turned to go.

"Take care," I called after her.

I watched her disappear through the door without another word. I'd never been dumped so quickly and with such finality. Now where were we going to get desserts? More important, did her departure have anything to do with Ivan's death?

I pulled out my phone and composed a message to McWilliam.

Hope Morris just came in and quit as my baker. Said she's leaving town tonight. FYI.

I sent it and trudged over to Danna at the grill. "Did you know it's snowing?"

"I've seen not a few people come in with white stuff on them. Too early, right?"

"Very."

"I wouldn't want to be Lou, out driving in the snow for a couple of hours and worrying about her dad at the same time," Danna said.

"I know. I hope she'll stop if it gets too blinding."

"I saw you talking with Hope. What did she want?"

"She wanted to tell me she quit," I said.

"What? She quit baking for us? Why?"

"No idea, except she mentioned bad memories and said she's moving away. Tonight, if you can believe it."

"That's nuts." Danna shook her head. "She's, like, in her fifties, isn't she? Doesn't she have a house or an apartment? And stuff and everything? She has another job, too. Adults don't just leave a whole life behind."

"It does seem crazy. Regardless, start brainstorming a new baker, okay? We don't have time to make desserts on top of everything else."

"We sure don't."

I pointed to the grill. "Sorry. I distracted you. Those need attention."

"Oopsies." Danna flipped a few meat patties and scooped a pile of scrambled eggs onto a waiting plate, then checked an order slip and poured out four disks of pancake batter. She lowered her voice. "Robbie, do you think Hope is trying to get away from the police? Maybe she killed Ivan Sheluk and thinks the authorities are getting close to arresting her."

"If that's the case, I'd have to say, good luck to her. I texted Juanita McWilliam about what Hope told me after she left a few minutes ago. With cameras everywhere, I doubt she could vanish into thin air. Plus, the county doesn't have any public transit unless you make an appointment for a ride. She'd have to take her own car to get out of here, and the police can easily track vehicles. None of it makes sense."

"It doesn't. She doesn't look like a murderer, anyway."

I'd unfortunately met more than one person guilty of homicide whose appearance made them an unlikely candidate. Even the sweetest face could mask a killer.

CHAPTER 48

We did manage to close a little early, at three o'clock instead of our usual Sunday three thirty. I plodded around, clearing tables and putting things away, while Danna scrubbed the grill.

"At least today we don't have to worry about how clean the floor or the bathrooms are," I said. "I still pat myself on the back for hiring a cleaning service to come in on Mondays and scrub the place down."

"It was a brilliant move, boss." Danna smiled over at me. "You're an amazing business owner and restaurateur. You really are."

"Aww, thank you. Much of our success is due to you, though."

"I appreciate that. We've come a long way, haven't we?"

"I'll say." I smiled back. "I still remember when you just showed up." Before I'd opened Pans 'N Pancakes,

I'd hired a helper who had quit before opening day. Adele and her friend Vera had helped out, but that wasn't a long-term solution. I'd placed an ad but had been too busy to check for responses. Danna had appeared at the door one afternoon, told me she wanted to work for me, and helped with that day's cleanup on the spot. She'd been my right-hand person ever since. "You saved my, uh, rear end from being a crashing failure."

"Sort of. Part of me telling you I wanted to work here was me following my dream. And part was sheer teenage rebellion. My mom wanted me to go to college. I wanted to cook. It was that simple."

"Right. Corrine thought you were taking a gap year, but you had other ideas."

Danna laughed. "I'll say."

"Do you regret not going to IU or Ball State or another college?" I loaded plates and mugs into the dishwasher. "You're smart enough, you could have gotten in anywhere."

"Seriously? I don't regret it for a minute." Danna brought the two grill spatulas to the sink. "Look at me, Robbie. I'm only twenty-three. I have my whole life to take classes if I want. Who knows, maybe I'll go to college at the same time as my baby." Her breath rushed in and she clapped her hand over her mouth.

Whoa. "Hey, you. Is there a second reason for the ring besides true love?" I set my armful of dishes next to the sink.

"Oh, man, did I ever blow that." Danna snorted. "We got a positive test last week, Robbie. I was supposed to sit on the news until, you know, after eleven or twelve weeks."

"A wise choice, and my lips are sealed. But now I know, let me say how happy I am for both of you." For the second time that afternoon, I extended my arms for a hug, but this time no tears were involved. I squeezed and stepped back. "Does this mean the wedding will be sooner rather than later?"

"It does. We're thinking in about a month, close to Christmas. Hopefully before I start showing, although actually I don't mind if anybody knows I was pregnant before I got married. I mean, who cares?"

"Totally."

"And in case you start worrying, Robbie, I don't plan on quitting and leaving you in the lurch. A bit of parental leave, sure, but I'll be back, and I won't be giving birth until you're well on your feet after your own baby."

"It sounds like a plan," I said. "How are you feeling? Any morning sickness?"

"I'm fine, which surprised me. I don't have any aversions or a queasy stomach at all."

"That's great. Everybody's different." I'd had my share of nausea in the first few months, but it had passed once I made it into the second trimester. "Have you told your mom?"

Danna grinned. "She went all ape about the news. She's super excited."

"I should think she would be."

"I was thinking about Hope leaving us," Danna said. "Why don't we make an arrangement with Buddy's Bread? He bakes cookies and brownies besides the artisanal bread."

I tilted my head. "That could work, if Buddy's willing. He might like the extra regular business, and his price might be lower, too. Good idea. I'll check with him tomorrow."

"Perfect. You know, with Len out, I hope Turner will be able to work on Tuesday."

"Good point. He did say his sister was on her way. They can probably trade off caring for Mona once she's home. Hospitals don't tend to keep people too long these days. And maybe his dad will come back early from his trip."

Danna nodded as she packed the condiment caddies into the box we stored them in overnight. "Robbie, I'm kind of worried about my own mom. The detective keeps wanting to talk to her, and Mom insists she didn't do anything wrong. What if they arrest her?"

"They can't arrest her if they don't have evidence." But if she doesn't have an alibi, she isn't automatically cleared, either. "Was she by herself Friday night?"

"Absolutely." Danna grimaced. "I was off with Isaac, and that guy Mom's seeing is out of town."

"You don't need to worry. According to Buck, they still don't know if it was murder. Now, let's finish up and get out of here."

"Okay, but shouldn't we put in an order for Tuesday before we go?" she asked.

"Yes, we should." I wagged my finger. "I'm warning you ahead of time, pregnancy brain is a real thing."

Because we were a good team, we'd done all the things. Danna had left via the service door by three thirty. I shut off the lights and took a quiet moment to myself before I headed home, sitting in the dim light near the door.

The snow fell softly outside as I thought. Danna, nine years younger than I, was starting a family with Isaac. Maybe we could open a day care in the apartment out back. I liked the thought of our babies being friends, growing up in a restaurant. I'd have to find a good replacement soon for Turner, and for Len if he moved on to other ventures. I had no plans for deserting or selling my business.

I texted Abe that I was leaving and tucked my phone into my left coat pocket. I stood, slung my bag across my chest, and pulled on my hat and gloves, snugging my coat as tight around me as I could.

CHAPTER 49

I let out a groan after the front door to the store clicked shut behind me. Three inches of new snow coated the porch and steps. The wet, heavy stuff was still falling. I wore comfortable pull-on boots, but they came only to my ankles and didn't include tread on the soles. My snow boots sat inconveniently at home.

In my heavy, off-balance condition, I had no intention of shoveling now or in the foreseeable future. So what if my feet got wet? I was going straight home to dry socks and warm slippers. I shuffled through the snow to the steps, then gripped the railing.

Except I didn't take a step. In a case of supremely bad timing, a contraction gripped me. I let out a different kind of groan as I waited, breathing, trying to calm myself. After the squeezing passed, I swallowed. That one had seemed longer than the earlier ones.

I picked my way carefully down the five steps. My

car was the only vehicle parked in the row of spaces facing the porch. Fresh snow had already begun to fill in the car-shaped spaces and tire tracks from the last customers, those who'd arrived after the precipitation started.

I made my way around the front of my car. I froze, staring a few yards away at the driveway to the side of the store. Danna always parked back there, but she'd left twenty minutes ago. Those tread marks in the snow were fresh. And nobody, but nobody, belonged in my driveway.

Prodding myself into action, I beeped open my car. My left hand was on the handle when a man's voice sounded behind me. Close behind me.

"I'm serious, Robbie Jordan."

I dropped the handle and whirled, my back to the car. Carter Kingsley glowered from under a forest-green watch cap and a bulky camouflage-patterned coat. He stood about four feet away, gloved hands at his sides. My baby was between us.

"About what?" I swore to myself as my throat thickened. I was trapped between him and my car. This was bad news, big-time. My right hand still held my bunch of keys, with the entirely useless fob between my thumb and forefinger.

"You know what." He took a step forward, his hands clenching into fists. "I warned you."

"Stay where you are." I swallowed, girding myself for whatever came, and slid my left hand into my coat pocket. "I don't know what you're worried about. If you didn't do anything wrong, you're fine. Right?"

"What kind of naïve fantasyland do you live in?" he

scoffed. "People are forced to serve time for things they didn't do."

My new mama bear self reared its head again, and I pulled out my phone. "Listen, Carter. The police have been running an extra patrol by here, and they're about due back. But I can have them here immediately."

He whipped his head toward the street, wearing an alarmed look.

"I'm leaving." I pulled open my driver-side door without taking my gaze off him. "If you know what's good for you, you should get in your car and go. And by the way? Stop threatening pregnant women, while you're at it."

He glared at me. Would he actually leave? I couldn't slide into my seat and lock the door fast enough to evade him if he moved forward instead of away. My heart thudded.

Carter took another step in my direction. I tossed my keys onto the dashboard and jabbed at my phone with an index finger. He didn't know the glove made my gesture futile. I hoped.

"Don't bother. I'm going." He spun on his heel and strode toward the driveway, disappearing around the corner of the building.

I wrestled myself into my seat. Closed the door. Hit the lock button. Stretched the seat belt out as far as it would go before clicking it shut around me. Started the car. Jacked up the heat. My adrenaline ebbing gave me the shivers.

I wanted nothing more than to be out of there before Carter drove away. Instead, another contraction set in. I groaned for the third time. If he backed out and continued his arc to ram into my car, I couldn't do anything about it.

Focusing inward was my only option. I saw his black sedan reverse all the way to the street, then drive in the opposite direction from my route. *Good*. But I was busy breathing. Inhale. Noisy breath out.

And then the pain was over. Which was great, except it had come so soon after the previous one. If this was the start of real labor, I'd better get myself home, and fast. I hoped my baby wasn't on her way out. Not yet. I didn't feel at all ready for many reasons, one being the matter of Ivan's death.

As the car warmed, my shoulders let go of the tension they'd been holding. My face relaxed. I needed to start driving, but I wanted to let Buck know about my run-in with Carter, and I didn't want to talk about it with Abe. I pressed Buck's cell number.

"You all right there, Robbie?" he asked without preamble.

"I am. But I wanted to let you know what just happened." I explained about Carter approaching me and his renewed threat. "I got him to back off and leave, though."

"You're something, you know that?" Buck's smile came through over the phone.

"It's this protective mother surge I've been getting, like I'm a mama bear. It's only the beginning of years of feeling like one, I'm sure."

"Tell me what exactly did old Carter say?

I thought for a second. "Basically he said he'd warned me, but it was his expression that scared me. Menacing and angry. His hands went into fists. When I said your department had been making extra patrols by the store and were due to pass in front any minute, he looked panicked for a moment, but he kept on coming. It was when I poked at my phone pretending to call that he left. I was wearing a glove, so it was a fake."

Buck chuckled. "Not the sharpest tool in the shed, that one."

"I guess not. Makes me wonder about the bank employing him, though."

"I might should have a word with the president. Him and me, we go way back."

"That's probably a good idea," I said.

"Listen, Robbie, did you take and tell McWilliam about this incident?"

"No. I thought you could."

"Will do, and right now. You take care, my friend," Buck said.

"I promise. Girl Scout's honor. You, too." I disconnected.

I put the car in reverse, then pointed the vehicle toward home, which had never felt so good. If driving home wasn't taking care, I didn't know what was.

CHAPTER 50

With a fire glowing in the wood stove, delicious smells emanating from the kitchen, and a loving man to greet me, nothing could have been more comforting—or more of a contrast with my workday and how it had ended.

I excused myself after Abe's strong welcome-home hug to wash up and change into a more relaxed version of the soft, roomy clothes I'd worn all day. I'd first heard the term "soft pants" from Danna last year. She'd said it meant sweatpants, loose yoga pants, or basically anything that wasn't jeans. I'd embraced it for at-home attire. I now wore soft clothes around the clock, which at work meant a large long-sleeved Pans 'N Pancakes T-shirt and stretchy pants.

After I'd petted both cats and the dog, I sank onto the sofa with an "oof."

"Tea, water, something else?" Abe asked.

"This baby is almost fully cooked. I'd like to sip a small glass of red wine."

He tilted his head. "Are you sure?"

"I am. Risa said it would be all right. Don't worry, I won't swig it."

Abe came back with a stemmed glass half full of a beautiful red wine in one hand and a pint glass of beer for himself.

"Cheers," he said after he sat next to me, extending his glass for a gentle clink. "So, what news, my love? I'm sure you have some."

"A little." I took a tiny sip and savored the flavor of the wine on my tongue and the warmth going down, something I hadn't felt since my last taste of alcohol in the spring. It was heavenly. Before pregnancy, I enjoyed a glass of an adult beverage on occasion. I knew how lucky I was not to be prone to getting addicted to the stuff. "For starters, my baker quit on me."

"Hope Morris?"

"Yes." I told him about Hope saying she was leaving town tonight.

"That's odd, isn't it?"

"Very."

"Did you ever talk to Mom about Hope?" Abe asked. "I think she knows her."

"I haven't. Do you know where she knows her from?"

"No, but she's like Corrine. She knows pretty much everyone."

"True. I'll give Freddy a call later." I set down the glass and cradled my belly. "I think I should call Risa, too."

Abe whipped his head over to stare at me. "Is something . . . has it . . ."

I laughed softly. "You should see your face. No, but I did have a couple of contractions earlier that weren't very far apart. I just want to check with her."

"Good idea."

A timer dinged in the kitchen. Cocoa raised his head from his bed and yipped.

"Dinner's in ten." Abe stood. "You already had yours, Cocoa."

I inhaled. "Lasagna?"

"You have the nose of a chef." Abe smiled at me before turning away.

I should certainly hope I could smell food like a chef. I'd been cooking professionally for nine years now. I took another sip of wine, then pulled out my phone. Ten minutes was plenty of time to talk to my mother-in-law, if she was free.

"Robbie, dear," she burbled. "Do you have news?"

"Not that kind, no." I rolled my eyes a little, glad she couldn't see me. Quite reasonably, my imminent labor seemed to be on everyone's mind. "Freddy, do you know Hope Morris at all?"

"A bit. Why?"

I repeated what I'd told Abe about Hope quitting abruptly. "She said she's leaving town tonight. It seemed odd to me, and Abe thought you might know her."

"It is odd. Let me think, now. In the past, we volunteered together at Grandma's Closet. You know, the thrift store in town?"

"Yes."

"But it's been a couple of years," Freddy said. "She

always seemed bitter, somehow, despite helping a good cause. All the proceeds from the shop go to benefit the Women's and Children's Center in Nashville."

"When I hired her to bake for the restaurant, she told me she had another income she wanted to supplement. I never asked her what her other job was. Did she ever mention what she did for work?"

Abe popped his head in wearing an inquisitive look. I mouthed, *Your mom*. He gave a thumbs-up and went back to dinner prep.

"Isn't she a midwife?" Freddy asked.

"Really? I had no idea."

"I believe so. A nurse-midwife, the kind who practices in the hospital."

Like Risa. I frowned, trying to puzzle this out. "And the job doesn't pay enough to live on?"

"I don't know, hon. Listen, I have to run. Howard and I are going out to dinner and a movie in Bloomington."

"Have fun, but drive carefully in the snow."

"We will. It seems to be ending, and our car does great in the white stuff, anyway."

"Good. Freddy? I wanted to thank you for your offer to be with us for the birth. It's very sweet, and I like the idea." I lowered my voice. "I haven't talked to your son about it, but I will tonight."

"Whatever works best for you, Robbie. Love you." She disconnected before I could return the sentiment.

I stared at the phone. Hope was a midwife? She'd never breathed a word about it, not even considering my near-term situation. She hadn't cast a professional eye on my enlarged midsection or asked where and with whom I would be delivering the baby.

"I'm going to phone Risa real quick," I called to Abe.

"Go for it," he said.

I pressed the midwife's number. She often didn't pick up, being at a labor or birth, but she always returned my call as soon as she could. This time she came on the line almost instantly.

"Robbie, what's happening?"

"Nothing." I cleared my throat. "I think."

She laughed. "Explain, please."

I told her about my two close-together contractions. "I haven't felt any more for the last hour or so."

"You'll know when your labor is for real." Her voice was gentle. "The contractions will be closer and they won't go away. You might have some fluid leakage, as well. In the meantime, your body is getting ready. When's your next appointment with me?"

"Wednesday."

"I'll check you then to see if you're partly dilated. Keep taking care of yourself, Robbie, and try to avoid stressful situations."

"I'll do my best." My stress at Carter threatening me wasn't exactly keeping calm or taking care of myself. With any luck, I'd have no more repeats of that kind of situation, as she put it. "Risa, do you know a nurse-midwife named Hope Morris?"

"I sure do. We trained together twenty-some years ago."

My eyebrows lifted.

"I don't think she's been working lately," Risa went on. "Or maybe it was only part-time."

"Why?" Part-time could explain why she wanted a second income.

"I might have heard rumors of some kind of legal problem with a birth she attended. Thing is, recently she's been working at the hospital in Columbus. Being as I practice out of Bloomington, I don't know the details."

"I see," I said. "Does Hope have a family? Children?"

"Sadly, no children. I don't know about a husband or partner. I say 'sadly' because she always seemed wistful, as if she'd wanted babies. I'm not sure why she didn't. Maybe she never found anyone she wanted to rear kids with. Lots of other women and their newborns benefited, though. Hope's a good midwife."

Or was. I heard noise over the line.

"Gotta run," Risa said. "Talk to you in a few days, if not sooner."

"Great. Thank you, Risa."

Wow. A good midwife in some kind of legal trouble. It could have been a malpractice suit or something else. Neither Buck nor McWilliam had mentioned being aware of Hope's issues. I hoped they knew and simply hadn't thought it was any of my business. Which, strictly speaking, it wasn't.

Risa had described the midwife as sad she hadn't had kids, but Freddy said Hope seemed bitter. Either way, my former baker was about to be on the run. To where, I hadn't a clue.

CHAPTER 51

Abe was off to work at eight the next morning, as usual. Being the angel he was, he brought me tea and toast in bed before he left, with dessert being a big kiss.

"My cell will be on and in my pocket no matter what I'm doing," he said. "And you're going to—"

"Call you if anything happens." I smiled at him. "I will. Including if it's Birdy throwing up on the entry-way rug?" My long-haired tuxedo had a bad habit of egesting icky hairballs exactly where the unsuspecting person stepped when they came in from outdoors.

He snorted. "Maybe not that."

"Have a good day, best husband in the world."

He pointed at me with both fingers. "You, too."

I lingered in bed, doing what stretches I still could. My morning crunches were a thing of the past. But I still had ab muscles in there somewhere, and I practiced tightening them along various dimensions. I'd need those muscles after the birth. I added a few dozen pelvic floor exercises while I was here.

Mostly I savored not having to get dressed and head into work.

My phone dinged with a calendar reminder. I grabbed it off the bedside table and grimaced when I saw the display. I'd reminded myself to take the deposit to the bank, but the bank was pretty much the last place I wanted to go today, especially if it meant running into Carter.

I'd do it later. Tomorrow I really needed to set Danna up with deposit slips and the account number. I should also give her the code to get into the safe in the apartment behind the store. The safe was the only secure place to leave cash for a few days. At least Abe knew the code, and my accountant had the account number. If something happened to me . . . No. I wasn't going to go there.

While I was downtown today, I could stop in and have a chat with Corrine. She might know something about Hope's past. I needed to talk with Buddy about baking for the restaurant. I should also cook a nice dinner for Abe, preferably something I could freeze portions of for us to eat during my confinement.

I giggled at the archaic term. Risa had explained that in older times, women stayed home with their newborn for a period of time, usually in bed, and the other women in the family took care of the pair. The practice let the birthing mother heal, establish a nursing bond with her baby, and adjust back to pre-pregnancy hormone levels, all while being coddled. I didn't plan to stay in bed for forty days or whatever. But the prospect of focusing on our much-wanted infant and not working for a couple of months sounded delightful. I was lucky to have such flexibility in my life.

I finished my tea and toast, satisfied I had a plan for the day. Thinking of Hope also brought Oliver to mind. Was he still behind bars? Had the detective found anything to actually charge him with, other than driving a stolen car he'd claimed not to know didn't belong to the friend he'd borrowed it from?

Asking Buck about Ivan's prison-mate got added to my mental list of downtown stops. Maybe by then the police would have the autopsy results, too.

I stayed in bed a bit longer with my phone, glancing through my email, social media, and several news updates. I did the couple of word games I liked, something I usually had to save for after work. I put the phone down when Baby Girl started kicking up a storm, which she often did when I was horizontal. I pulled up my sleep shirt and laid my palms on my bare belly, smiling when a little heel pushed against my hand. Nothing wrong with this kiddo's activity level.

I'd kept her safe all this time, despite encountering more than one murderer.

"A few more days, little one," I murmured. "Maybe a week or two, but we'll meet up soon, and won't we have fun?"

I received an elbow in the kidney for my trouble and grinned as I rolled out of bed and got myself ready for the day.

CHAPTER 52

I made my way out of Buddy's Bread at about eleven. My tote bag from WFIU, the Bloomington NPR station, now held a fragrant warm baguette and a crusty boule and my belly a cranberry-walnut muffin, all on the house. Buddy had been more than willing to set up a cookie-and-brownie delivery to Pans 'N Pancakes. He said he could manage three times a week—Tuesday, Thursday, and Saturday mornings—and we'd struck a bargain both of us were happy with.

On my way to the bakery, I'd stopped into my store to pick up the bank bag. I decided to get the deposit over with before the rest of my errands. All I had to do was take the money straight to the counter and leave with a receipt for the amount. Other workers and customers would be there. Still, the prospect of encountering Carter made me nervous. I squared my shoulders and told myself I had nothing to worry about.

Inside First Savings Bank, there was no sight of the manager. I gave a quick glance into his office as I passed. The light was on, but the room was empty. Fine with me. A couple of minutes later, I pushed out through the heavy door, receipt in hand.

I resettled my sunglasses on my face. Today wasn't as cold as yesterday, and the November sun shone as brightly as it gets at this time of year. Last evening's snowstorm hadn't lasted long, and whatever was left had already melted. I made my way toward Town Hall, where I could grab a pit stop before I looked for Corrine.

Personal business accomplished, I trudged up the wide interior stairs and poked my head into Corrine's assistant's office, which was in front of hers like a guard station. The door to the mayoral lair stood ajar a few inches. It wasn't enough for me to see in as far as her desk, which faced the door.

A fresh-faced young man sat at the outer desk, but he wasn't her usual aide. "Can I help you with something today, ma'am?"

"I'd like a quick word with Corrine, if she's in."

"Your name, please? What would you like to speak with the mayor about?"

"My name is Robbie Jordan. We're friends." I left it simple. This kid didn't need to know I wanted to pick her brain about a possible homicide suspect.

"Please have a seat, ma'am. Let me see if she's available." He rose and stuck his head around the partly open door.

I stayed standing. If she was busy, I'd come back later, or never.

"Robbie's here?" she said in a loud voice. "Why sure, hon, send her the heck on in."

Young Dude stood back and gestured me toward the door as he pushed it wide open. I skirted his desk and stopped abruptly at what I saw.

Oliver Stanganelli sat on the other side of the desk from Corrine. His back was straight, his hands were clasped in his lap with nearly white knuckles, and one knee jittered up and down.

"Robbie, darling, come in, come in." Corrine waved at the empty chair. "Take a load off."

"I can come back," I began.

"No, no, it's fine." She gave me the full mayoral beam. "You've met Oliver."

"I have. Good morning, Mr. Stanganelli."

He jumped to his feet and motioned me to his seat. "Please. I was about to leave."

"I won't hear of it," Corrine said. "I got a second chair right there. Sit down, now, Robbie. You, too, Oliver."

"Thank you," I said to Oliver as I sat. "So, you've been released from custody."

He looked reluctant, but also resumed his seat. "Yes, ma'am."

"They didn't have a lick of evidence to up and hold him," Corrine said. "We were just catching up on old times, weren't we?"

This was a turnabout. Earlier, she'd expressed nothing but negative memories of Oliver.

"Yes." He clasped his hands again and pressed his lips together.

Why was he here if he was so uncomfortable? Maybe

it was a command appearance by Corrine. She did run the town, after all.

"So where you headed next, Ol?" Corrine folded her own hands on the desk. If she'd meant to mirror his clasped hands, hers was a completely relaxed, casual move.

"Frankly, I have no idea," he said. "Prison doesn't do a good job of preparing inmates for after we get out, at least not in terms of practicalities."

"They don't give you job training or nothing?" Corrine asked.

"Actually, I did do a lot of cooking during my incarceration. They found out I was good at it, and that I wouldn't steal the sharp knives and hurt anyone."

I had a little light bulb moment. "What kind of cooking?"

"Well, food inside isn't fancy, but I did plenty of line prep and grill work. I enjoyed it, and it took my mind off my situation." His situation being doing time for robbing a bank.

"I am going to be short one cook in my restaurant come January. What we serve isn't fancy, either, and it's breakfast and lunch only." I tilted my head, regarding him. "As long as your record stays clean, and if my crew is okay with the idea, I'd be willing to hire you on a trial basis."

Corrine gaped, but not as wide as Oliver did.

"You would hire *me*?" he asked, his tone incredulous. "A convicted felon?"

"We can give it a try. See how you do." I shrugged. This might have been the stupidest offer I'd ever made. Or it might be brilliant and a kind of public service. Released felons must have a terrible time landing decent employment.

"Thank you, Ms. Jordan." He let go of his hands and his shoulders relaxed. "You don't know how much your generosity means to me." He rose.

"Let's be in touch," I said. "But Ms. Jordan is my aunt. Please call me Robbie."

"All right, Robbie. Now, if you ladies will excuse me, I met someone who'll give me a ride to go visit my family. I have more than a few apologies to make."

"Sounds like things are falling into place for you, Oliver," Corrine said.

He nodded his acknowledgment without speaking.

I handed him one of my store business cards. "Text me at this number and let me know how to reach you."

"I will." He pocketed the card. "Thank you again. I'm more grateful than you can know."

We watched him leave.

"Well, well, well." Corrine leaned back in her swivel chair. "Are you sure hiring him is a good idea?"

"Not entirely. But he's not a car thief, and he served his original sentence. As long as he gets cleared of involvement in Ivan's death, I'm willing to give him a try, but only if Danna and Len agree. Having a fourth crew member is important to the sanity of the rest of us."

"I'm sure it is." She winked. "And it'll help later in the year."

"Yes, Grandma, it will." I smiled.

"Danna told me she let it slip to you."

"She did," I said. "It's such exciting news for all of us, but for you in particular."

"Right?" She chuckled. "Who knew my baby would be having a baby? I sorta like never even thought about it."

The assistant gave a knock on the door. "Ma'am, your eleven-thirty is here."

"Sorry, Robbie," Corrine said.

I stood. "No problem."

"What in heck did you stop by for in the first place?" she asked. "It wasn't to see old Oliver. I saw how surprised you looked when you saw him setting there."

"I had a question about Hope Morris. I'll text you."

"Perfect."

I ambled away, my thoughts going straight to picking Buck's brain about not only Hope but now Oliver, too.

CHAPTER 53

My tote bag slung over my shoulder, I trundled down the block thinking about Oliver. I hoped Danna would be down with the plan to try him out on our crew. She got along with everyone and had a generous heart—like her mom. I doubted Len would have an objection, either.

It all depended on Oliver not being linked with Ivan's death in any way, or committing any new crime, for that matter. Buck or McWilliam should be able to set my mind at ease about Oliver being cleared of suspicion.

Buck was trotting down the front steps of the police station when I approached. A gust of wind almost blew his hat off.

"Well, good night nurse," he exclaimed. "Was you coming to see me, Robbie?"

"I was. You're exactly the person I wanted to talk with. Where are you off to?"

"Gonna take and grab me a sandwich, seeing as how Monday is the day your place is closed up tighter than a nun's knees."

"Buck!" I shook my head. His colorful expressions didn't usually run to the borderline racy.

"Shoot, sorry. Anyhoo, treat you to lunch?"

Huh. Could I eat again? As an old pickup truck rattled over a pothole, I assessed my state of hunger. Yes, I could grab a bite of lunch with my favorite police chief.

"I had a muffin an hour ago," I said, "but I'd love to get a bite with you."

"Eating for two and all, am I right?"

"You certainly are, and number two of the pair is getting bigger and bigger." As was I, but the weight was temporary and didn't worry me. I planned to breastfeed the baby, and Risa had said doing so would make the pregnancy pounds melt away. Let it be so. Once I went back to work and was able to go cycling again, I hoped my activity level would help me regain my strength and my former physique.

"Come along, then," he said. "My treat."

Soon enough we sat across a table at Strom and Pete's. Buck had ordered a salami and mozzarella stromboli. The specialty of Pete's shop, the sandwich was basically a rolled-up pizza. I'd opted for a salad topped with their marinated grilled chicken, always a delicious choice, and it came with soft, homemade pita bread. The aroma in here of tomato sauce, the scent of crust baking, and the tangy smell of pickled peppers and olives made my stomach growl out loud.

I glanced around, not seeing anyone I knew, and spoke in a low voice. I told Buck about seeing Oliver in Corrine's office a few minutes ago.

"Does him being there mean he's no longer a person of interest?" I asked.

"Seems so. The local authorities where Stanganelli borrowed the vehicle brought in his friend, who admitted to having stolen it. We believe Stanganelli was telling the truth when he said he didn't know it was a hot car."

"What about Ivan's death?"

Buck flipped open his hands. "Can't arrest a man for homicide when we don't know if that was how Sheluk died, now, can we?"

"I guess not." I glanced at the wall next to our booth, which had a faded photograph of a conical mountain with smoke or steam coming out of the top. Under it a caption read Mount Stromboli. I pointed. "Whoa. Take a look at this, Buck."

The young woman working the counter brought over our meals.

"What's that, a volcano?" Buck asked her.

"It is," she said. "It's on an island near Sicily in Italy. The island is also called Stromboli. Isn't that funny?"

"Wow. I had no idea. Thank you." I smiled up at her before she turned away. "I feel like I've never seen the picture before."

"Sure fits for this place, don't it?" Buck took a big bite of his stromboli, barely catching the sauce before it dripped down his chin.

"Did I tell you Turner is leaving to go to culinary school in January?" I asked before attacking my own lunch.

Mouth full, Buck shook his head.

"Oliver told me he did line cooking in prison. Since he has experience and is apparently innocent, I offered him a job starting in the new year."

Buck's eyes bugged out. He swallowed his mouthful. "You what, now?"

"I told him if my crew was okay with the idea, I wanted to hire him. I need another cook, Buck. He needs a job."

"Welp, I s'pose that is a kind of public service, Robbie." He seemed to give the idea some thought. "I'm thinking you're right. I don't see nothing wrong with hiring the man. It's not like his first crime was violent or nothing. Long as he's cleared of having anything to do with Sheluk's death."

"Exactly." I savored a couple of bites of salad with chicken. "To change the subject, I'm interested in Hope Morris's past. She quit on me yesterday and said she was leaving town last night, for good."

Buck wiped his mouth. "You're full of surprises today, my friend."

I added what Risa had mentioned about Hope's possible troubles.

"I can't say I'm aware of any issues she's got, but I'll check into it." Buck took another enormous bite.

"I was in the bank a little while ago, and Carter wasn't in his office. Was that your doing?"

"Might could be. I did have the chance to slip a word to my buddy, the president. He was surprised in a big way to learn of his employee's past with the symphony finances. I do believe the president planned to encourage old Carter to take a little bit of time off, possibly on a permanent basis."

"Thank you." I smiled fondly at him, sipping my water.

"Can't have nobody threatening my favorite chef, now, can I? I took and told McWilliam, too, just so's you know."

"Thanks. I wasn't up for letting her know yesterday."

We ate in companionable silence for another couple of minutes. I realized Lou had never gotten back to me about if her aunt had information on Oliver. Maybe it didn't matter. Lou's father's health took priority.

I set down my fork. "It's been a week since Ivan died, or nearly. You still don't have any word from the coroner?"

"Mmm." He swallowed his last bite. "Said he'd have a verdict this afternoon. Stand by for news, as they say."

"It'll be a relief to know what you're dealing with, won't it?" I asked.

"I should say. Especially for old Juanita. She's been pretty much tearing her hair out."

"Wouldn't want that. She has great hair." I hoped my own dark, full head of hair would gray in the same distinctive way as hers.

"You know what I mean. More information is always a good thing when it comes to murder."

That was possibly the understatement of the year.

"Speaking of information," Buck continued, "we dug up something useful from the only local taxi company. Seems a driver delivered old Sheluk to Adele's farm that night."

"When I went out to see Adele that morning and I didn't see any strange cars, I wondered how Ivan got there."

"Driver said she thought it was a mite odd, but he paid the fare and a big tip, and she didn't think it was her place to ask no questions."

"That's too bad, but I can see her point." I shook my head. Poor Ivan had taken a one-way taxi ride to his death.

CHAPTER 54

After lunch, I puttered in the restaurant. Breakfast prep for the next day always needed doing. I savored the quiet and the temporary tidy orderliness of a place that tomorrow would be hopping with diners chatting and dishes clattering, the air filled with the fragrance of meat frying and biscuits baking.

While I worked, my curiosity about Hope rose up again. Being alone, I was able to take plenty of sitting breaks. After the pancake mix was ready, I sat and poked around on my phone.

Risa had said Hope practiced out of the hospital in Columbus, Indiana. I'd gone there a few years ago before Christmas to check into a person of interest in a double murder investigation. I wouldn't take that trip now, but an online search couldn't hurt.

I found an article about the midwifery practice associated with the hospital. "Ooh," I said aloud. The story said the entire labor and delivery department was about to close.

Yikes. What were women in the area supposed to do? Drive to Bloomington or Indianapolis, I supposed. That was a long way for someone in the throes of labor. My own forty-minute drive to Bloomington was far enough, even if Abe drove with a heavy foot.

I kept looking, searching for Hope's name paired with the hospital. The OB department had had several waves of layoffs, and she'd been in the first round. My eyes widened as I drilled down. A previous story mentioned her in association with a malpractice suit that named her. That was kind of the definition of legal trouble. The parties apparently had come to an agreement. I knew many such cases were settled out of court, but it made me wonder if the suit was part of the reason the hospital sent her packing.

Baking a few trays of desserts for my restaurant several times a week couldn't have provided enough income for her to live on. Risa hadn't mentioned Hope applying for a midwifery position with the Bloomington practice.

I wished I'd asked Hope more about her life. I must have her address in my files, but right now I didn't know where she'd been living. Maybe having the police ask her questions about Ivan had been the last straw for staying in South Lick, Nashville, or surrounds. McWilliam might still need to find Hope to further question her about her past with Ivan. I'd done my due diligence and reported Hope's departure. It was up to the authorities to track her down.

About to rise and continue prepping, I stayed where I was when my phone rang with a call from Lou.

"Lou, how are things going?"

"Our dad died this morning." Her voice was low and subdued.

_Oh_. "I'm so, so sorry, my friend."

"Thank you." She sniffled. "Len and I were both at his side here at home."

"Good. That's as it should be."

"My brother wasn't up to calling you, but he—"

"He won't be in to work," I finished. "Of course he won't, and neither will you. You're both where you need to be for as long as it takes. We'll be fine here."

"Thank you. I . . ." Her voice trailed off.

"You go be with Len and do all the things. Let me know about a service, okay?"

"I will. You're a good friend, Robbie."

"Love you."

"Love you too." She disconnected.

I sat back. Her father's death had come a lot sooner than Lou had expected. The poor thing. Both she and Len. At least he'd had a reconciliation with his father, and Lou had gotten to the bedside in time. Small blessings were blessings, nevertheless.

If Turner couldn't resume his shifts, Danna and I would have to scramble. Maybe I could twist Adele's arm to help out, or Freddy might be willing.

I whipped my head around at a noise from the side of the building. The service door creaked. My pulse started going double time. _What the—?_

Turner appeared in the opening. "Hey, Robbie." He let the door shut behind him.

I let out a noisy breath and fanned myself with my hand. "Hi."

He frowned and hurried toward me. "Are you okay?"

"I'm fine. You startled me is all."

"Whew." He sat opposite me. "I'm sorry, I should have texted first, but I saw your car out front."

"It's not a problem. How's your mom?"

"She's home and my sister's with her. My dad is on his way back, too."

"That's good. Is Mona in much pain?"

"She's doing okay. She's allergic to opioids and they don't want her to take things like ibuprofen, but she's doing acetaminophen and meditating." He gave a lop-sided grin.

"As she does." I smiled back.

"Exactly. I stopped by to tell you I'll be back on shift tomorrow."

"Thanks. That's great." I explained about Len and Lou's father dying.

"That's really sad." His mouth turned down. "I can't imagine losing my dad."

"I hear you. Anyway, until Len comes back, it'll be a big help if we can count on you."

"You can, but we'll be back down to two of us here when you go into labor, right?"

"I have a bit of news about that."

His jaw dropped. "Has it started?"

I gave a laugh and shook my head. "No. I mean news about staffing here." I explained about Oliver and his experience cooking. "I thought it might solve one problem for us, and he needs a job."

"Hmm. I heard of a restaurant in Los Angeles somewhere that hires convicted felons who've served their sentences."

"Are you willing to work next to one?"

"I can do that."

"Fantastic. Thanks, Turner. I had asked Oliver about starting when you leave in January, but he might be willing to get his feet wet here earlier than that."

"I hope it works out so you'll have a replacement for me in the new year," he said. "What does Danna think?"

"I haven't had a chance to ask her yet. Mind if I call her right now?

"Go for it."

I put her on speaker and went through the Oliver proposition. "Turner's here, too. What do you think?"

"Are you in, dude?" Danna asked him.

"Sure," he said. "Would hiring be, like, provisional, Robbie?"

"Of course. I can give him a trial of two months," I said. "If we're all in agreement that he's a good fit, I'll get a contract drawn up for ongoing employment."

"Sounds like a plan," Danna said. "Turner, your mom's going to be okay?"

I let them chat about that for a minute.

After the call was over, Turner looked at me. "You look beat. Let me finish breakfast prep while I'm here, okay?"

"Seriously?"

"Yes, boss, seriously. Go home and put your feet up."

I pushed to my feet. "I'd better get out of here before you change your mind."

"Not a chance." He smiled and grabbed an apron.

I talked him through what I'd done and what was left, then gave him a quick hug.

"I'm really going to miss you when you head off to school."

He winced. "I'm sorry, Robbie."

I held up a hand. "And I'm super glad you get to do it. No regrets, my friend."

"Deal." He turned away, then turned back. "I'm going to miss you, too. And Danna and this place. Working here has been some of the best few years of my life."

I swallowed away sudden tears. "Then you're just going to have to come back."

I pulled on my coat and slipped out the front door. He wouldn't come back except to visit. Turner had higher ambitions, and I was glad of it.

CHAPTER 55

"This is adorable, Adele." I held up the tiny knit-ted hat she'd brought to my house at about four that afternoon. "It's so soft."

She'd used a yarn with colors shifting from blue to purple to green and the cap featured little ear flaps ending in braided yarn strings. Leave it to Adele not to automatically knit a pink hat.

"Figured our girlie's gonna need to keep her head warm for the winter." She beamed as she sat on the sofa with Birdy and me. "It won't be itchy, either. Thought you'd like it. I'll keep knitting them for her as she grows."

"I love it. Abe will, too." I leaned over and kissed her cheek. "Thank you."

"Any action in there?"

"If you mean has my labor started, the answer is no." My lower back was achy, but I figure it was from lack of rest. "Were they able to sample the dried blood on Aries III's horn?"

"Sure enough. Got that accomplished end of the day yesterday." She stood. "I'd best be going. Samuel's making me dinner tonight. He said he'll make extra portions and freeze them for you and your man to eat after the baby comes."

"How sweet of him."

"The man is the true embodiment of sweet, don'cha know?"

I hoisted myself to my feet and walked her to the door.

"You promise to call with any news?" Adele peered into my face.

"I promise."

She opened the door and frowned. "Looks like a doozy of a storm is blowing our way."

She was right. Massive dark clouds loomed to our west and were gusting toward us in a hurry. The air smelled like rain even though it hadn't started falling yet. Cocoa trotted over and barked at the wind.

"Drive carefully," I told Adele, then looked down at the dog. "Why don't you go out now, while you can?" I let him into the yard. He'd let me know when he was ready to come in.

Speaking of dinner, it was about time for me to start preparing ours. I always tried to cook for Abe on my day off. He did most of our other dinners, since I worked with food all day. For tonight I'd planned large pasta shells stuffed with a ricotta mixture and baked with a homemade roasted tomato sauce, which I'd made in the summer and frozen. I picked up the rest of the ingredients on my way home from downtown.

On my way into the kitchen, my back began aching more. I held on to the counter and tried a few figure-eight belly dancing moves. When my belly seized up, I stopped, glancing at the clock. The pain lasted about twenty seconds.

I filled the big pot with water and started it heating on the biggest burner when another pain began. *Uh-oh.* It had been less than three minutes since the previous one. This contraction was more intense and lasted thirty seconds. I pulled the ricotta, mozzarella, and eggs out of the fridge. If I was in real labor, I'd better move fast to get our dinner assembled.

A new contraction gripped me after only two minutes. I swallowed and tried to do the slow, regular breathing Risa had taught me. Easier said than done. This pain hurt in a dull, insistent kind of way, and seemed like it lasted a whole minute.

It was time to call the midwife, and Abe right after her. First, I turned off the burner under the pasta pot. Dinner was not happening, not now.

"Risa, I think it's started," I began when she picked up. "Contractions are coming fast and furious." I moaned as another one began.

"Stay with me Robbie. Focus on your womb."

I tried until it ended. "Okay, the contraction's over. They're coming every two minutes and lasting nearly a minute."

"No bleeding, no waters broken?"

"Neither."

"Is Abe with you?"

"No, he's still at work."

"Call him." Her voice was low and calm. "I'll get

there as soon as I can, but I'm up in Morgantown. It'll take me fifteen, twenty minutes to reach you."

A rumble of thunder was punctuated by a loud crack of lightning. I let out a yelp. Adele's doozy seemed to have arrived.

"Yes, we're about to be hit with a big storm," Risa said.

"Can you even get here?"

"Yes." Her voice was firm.

A creaky sound came out of my throat as another pain started.

"Whatever you do, don't push, Robbie. All right?"

"Mmm."

"Listen, I'll call Abe. See you soon." She disconnected.

I listened to the pouring rain, cringing every time the skies split with more lightning. I let out a whimper. What if Risa couldn't make it to the house? What if my beloved Abe's car was hit by lightning?

"No," I scolded myself out loud. "They'll be here. We'll all get to the hospital. Everything's going to be fine. I'm going to meet my daughter. It'll be fine."

I didn't convince myself, but my self-pity went out the window when the next contraction gripped me. I had no choice. For tens of thousands of years, women had been giving birth, sometimes alone. If I was forced to be one of them, so be it.

As it turned out, I didn't have to do it by myself. Risa bustled in before her predicted fifteen minutes, with Abe on her heels and Cocoa on his.

I let out a raspy post-contraction breath. "I've never been so happy to see anyone."

CHAPTER 56

Abe showed Danna and Corrine into the living room two days later at the end of the afternoon as I sat in the gliding rocking chair holding our baby girl. Both cats and the dog were keeping us company in various spots around the room.

"We won't stay long, Robbie," Corrine said. "But we had to come and say a big Hoosier hello to your little one."

"Please," I said. "I just finished feeding her a few minutes ago. Sit down, you two." Abe had texted the news to Danna after the birth, adding it was fine to close the store the next day if she and Turner didn't want to manage with only two of them. Adele and Sean had also gotten the news the first evening. Adele had stopped by yesterday to meet her grandniece, and I'd called Lou and Turner about the baby.

Instead of sitting, Danna knelt in front of my chair,

her eyes wide with wonder. "Look at her tiny little hand."

"She's a peanut, but she's all there." Abe beamed.

"How much did she weigh?" Corrine asked.

"Seven and a half pounds," I murmured. "And I felt every ounce of it."

"Robbie had one of the world's fastest labors, apparently," Abe said. "She gave birth in our bedroom four hours after her labor started."

"What?" Danna's face paled.

"It's true." I stroked the baby's soft dark hair. "She started coming out as soon as the midwife got here. With the massive storm we had, no way were we making it to the hospital in Bloomington."

"You done good, Robbie." Corrine beamed. "Now, spill the news. What's our newest South Lick resident's name?"

"She's Gianina Frederica O'Neill," Abe murmured.

"I love it." Danna sat next to her mother. "It honors your mom, Jeanine, and your Italian dad, plus Abe's mom and his family."

"That was our goal," I said. "We debated using O'Neill-Jordan or Jordan-O'Neill, but it seemed like too much to saddle her with."

Gianina let out a couple of squeaks.

Abe held out his arms. "I'll take her. She might need a fresh diaper."

Happy tears trickled out as I handed Gianina to her father. Abe couldn't feed her, but he could do everything else—and already did. I swiped at my cheeks.

"Your emotions running all whackerdoodle, Robbie?" Corrine asked.

"Definitely. Risa said crazy mood swings are normal for the first couple of weeks. Hormone levels and stuff." I gazed at my longtime co-chef and younger friend. "Danna, I didn't mean to scare you by saying she was born at home."

"It's okay. Isaac has been making noises about us planning a home birth." Danna shook her head. "My idea is to pitch a tent on the hospital grounds a month before my due date. I want the drugs and the operating room and everything close by, just in case."

"Listen, hon, Danna cooked up a hearty beef stew for you two," Corrine said. "Abe took it when we came in. You gots to keep your protein up for making milk. A glass of dark beer don't hurt, either." She stood. "We'll be getting ourselves along. We don't want to tire you out. I remember what postpartum felt like."

Danna rose, too.

"Thank you both so much for stopping by, and for the food." I smiled at these two women who had been so important to me for years. I was lucky to have moved to this community. I'd created a found family, and I knew the coming years would be rich as I raised Gianina in the store and among beloved friends.

The doorbell pealed. Cocoa yipped. Maceo dashed out of the room. Birdy opened one eye and closed it again. I began to push myself to my feet but winced. My fast labor had done a number on my lady parts.

"You stay put." Danna jumped up. "I'll get the door."

Before she could leave the room, Abe, holding the baby, ushered in Buck. My favorite policeman was also a member of the found family. Today in jeans and a flannel shirt, he held a bunch of flowers and a heavy-looking tote bag.

"Hey, there, mama." He proffered the bouquet of red and yellow carnations. "Brung you these, and my Melia cooked up a casserole for y'all."

"Thank you, Buck," I said. "How lovely. Please sit down."

Abe handed me Gianina. "I'll put the food away and get the flowers into water."

The baby let out a tiny cry at the transfer. I shifted her to my shoulder and gently stroked her little back.

"What, they give you the day off?" Corrine gave Buck a fake frown.

"You know very well I'm taking the week off. Even more so, now we got the last loose end tidied up." Buck perched on the edge of the easy chair.

"The loose end of the case?" I asked him. *Finally*.

"Yup."

Corrine gave a slow nod, as if she already knew.

Danna gave her mom the side eye. "And you didn't let me know?"

"Not my news to share, hon." Corrine sank back onto the couch. "Set yourself down again for a sec. Buck's got him a story to tell."

Danna folded her long legs to sit cross-legged on the floor. Abe returned, placing a vase full of the cheery blooms on the bookshelf.

"It's story time, Abe." Corrine patted the couch next to her.

Abe glanced at me with raised eyebrows. I shrugged. He joined her.

"Welp, once upon a time," Buck began. "Only kiddin'—it ain't such a long tale."

Corrine made a rolling "Get on with it" motion with her hand.

"It's this way." Buck leaned forward, elbows on knees. "The coroner determined cause of death was accidental, not homicide."

Wow. Nobody killed Ivan. He hadn't confronted a murderer in his last minutes of life. I was glad.

"What a relief." The baby stirred and I shifted her to the crook of my other arm. When I looked up, all eyes seemed to be on me. "What?"

"We all know you were working hard on figuring out Ivan's death," Danna said. "You don't sound surprised at the outcome."

"I guess I'm not, really." I glided back and forth, hoping to keep Gianina happy. "Adele found dried blood on her ram's horns. I thought Oliver was too well-intentioned to kill his friend, despite having that defaced photo, which I suspected was from long ago. I knew Adele didn't kill Ivan. I did wonder about Carter, and Hope's quick disappearance was strange."

"Old Carter's got his problems, but I had me a little chat with him. It turns out he was down to Louisville with his sister all that night."

"So he had an alibi all along," I murmured, more to myself than anyone else.

"And get this," Corrine said. "I learned him and Ivan were cousins."

Buck nodded. "That's how Sheluk knew about Carter's little problem with embezzlement."

"Amazing. What about Hope?" I asked Buck. "Did you learn why she left so abruptly?"

Corrine looked at me. "After you texted me about her, I checked in with an old friend. He grew up with her, and said she has a history of leaving wherever she is when the going gets tough. He also told me she was burned, hard, by Ivan dumping her all them years ago. I think she probably headed out to make a new life. It's not like she hasn't done it before."

"How sad," Danna said.

I nodded. Except splitting was no way to build stability, either.

"Buck, do you know for sure what happened to the man in the paddock?" Abe asked.

"Final verdict was that Sheluk had a heart attack of a sort," Buck said. "He musta been leaning over the fence to say hello to the ram and fell in once he got unconscious. Old Aries III butted him after he was alone in the field, and the man plum expired."

"But why would he be at the paddock at all?" Abe asked.

"Might never know," Buck said. "Maybe the man liked sheep."

Corrine snapped her fingers. "Just remembered. Ivan grew up on a farm. Could have been a nostalgia trip for him to greet the livestock."

"The fence is labeled with yellow caution stickers warning that it's electrified," I said.

"He could have figured out the switch was in the barn," Corrine said. "Probably headed himself in there and turned off the juice. Ivan had his problems, but dumb wasn't one of them. The man was sharper than a box of tacks fresh from the factory."

"If he did that, he might have already been inside the fence when his heart failed, or the ram butting him caused it," I said. "Ivan was on his way to visit Adele to make amends, according to her." I thought back to when I'd met Ivan. "Buck, did the autopsy also find that Ivan was ill? He'd seemed out of breath when I met him at the bank, and when he was in the restaurant he'd struck me as unwell."

"As a matter of fact, it looked like he might coulda had cancer," Buck said. "ME's still checking out the facts, and Juanita's trying to get his health records from prison."

"He must have been dying," Abe murmured. "Having the end of your life in view would prompt anyone to make amends for the past."

My eyes brimmed over. The poor man. Abe gave me a sympathetic look. The baby let out a little cry. I sniffed back the tears and lifted her so our cheeks touched. I inhaled her delicious baby scent, then held her close.

"You're okay, sweet girl," I whispered. "Mama's got you." For now and for always.

CHAPTER 57

I sat in the corner of the long sectional in my in-laws' living room three days later. The air was redolent this afternoon with aromas of turkey and squash roasting, freshly baked pies, and potatoes on the simmer. That is, full-on Thanksgiving.

Abe and I contributed a pan of olive-oil-drizzled Brussels sprouts ready to roast after the turkey came out, plus rolls Abe baked this morning. After we arrived, he tucked Gianina into our wraparound carrier on his chest and went to help his dad in the kitchen.

"I promise I won't work near anything hot while I'm wearing her," he said.

I only smiled. I knew another draw of the kitchen was the IU football game playing on the big screen in the adjacent family room.

Freddy approached carrying two Manhattan glasses. "I invented a Celebrating Baby cocktail, which also works for Thanksgiving." She handed me one of the glasses and sat at the other end of the couch.

I thanked her and took a sip, rolling the flavors on my tongue. "Mmm. Cranberry, orange, bitters, and what, rum? Plus bubbly."

"You got it. The orange is from the Grand Marnier."

"It's a delicious combination, but I need to take it slow."

"You haven't been drinking for most of a year." She sipped hers.

"Right. More important, the last thing I want is alcohol getting into my milk." I'd done my research and knew sipping a single drink right after I'd nursed wouldn't harm my little one. "I won't feed the baby for another couple of hours, so a few sips will be okay."

"So," Freddy began, "I heard the case of that man's death is all resolved. They concluded it wasn't murder after all."

"Yes. Buck told us a couple of days ago."

"The news must set your mind at ease."

"For sure. Nobody wants to think about someone actually committing murder." I took one more small sip and set down the glass.

"I have to say, I'm glad it wasn't Carter. The man's a petty crook, but he never struck me as a killer."

The front door opened, admitting a beaming Adele and Samuel, followed by Abe's brother and his wife. Greetings all around ensued. Adele plopped down into the armchair nearest me, while everyone else went off to watch the game. Freddy also disappeared into the kitchen.

"Where's that girlie of mine?" Adele glanced around.

She'd stopped by the house to meet her great-niece the day after the birth but hadn't seen Gianina since.

"Abe's got her for the moment."

"And how are you making out, sugar?" she asked.

Freddy returned with a drink for Adele.

"Thank you, hon." My aunt took a sip. "Yum. Sure as heck smells good in here."

"Good smells are pretty much all Howard's doing." Freddy sat. "He's a much better cook than I am."

"Something he passed down to Abe," I said.

"I was asking Robbie how's she's doing," Adele said.

"Well, yesterday my milk came in, big-time." I winced a little. "So Gianina and I are figuring out how to deal with feeding."

"I remember those days." Freddy shook her head. "Seems like it was yesterday. Let me know if you need any help learning to nurse her, okay?"

"Thank you." I gave her a grateful smile. My labor had happened way too fast to call her for support. Taking my mother-in-law up on this offer seemed like a good idea. "She'll want to eat again while we're here. Maybe you can sit with us and give me a few pointers."

"I'd love to," Freddy said.

"All's I know about that business is lambs suckling the ewes." Adele guffawed. "Only problem they run into is when the mama rejects one of her babies."

"No danger of rejection here," Freddy said.

"If a ewe pushes away a lambkin, I just take and bottle feed the little one," Adele said. "They turn out fine."

"Adele, I assume Buck told you about the resolution of Ivan's death." I gazed at her.

"Sure as shooting. He stopped by himself to deliver the news." She swigged the cocktail and nearly choked. "Whoa, Nelly. This is more for sipping than for chugging, I think."

"You would be right, my friend." Freddy laughed.

"Anyhoo," Adele went on. "I got a letter from a ghost yesterday."

"A ghost?" I asked.

She nodded, in all seriousness. "From Ivan."

A chill went through me. Freddy gaped. Adele stared at her hands.

"Written before he died," I whispered.

"Yes." My aunt looked up. "He'd already said he was coming to see me. This note said it was to apologize, but that if he didn't make it . . ." Her voice trailed off.

I reached for her hand and held on.

She took in a deep breath and continued. "If he didn't make it, he wanted me to know some stuff."

"He knew he was dying," Freddy murmured.

"He must have." Adele seemed to go inward with her memories.

The three of us sat in silence for a few moments. Freddy looked pensive and at the same time warm and supportive toward Adele. I was full of thoughts about life ending, about seeking resolution, and about life beginning.

I was roused from my meditation by my phone alerting me to a video call with the ring tone I'd set for Sean.

"Sean, honey." I smiled into the screen.

Roberto—my father—appeared behind him. "Happy Thanksgiving!"

"You're together?" I asked.

Freddy jumped up and called for Abe to come in.

"We wanted to surprise you, Mombie."

"I told him one still photograph is not enough of my new granddaughter," Roberto added with a flourish of his hand.

Abe had sent him the news and a picture, and we'd had a phone call with Sean, but neither had seen Gianina on video yet.

Abe hurried in and snuggled in next to me. "It's so great to see you both." He lifted the baby out of the wrap and cradled her in his left arm. "Here she is. Gianina, meet your brother and your *nonno*."

By some miracle she stayed asleep. Roberto murmured endearments in Italian.

"Happy Thanksgiving, baby sis," Sean said.

"How did you two get together?" Abe asked. "Do you have a few days off for traveling, Seanie?"

"No," he said. "I just took them. I'll make up the work."

"I am a professor." Roberto flipped open his hands. "I can write him a *scusa*, saying he came for research."

Which would be stretching the truth since Sean was still a high school student.

"I can't believe I'm missing this." Sean swiped away a tear.

Roberto laid his arm lightly over Sean's shoulders.

"Oh, honey," I said. "You'll meet her soon." Gianina was his first sibling. We'd urged him not to miss this exchange-student year. The program discouraged visits from home during the year, but maybe we could plead extraordinary circumstances and bring the baby to meet him in the spring.

Gianina let out a whimper. Abe brought her up onto his shoulder and gently patted her back. Adele greeted the Italian contingent, as did Freddy.

We all chatted about Sean's studies, about Roberto's latest publication, about anything but murder. We didn't need to. That chapter was over, that book closed. This time, the death hadn't turned out to be homicide at all.

I would be just as happy if my life stayed homicide-free from here going forward. I'd showed a knack for solving murders, but that had no place in a baby's life—or in mine.

Recipes

Pecan Scones

I adapted this recipe from one I saw in the *Boston Globe* by Sally Pasley Vargas. It was a popular breakfast special in Robbie's restaurant.

Ingredients
¼ cup granulated sugar
1½ tablespoons ground cinnamon
3 cups flour
¼ cup granulated sugar
1 tablespoon baking powder
¼ teaspoon baking soda
¾ teaspoon salt
10 tablespoons (1 stick plus 2 tablespoons) cold
  unsalted butter, cut into small cubes
1 egg
1 cup heavy cream
1 teaspoon vanilla extract
2 tablespoons melted butter
½ cup pecans, finely chopped
  Extra flour (for rolling)
  Extra heavy cream (for brushing)
2 tablespoons turbinado sugar or raw cane sugar
  (for sprinkling)

Directions
  Line a baking sheet with parchment paper.
  Mix ¼ cup sugar and the cinnamon and set aside.
  In a large bowl, whisk the flour, ¼ cup sugar, baking

powder, baking soda, and salt to blend them. Add the butter cubes and toss to separate and coat them. With your fingers, pinch the butter cubes to flatten them.

In a small bowl, beat the egg, cream, and vanilla with a fork until blended. Pour it over the dough. Use a rubber spatula to mix them until it forms a shaggy dough. If there are dry crumbs in the bowl, add more cream, 1 teaspoon at a time.

Scrape the dough out onto a lightly floured counter. Press it together to form a cohesive dough. Roll it into a 10-inch square.

Brush the square with melted butter. Sprinkle it with the pecans and about 2 tablespoons of cinnamon-sugar. With the rolling pin, lightly roll over the dough to press the pecans into it.

Fold the dough in half to form a rectangle. Position it so the short side of the rectangle is facing you. Flatten slightly with the rolling pin. Brush with more melted butter and sprinkle generously with more cinnamon-sugar. Fold the edge closest to you up to meet the top edge. You now have a square again. Roll the dough into an 8-inch square that is about 1-inch thick. Set it on the parchment-lined sheet. Freeze for 30 minutes.

Preheat oven to 400 degrees.

Using a bench scraper or a large chef's knife, make 2 evenly spaced cuts in both directions (4 cuts total) to form 9 squares.

Place the scones $\frac{1}{2}$ inch apart on the baking sheet. Brush with cream and sprinkle with turbinado sugar. Bake for 22 to 25 minutes, or until the tops are golden brown. Cool for 5 minutes on the baking sheet. Transfer to a wire rack. Serve warm.

Italian Wedding Soup

This Italian-seasoned meatball soup was a big hit on a chilly November day in Pans 'N Pancakes.

Ingredients
2 tablespoons olive oil
1 medium yellow onion, diced
2 large carrots, diced
2 stalks celery, diced
3 cloves garlic, minced
6 cups chicken broth, homemade or commercial
2 cups water
1 habanero pepper (keep whole)* or a few drops of
    hot sauce (optional)
2 tablespoons minced fresh rosemary
½ teaspoon dried oregano
½ teaspoon salt
¼ teaspoon pepper
½ cup small pasta such as orzo
1 15.5 ounce can small pink or white beans, rinsed
8 ounces fresh spinach, stems trimmed and leaves
    roughly chopped, or one package frozen, thawed
2 tablespoons basil pesto
20 small meatballs (any meat, pre-made or from the
    recipe of your choice), uncooked
Parmigiano Reggiano, for serving

*The whole pepper is optional, but it adds nice flavor in the background while barely increasing spiciness. Just make sure you don't chop or squeeze it.

Directions

Heat olive oil on medium heat in a heavy soup pot or Dutch oven. Sauté onions until they begin to soften. Add carrots and celery and continue cooking until all are soft. Add garlic and sauté one more minute.

Add chicken broth and water. Enclose habanero in a tea ball and add to the pot. Add herbs and salt and pepper. And stir.

Increase heat until the soup boils. Stir in the pasta and reduce to a simmer.

After the pasta is al dente, add beans, spinach, and pesto and stir well. Add meatballs. Bring to a simmer and cook gently for an hour or until flavors are melded. Correct seasonings.

Serve hot with grated cheese on top.

Chicken Fajitas

Abe whips up this easy meal for a weeknight supper.

Ingredients

1 pound boneless, skinless chicken thighs, cleaned
    of excess fat
1 teaspoon chili powder (less if you find it too
    spicy)
1 teaspoon cumin
½ teaspoon salt
¼ teaspoon pepper
1 onion, slivered
1 green pepper, seeded and slivered
olive oil
flour tortillas
Options: grated Monterey Jack cheese, hot sauce,
    salsa

Directions

Prepare all ingredients first.

Mix spices in a pie dish or dinner plate. Rub mixture on both sides of chicken thighs and set aside.

Wrap tortillas (two per person) in a damp towel and place on a plate in microwave or warm oven.

Heat 1 tablespoon oil in a heavy skillet over medium heat. Sauté onion and green pepper until wilted. Remove from pan and keep warm.

Add 1 tablespoon oil to same skillet and turn heat to medium high. Sauté chicken thighs on both sides until done. Slice in narrow strips. Add back to skillet with vegetables and turn heat to low. If using microwave, zap tortillas on low until warm.

Dish up plates and serve with guacamole and warm tortillas on the side for wrapping. Some might like to add grated cheese and/or hot sauce or salsa.

Robbie's Guacamole

Robbie makes a quintessential Cali-Mex topping to go with Abe's fajitas.

Ingredients
2 ripe avocados, pitted
1 teaspoon fresh lime juice
1 teaspoon chili powder
1 teaspoon ground cumin
2 tablespoons salsa
hot sauce to taste
salt and pepper to taste

Directions
Scoop out avocados into a medium bowl and mash with a fork. Mash in other ingredients. Correct seasonings and hot sauce to your own tastes.

Serve atop any Mexican food or as a dip with tortilla chips.

Apple Cider Muffins

These fall muffins were a popular breakfast special in the restaurant.

Ingredients
2 cups flour
½ cup sugar
1 tablespoon baking powder
1 teaspoon cinnamon
¼ teaspoon ground cloves
½ teaspoon salt
2 eggs
1 cup apple cider
½ cup oil

Directions
Preheat oven to 375 degrees F. Grease a twelve-cup muffin tin.

Mix dry ingredients in a mixing bowl. Make a well, add the eggs, and use a fork to combine. Stir in cider and oil with a fork until barely mixed.

Fill tin and bake for 20 to 25 minutes until muffins are lightly browned. Cool in pan on a rack for fifteen minutes before turning out.

Enjoy warm or at room temperature with butter, a slice of sharp cheddar cheese, or plain.